D1527751

My GRL

By John W. Howell

Martin Sisters Publishing

Published by
Martin Sisters Publishing, LLC
www. martinsisterspublishing. com
Copyright © 2013 John W. Howell
Martin Sisters Publishing, LLC, Kentucky.
ISBN: 978-1-62553-059-2
Editor: Cassy Kost
Printed in the United States of America
Martin Sisters Publishing, LLC

Dedication

My GRL is dedicated to William McCormick (1925 – 2007) who was not only a loving father, grandfather, and husband, but also a voracious reader of books. Bill taught me the love of the written word through a very practical lifelong dedication to continued improvement of the mind. He spent his working life as a marketing person for the *Pittsburgh Press* surrounded by meaningful words, finishing his career as Vice President. He and his wife Mary Kay were inseparable in life and are now together. They raised the beautiful woman who steadfastly remains my spouse. Bill was the first person to actually say he liked my writing.

Acknowledgements

MY GRL is a piece of fiction written out of the author's imagination. Port Aransas is a real place with real people, but the events described and places visited are purely fictional with no intent to depict reality. I want to thank Randall J. Pawelek for letting me include the words to his song *Crazy Fun* which he composed and recorded on the CD titled: *A Moment in Time* by the Jaiy Randy Band, © Big Ram Records 2012, Bill Green Music - BMI. Big thanks to Melissa Newman Senior Editor of Martin Sisters Publication for her support. Finally, thank you Molly for being there the whole way.

Chapter One

Gerry and I finish our beers at the Sandbar and make a move to cross the crowds toward the front door. Before the karaoke noise starts, we agree to go to another place for some pizza. She directs something to me which I can't understand, so I hold my hand to my ear and try hard to hear her. She looks a little upset. I signal we should wait until we get outside to talk.

She nods and I take the lead, reach back, grab her hand, and act like a bulldozer while I separate the crowd as we pass through. It becomes harder since everyone has begun to pay attention to the drunken girl singing what sounds a little like a slurred Avril Lavigne song to the karaoke machine on the stage up front.

We make it to the door and go out into the humid night. I drop Gerry's hand and notice there are two guys walking toward us. I tell her to stay close and figure the guys will eventually make way and go into the bar. I am about to ask her what she was trying to get me to understand in the bar, when I feel a rush of air behind me and hear what sounds like someone thumping a watermelon. That was the last thing on my mind when the lights of the world go out.

"Where am I, and how did I get here?" I ask the nurse who's standing next to the bed.

"You are in Corpus Christi Memorial Hospital, and you have had a severe blow to the head." She casually yet crisply replies. "I am Nurse Quinlan." She continues unprompted, "you will need to rest now. The doctor will be coming around shortly, and I don't want you to be too tired to answer his questions."

"He has questions? What kind of questions?" I am trying to disguise the tinges of panic I feel since I have no idea how I got here. Unfortunately, I'm not too successful.

"He wants to figure out what happened so that he can determine a course of treatment. You have been unconscious for a few hours, and I believe the doctor will want to assess whether or not you are going to require treatment other than rest."

"I was unconscious for a few hours? My God! I have absolutely no idea what happened. What other kinds of treatments are there?"

The nurse smiles and gives me the old, "let's see what the doctor says, shall we?" This is the verbal indication she will not be offering any more information regarding my case.

She turns to leave, "when the doctor will be in to see me?"

"I have no idea but I assume it will be sometime soon." I sigh and decide to start to try and connect the events which caused me to end up here.

"Can you tell me what time I was admitted to the hospital?" I ask as she moves closer to the door.

"Oh yes, I believe it is in your chart. You came into the emergency room about quarter of six and were admitted to a regular room at eight forty five last night." She pauses and looks up from the chart. "Do you need to know anything else? If so, your doctor can provide the details." She snaps the chart shut and shoves it back into its slot.

"Can you tell me what time it is now?"

She glances at her watch. "It is after one in the morning."

I had, indeed, been out of it for several hours. She dims the lights in the room and allows the automatic door to close very gently.

My thoughts go back to earlier in the day. I remember having toast for breakfast along with some Greek yogurt. I can't remember the kind of yogurt or what I had on the toast. I wonder, is it important to be able to remember what you had on toast? I think it is more important and more critical to recall what went on the rest of the day. This is causing me to worry, as I am drawing a total blank on the entire day and how I got here.

As I am beginning to feel another panic attack rising, the door swings open and in walks a young man in a white coat with a stethoscope casually lying around his neck.

"Hello, I am Dr. Samuels and I treated you when you came in. I am checking on you before I go home."

I give him a weak hello and proceed to bombard him with questions. He smiles and holds up his hand with a traffic-cop-like gesture. I stop asking and take a deep breath.

"How do you feel?" He pulls my chart from the wall.

"My head hurts."

"I am not surprised that you have some pain you took a hell of a hit to the head, and I must say the hit was localized and although I'm not an expert in these things it looks like it was done by someone who knew what they were doing."

"What do you mean *localized*?" I ask the question softly. "What do you mean *knew what they were doing*?"

He smiles and says, "I apologize. It might be helpful for me to let you know what happened to you last night. By the way, it is not unusual to have some temporary short-term memory loss after a blow to the head. So, relax and let me fill you in."

After about five minutes discussion with the doctor, I now understand I had been hit on the head by a soft object specifically designed to knock someone out, but not cause serious contusions or brain damage. The term "black jack" was mentioned. Even though the doctor is still talking, I am hardly listening since I have a big question brewing. I want to ask why the hell someone would want to knock me out when my mind is flooded by a flash of memory. *Shit*, my inner self is talking. I was walking with Gerry when a couple of guys came up to us. I don't really know what happened next. I'm sure we were approached by the two guys, but that's all I remember. I need to ask the doctor a bigger question than whom or why would someone want to knock me out.

"Where's Gerry?"

Dr. Samuels stops talking and looks at me as if I had just fallen through a hole in the roof on the end of a repelling line, dressed in a Ninja outfit.

I ignore his petrified look and continue, "I was with Gerry . . . Gerry Starnes last night, and I just remembered she was there when the two guys came up to us." I know I am beginning to ramble. I need to know where she is. "She will be able to tell me what happened."

Dr. Samuels looks down at the chart on his lap and I immediately know something is wrong.

"What's the problem?" I ask softly.

Dr. Samuels looks up with a crinkled brow. His mouth opens a couple of times before he says anything. He finally allows the words to escape, "I am very sorry to tell you that Gerry was shot and did not make it. She was shot outside the Sandbar."

I cannot process what the doctor just said and ask him to please repeat what he told me. He is very embarrassed and again tells me Gerry has been killed. I cannot believe my ears. I am trying to understand, but can't put together why anyone would want to kill Gerry. She is . . . was a really sweet person, and we met a month ago while I was looking to buy a boat when I first arrived on the Island.

We would get together now and then and have a drink or dinner. There was nothing going on between us, yet we always had really nice conversations. I always looked forward to the times we spent together. Her sense of humor was pretty much the same as mine. Like me, she was not a native of Mustang Island, but a transplant. She was a loan officer in one of the big banks in San Francisco and pretty much quit that career for the same reasons I took a leave from the law firm and looking for the satisfaction of doing her own thing. She came to the Island on vacation like me and returned to get a job at Premier Yacht brokerage. Gerry was very good at selling boats and had a pretty loyal following among the kinds of folks who needed a boat. I am lost in thought about Gerry as Dr. Samuels gets up and begins to leave.

"Do they know who did it?"

"They are unsure; but the police told me very little. They did ask me when you would be ready to answer a few questions. I told them you would probably be ready to answer some questions in the morning. I think that is still true since you seem to be regaining your memory. Please try to get some sleep now. I have ordered something that will help. I'll be back in the morning and will let the police officers know if you are ready to talk to them."

"Thank you doctor." He leaves and a nurse takes his place. She gives me a shot of something and almost immediately I am out.

"Good morning." It is a cheerful greeting from a heavyset woman, as she places a food tray on one end of the table. "You enjoy," she chirps. "There's a menu selection under the tray that needs to be filled out for lunch and dinner. You don't want the kitchen staff to make those decisions for you. It's okay with breakfast since there are not a lot of ways to mess that up, but lunch and dinner are a different matter." She bids me goodbye and leaves with the promise of coming back for my breakfast tray and selections.

Before having any breakfast I need to find the toilet. There would be no room for coffee or anything else until I took care of the uneasy pressure from within. I look around and see a door off to my right. Unfortunately, the tray and table are in the way so I exit the bed to the left. When I place my feet on the cold floor and put the weight of my upper body on them, I realize my legs are like rubber. I manage to hold onto the bed, the tray, and a chair while I do a hand-over-hand balance and foot shuffle to the bathroom. I am reminded of the old wing walker rule of "don't let go of what you got until you got hold of something else."

I finally make it to the bathroom, close the door, and look in the mirror which seems to be too low to accommodate my five foot eleven inch height. I stoop down to position my face so I can see it. Gazing at the reflection, I actually look better than I thought. All in all I vainly conclude I look no worse than if I had too much to drink the night before. I hold myself steady on a handy bar built for this use and take care of business. I splash water on my face, and then wipe it with a paper towel.

While I'm wiping my face, the memory of what happened to Gerry rushes back into my consciousness. I feel saddened all over again. I finish and make a vow to find out what happened, and another vow to help put the person who did this horrible thing away for life. Of course, all vows tend to make us feel better at the time, but the effectiveness of the vow will be carrying it out.

When I step out of the bathroom, I am greeted by yet another nurse who looks upset. "You are not allowed to get out of bed until the doctor gives you permission."

"I needed to use the bathroom."

"You need to use this buzzer and call for a bed pan next time."

"Okay I will do that. I promise," I say. At the same time I am promising myself there is no way in hell I will do that. I think, "Besides I should be out of here before I have to use the bathroom next." As I get into bed, Dr. Samuels enters the room. He looks refreshed and relaxed like he does not have a care in the world. It could be his youth, or just a good night's sleep. Either way he looks great. "Good morning Mr. Cannon," he says.

"Good morning Doctor and you can call me John."

"Very well. Good morning John." He starts to examine me. He takes my pulse, listens to my lungs and passes a light back and forth in front of my eyes. His expression does not change as he makes notes on my chart.

"So how does it look?" I say.

"I think all is well, given the circumstances, and you should not have any permanent damage. I believe it will be okay, health-wise, to talk to the police. Do you think you should talk to the police without a lawyer?"

"Why?"

"Gerry was shot in the back of the head, and while you were unconscious some officers took samples of your DNA."

"Do you know what they found?" I ask while looking directly into his eyes.

"No," he says. His eyes never leave mine.

"Well, then . . ." I pause to think my statement through. "I will represent myself until such time that I believe I have a fool for a client."

We both chuckle, and he leaves saying goodbye over his shoulder.

I am sitting on the edge of the bed thinking about Gerry, when the door opens and two men walk in. They look like they have just walked out of a casting call for *Gilligan's Island*, minus the sailor's hat and captain's cap.

The older man is tall and dressed in khaki Dockers shorts, boat shoes, no socks, and a patterned Hawaiian shirt with a giant hibiscus print which looks like it should cover a table in a Tiki lounge. The lump under the shirt cannot be missed, as it is clearly some kind of handgun. He has silver hair, cropped short, and a silver mustache which contrasts nicely with his tanned skin. His rounded chest causes the buttons on the shirt to appear to be under stress trying to keep everything in place. His muscular arms and generally fit condition gives the outward appearance of having been a professional fighter at some point in the past. His color of hair and the lack of weathering of his skin make figuring out how old he is very difficult. The range could be from forties to near sixty.

The shorter, younger man is dressed somewhat the same, but instead of a Hawaiian shirt he has a coral-colored polo shirt tucked into his walking shorts. He is wearing a pair of flip-flops, which might be difficult to run down and tackle a crook. I surmise there must not be that much running by the police on Mustang Island. The young officer has blond hair, trimmed short in the style of recently released military. He is wearing his handgun on the outside of his shirt, an automatic pistol which I guess to be a Glock 9mm.

"Excuse us," says junior. "The doctor said you were well enough to answer a few questions about what happened last night."

Before I can answer, the older man adds in a kindly way, "It shouldn't take too long Mr. Cannon and we will try not to tire you out."

"I will be glad to tell you anything I know," I say. I do caution them that my knowledge of the event is somewhat limited because I was knocked out by one of the two men who approached us. "Also you can call me John."

The older man, who tells me his name is Ned, asks me, "How do you know it was two men?"

"Gerry and I left the Sandbar after a few drinks to go to the Cove for pizza. We had just left the bar and these two guys were outside the bar walking towards us. I figured they would just pass us when one hit me from behind."

Ned continues, "Did you see the guy who hit you?"

"No. As I said, I was hit on the back of the head. Right here." I say this with some degree of impatience while pointing to the back of my head.

"You said there were two men who approached you. Did you see the guy slip past you? The one who hit you I mean."

"Come to think of it." I pause to really think about it. "I did not see anyone slip past me. There was the shingled storefront on my right, and the guy would have had to pass me to the left. Had he done that, I would have known he was trying something and maybe would have had a clue that I was going to be hit. Believe me, I had no clue; it just happened."

Ned nods. "I believe you John." He paces back and forth, his brow furrowed in deep thought. Then he says, "I think there was another guy that you did not know was behind you."

"I wish I knew for sure." This is my summary of events.

Ned and the young officer ask a few more questions along the lines of how well Gerry and I knew each other and did she have any enemies. I tell them all I know, which is Gerry and I were only friends and I did not think anyone disliked her. The two of them seem satisfied with the answers.

"One final question and then we will let you get back to healing." Ned looks through a file folder. "Have you ever seen this gun before?" He then thrusts a picture of what appears to be a revolver in front of my face. I take the picture from him so I can actually focus my eyes on it.

"No," I then pause to think and assure myself the next statement is true. "I've never seen this weapon before." I am curious and wonder what this weapon has to do with me. "Why do you ask?"

Ned bluntly responds, "You were lying on top of it at the scene of the crime."

Holy shit. I think and almost say out loud. "Say again?" pops out of my mouth instead.

Ned goes on to explain when the EMTs placed me on a gurney; they found the gun underneath me. How it got there he did not speculate, but he did assure me I was not the one who fired the .22 caliber revolver. He explains when someone fires a pistol there is gunpowder residue left on the hands and clothes. He admits his investigative team already tested me and found none on me. He also tells me that they took a cheek swab.

He apologizes for not getting my permission. "You were out cold, and I really didn't believe there would be any harm in collecting the DNA since I want to believe you're innocent anyway." He goes on to say he doubts when the DNA testing is done there will be anything of use anyway. "I would appreciate getting your permission, after the fact, though."

I assure him it is no problem. Even the worst lawyer would advise to cooperate with the police, especially if you believe yourself innocent. I have no cause to think I had anything to do with Gerry's death.

Ned and the young officer get up to leave. "Let me give you my card." He pulls one out of a little leather case which serves this only purpose. "If you think of anything, please give me a call." He smiles, what I am sure is his version of a warm smile. To me, it resembles the facial gesture of a fairly dangerous crocodile.

"Oh!" he adds as he hands me the card, "please let us know if you intend to leave the area. It's just protocol. I am sure you understand."

I guess I do understand I am still a suspect. Not wanting to let him know I am on to the subtlety of what he just said. I merely respond I will keep his office informed if I remember anything or intend to leave. He seems pleased I am the paragon of cooperation. I have read police consider a passive suspect the best kind. There are no real worries about having to explain to superiors how a suspect got out of control, was injured, or worse, disappeared. Ned nods goodbye and junior follows suit. As they leave, it occurs to me I don't know junior's name. I guess it is not all that important since, after looking at his card, I realize I now have Ned Tranes, the Chief of Police of Port Aransas on my case.

Chapter Two

I lie back down on the bed and search my memory to see if I do have anything to worry about relating to the unfortunate situation with Gerry. Even as I think about it, I am a little confused as to why I have difficulty thinking about Gerry in terms of murder instead of "unfortunate situation." I attempt to rationalize it is such an unpleasant subject I want to avoid it even in my own mind. The rationalization seems logical until I start to think of alternatives. One alternative which creeps me out is maybe somehow I did have something to do with Gerry's murder.

Not that I pulled the trigger. I know that did not happen, but what if there is something going on between me and someone else, and Gerry was merely collateral damage? I know I have created a lot of hard feelings in my career. I suddenly remember an incident in the elevator the day I found out from my accountant, two months ago, I could afford to live my life as I wanted to live it.

I remember leaving the accountant's office and stepping inside the elevator next to a man who looked at me without a smile and he took a step back. I pushed the lobby button, and as we descended the few floors, I had a feeling I knew the guy. I was at a loss as to how or where. I had a feeling he was looking at me and I didn't dare turn around.

We reached the lobby, and as I stepped off the elevator it hit me. The guy was the opposing council on the Taft lawsuit. I turned to introduce myself, but I was too late as he pushed by me. "Didn't you represent Taft in the suit with Avery?" I blurted the question out to his back.

"Fuck you, Cannon." I stood watching as he walked away without turning or breaking stride. I remembered the lawsuit was very acrimonious and I was totally surprised by his lack of professionalism as demonstrated by his reaction. I guessed he felt his loss was personal, which was a dumb feeling, given the nature of lawsuits. I never took losses personally.

I'm sure that guy wasn't the kind to actually kill someone to get to me. Staying with this thought process brings me to another question as to the killer's motivation. Did the killer think Gerry and I were involved, and by killing her he was somehow sending me a message? Man! If so, I sure miss the point.

The memory of the elevator interchange brings back some others as well. I am lost in thought, thinking about each case I worked on. I want to check the possibility someone on the losing side might have some reason for revenge. I come up blank and conclude my nostalgic tour right back to the elevator scene where I started.

I remember clearly the case of Taft vs. Avery involved the CEO named Matt Jacobs and he was very angry when he lost the case. I also remember the partners of my firm were a little concerned about Jacob's anger. He was an important business person and I really pissed him off. Jacob's company headquarters was in San Francisco and since our firm was in the same city, the partners were reluctantly writing off any opportunity to do business with him and I think blaming me.

I can't specifically recall the details of why he was so pissed off, so I need to check some of the facts. After making a mental note to look up the particulars of the case of Taft vs. Avery, I revisit the next morning after seeing my accountant.

Since it was less than two months ago the details are pretty clear. I remember I woke up early with a full-fledged case of excitement. I was going to go into work and meet with Gerome Peters, the senior partner, and tell him I was intending to request a leave of absence under the HR practice which governs personal exploration. The policy is clear and allows any partner a twelve-month personal leave without pay to pursue an avenue of personal study or exploration. The only restriction is the partner must be in good standing and have spent at least ten years in a specialty. I have been with the firm for twelve years and am in good stead so I had both covered.

The only other requirement is there needs to be in place others trained to assume the partner's caseload for the duration of the leave. The policy was actually put into effect after a partner became unduly stressed and killed himself. The resulting investigation pointed to overwork as the root cause. The other policy put into effect after the investigation was each partner is required to take at least two weeks continuous vacation once a year.

I had not prepared a statement or letter, but had rehearsed a little of what I wanted to say. I knew Peters would be taken aback. He was not the kind of person to show any emotion, but I was reasonably certain he would try to talk me out of my decision. He would at least question me on how long I had thought about this move, and if I fully understand the ramifications to my professional and personnel life. I was also certain he would not ask what I intended to do with the time off. This would be too much of a personal conversation, and Peters avoided these kinds of conversations like the plague.

The meeting with Peters went pretty much the way I anticipated. He tried to talk me out of my decision and did so in such a condescending manner I was sure his motives were all about the lost billing revenue and nothing about his concern about my future. In so many words, he told me I was making a big mistake and should take some time to think about what I was doing. I told him I had thought it through and my mind was made up. We talked at length about who would take my cases. He seemed somewhat appeased as I demonstrated that all cases were being covered by experienced attorneys.

We also talked about timing. We came to agreement on a three-week transition period. The discussion ended with his wishes for an enjoyable leave. He advised me to contact HR and get the paperwork completed. He said he would approve the leave of absence for twelve months. Before leaving his office, I shook his hand and expressed gratitude for his support. He blushed at my acknowledgement of his help. This blushing, which I had never seen before, indicated to me his support was very shallow and possibly transitory and he was embarrassed by it.

I spent the next three weeks helping the team on all the cases. Many of the associates could not understand why I was taking a leave. Others quickly understood and expressed envy over the opportunity that I would be taking. There were a few rounds of dinners and lunches. Most turned into maudlin expressions of staying in touch and how much I would be missed, since there will be no way to replace my ability to accomplish the impossible. Luckily, I was well aware my time at the firm would be well forgotten within a couple of weeks.

Human beings, in my experience, have the ability to quickly adapt to compensate and fill the void of a seemingly indispensable worker. I never took all the expressions of fidelity and respect too seriously and was not disappointed when all phone calls and contact ceased after three weeks. It was just as well, since if I ever did come back to the firm, it would be nice knowing all the work was being handled in the meantime.

After packing my stuff, I left the office with another round of good wishes. There was a cake and speeches. When it came to my turn, I thanked everyone for the outpouring of feelings and summarized by reminding them I would be back in twelve months. I also said they should try very hard not to screw up my clients while I was gone. I got a big laugh and after the final handshakes, I grabbed my things and left the office.

The next day I was totally regretting my decision. I woke up about twenty times during the night with the fear I had really messed up, accompanied by serious bouts of night sweats. I thought back to all the good wishes and couldn't help the feeling that everyone was happy to get me out of there. Those sons of bitches succeeded, because there was no going back now. I could not return early after all the bravado, and I was now in a position to live my life the way I thought I wanted to live. I remember feeling the first morning that the only way I wanted to live my life would be to stay in the comfort of the routine I had come to know and hate.

Notwithstanding the fear and loathing occupying my every hour, I booked a flight to Corpus Christi. I prepared my condo for a long-term absence. I notified the superintendent I would be back on an interim basis. I turned off the water at the meter's central shut off, and since I had an all-electric apartment I did not need to worry about any gas leaks. I turned off the icemaker but kept the refrigerator and wine cooler on. The wine cooler needed to protect my wine, and the refrigerator needed to run so the seals would not dry out and leak. I set the main heater thermostat on 50 degrees, and since I lived in San Francisco where daytime temperature was pretty moderate, I did not have air conditioning. The only adjustment necessary was the heat if it got really cold. Very seldom did I need to run the heat, and very rarely would the inside temperature get down to 50 degrees even in the coldest weather, so I felt I was pretty safe at the setting.

I cancelled the New York Times and San Francisco Chronicle and had my mail held until I could arrange a forwarding address. I left my AT&T U-verse video, Internet, and landline service in place. I really did not want to go through the hassle of returning my equipment. The service was inexpensive enough, and I felt it would come in handy should I return to the condo now and then. I had remote access to my voicemail, so leaving everything in place seemed like a good idea.

I decided to pack lightly since I couldn't imagine needing too much more than polo shirts, T-shirts, shorts, Columbia shirts, underwear, swim suits, and a pair of boat shoes. I figured I could shop for more if needed. I shoved everything into a compact gym bag which met airline requirements for overhead bin and under the seat. I also packed a small personal bag with my iPad, iPhone, and iPod. I was carrying everything I needed.

I almost forgot to rent a car in Corpus. I settled on a Ford Fusion but really would have liked a Range Rover. To confess, I did not even ask for a Range Rover. I asked for a compact with a cheap daily rate, and the Fusion was what Budget had to offer. I was not too sure how long I would need the car, so I booked a weekly rate which was renewable. It also had unlimited mileage so I would have the flexibility to go wherever I needed.

Finally landing in Corpus I picked up the rental without an upgrade. I don't know why the rental agencies always ask if you want to spend more money on an upgrade. I guess they think you won the lottery since you booked your car. It is annoying to say the least. I drove the fifteen minutes down what everyone calls SPID. It sounds like a potato and means South Padre Island Drive. I turned left at State Route 361 for the fifteen minutes to Port Aransas. I checked into the Holiday Inn Express and planned to try and find more permanent accommodations as soon as I got my bearings.

My first stop on the Island was the local food store. I wanted to buy a paper and some bottled water. I quickly learned this store is the place to stop to find anything you need. Not only are there groceries, but there are movies to rent, fishing licenses, hardware, newspapers, lotto tickets, and beer and wine. In addition, there is a very interesting bulletin board with every manner of announcement ranging from help wanted ads to business card postings.

The newspaper had an advertisement and the phone number of a realtor. I gave them a call, and in short order I was the proud occupant of a three-bedroom home on Oceanside Drive. It had everything I needed and was available for a twelve-month lease. It also had a significant view of the Gulf of Mexico. This view was not on my must-have list, but there was no way I would give it up.

My second objective was to find a vehicle which would be a little more serviceable. The Fusion was fine for town, but could not be taken to the beach. Its profile was too low for the soft sand, and ripping off the air dam on a rental was not on my shortlist of life objectives. The next day after settling the house lease I was looking at the message board at the store while waiting for my salami sandwich. Since each sandwich was custom made, there was plenty of time to read the bulletin board next to the deli. There was a three-by-five index card with a description of a vehicle that might fill the bill. I gave the local number a call and went to look at it.

It only took a couple of minutes to be totally enamored with the 1978 Toyota, FJ40 Land Cruiser. It was painted what they call "Smurf blue" and had a removable top, six-cylinder motor, four speed manual transmission, and driver controlled four-wheel drive. It was also equipped with roll bars, and had two jump seats in the rear. I did not know much about this vehicle other than it was considered a classic and the fact it would be perfect for maneuvering the sandy beaches around Port Aransas. I did not realize it at the time, but the $4,900 price tag was extremely reasonable, especially since it was actually running and had all its original equipment and emblems.

I took the hardtop and doors off and was very happy with my purchase. The body had a little rust in places, and I needed to replace the starter and hydraulic clutch, but it was a sweet ride. The previous owner gave me a repair manual so I used it to do the repairs myself in under a half a day. This was the essence of the desirability of this machine; the average Joe could actually do repairs successfully. When I got the FJ, none of the lights worked. I managed to get them all working as well as the horn, windshield wipers, and washer. It took me three trips to the safety inspection station, but I finally got everything right and now my car is street legal and fully safe.

When the mechanic finally signed my inspection sticker he said, "We should charge by the trip instead of flat fee." I couldn't have agreed with him more.

I met Gerry in the process of buying a boat. I saw one online I was interested in. It was a 1982 flying bridge cruiser, thirty-one-foot twin, and sounded like it might be a buy at twenty-nine-thousand-dollars. I called the brokerage, and the pleasant female on the other end said she would be happy to show it to me. I went over to Premier Yacht Brokerage and met Gerry. I was surprised at how slight she was and the way her brown eyes seemed to grab a hold of whoever she was talking to at the time. She was dressed casually but you could tell her clothes were designer labels just by the way they were proportioned to her small frame. She was very friendly and seemed to be genuinely interested in helping me find the right purchase, and not just trying to close a deal.

"So what kind of boat do you think you are looking for?" she asked me after some discussion of the cruiser.

I was a little embarrassed. "I'm really not sure."

"Oh I understand. Sometimes we start looking and don't really have a firm idea of what we are looking for. Why don't we go ahead and look at the cruiser and we can talk about the pros and cons to that kind of craft. I have a belief most people have a better idea of what they don't want as opposed to what they do." I agreed and we set out. The cruiser was in a slip in the marina, owned by the University of Texas at Corpus Christi. It was low tide, so we had to jump from the dock, which was higher into the boat. Gerry unlocked and swung open the door that led below deck. After looking over the boat and at the two three-hundred and fifty horsepower gas engines located under parallel hatches in the rear, I wondered aloud how much it took to operate. Gerry explained that the fuel would run about five dollars a gallon and this boat at medium power would burn about twenty gallons an hour.

"So you are talking about a-hundred dollars an hour."

"The other important point is the fuel capacity is about two hundred gallons, so the effective range of this particular boat is no more than nine hours with about twenty gallons to spare," she said.

She wrapped up her assessment with the fact that this kind of boat would be good for cruising but not really appropriate for fishing since most of the great fishing was found outside the effective operating range of a boat like this one. I really appreciated her honesty, and after about three or four more days of looking we finally found the boat that would be just right.

It was a 2002 sixty-five-foot Hatteras Convertible Sport Fisher. Since I had designs on starting a charter business I needed to consider a boat which had well rounded functionality. The Hatteras seemed to fit the bill. It would be serviceable as a charter craft for fishing and could also function as a pleasure boat. It had a full downrigger set up as well as spacious cabin that could sleep six people. It was diesel powered, so it came with the economies of scale that would allow a twelve-hour operation with plenty of margin for safety. My only concern was to question whether or not I had the chops to learn how to captain this beast. Gerry explained there was a school in Corpus which would teach the fundamentals of navigation and seamanship. The manufacturer of the boat would teach me to operate the craft safely. It all seemed too easy. Gerry left me alone to call the owner to check on some of the questions I had about rust, dripping pipes, and stain on the deck. I started to second-guess my path forward. I was a complete novice contemplating a move to take on the Gulf of Mexico, and there seemed to be an infrastructure which would accommodate my dream. The only fly in the ointment was I would not be able to hire out the boat for pay until I had a captain's license. This will take about a year to attain. I decide in the meantime I would build experience. I didn't need the money so I figured it would be okay.

Something is bound to go wrong, I was thinking when Gerry came back and interrupted my thought.

"The owner of the boat is anxious to sell and just cut the price," she said

Of course he is anxious, the doubting voice inside me cried to be heard. He wants to unload the barge before it slips below the surface. I did my best not to give in to the voice and asked, "where did the price end up?" Gerry said. "I feel there might still be some room for negotiation, but that the boat was priced at nine-hundred-thousand-dollars down from one million-two-hundred-thousand."

Hearing this buying incentive, the voice screamed at me to stop the madness. "Let's offer a flat eight-hundred-thousand" I said above the din of the inside protestations. I figured this price could kill the sale.

To my surprise, Gerry agreed the offer was fair and left the office again to call the owner. I was now left at the mercy of the demon inside me. I got up and paced the room wildly in an effort to calm or at least quiet the raging beast trying to hold sway over the arrangement. I was breathing hard and a small amount of sweat beaded on my upper lip. I never realized how traumatic a purchase could be until that moment. I was quickly starting to regret my decision, and I was about to tell Gerry to stop the process when she came back and said, "Deal is done."

My knees were weak. I smiled faintly and said, "Good." Gerry laughed, as my buyer's remorse countenance showed through without a filter.

"You just got the best deal on a terrific craft," she said. Maybe she was trying to either save the deal or make me feel better.

I could not tell which, but the words did seem to make sense. I actually got this dream boat for about half price. I told my inside voice to take a big cup of shut-the-fuck-up and then asked Gerry if she would like to join me for a drink.

We went to Gerry's favorite place called The Sand Bar, had a couple of beers, and talked about the purchase. While we drank our beers, we talked about all the great things about the boat: two 1400 horsepower Detroit Diesel marine engines, 1800-gallon fuel tanks, full salon, stereo sound throughout, laundry, fully equipped galley, air conditioning, fully auto navigation equipment, radar, four bedrooms, and three full baths. Those were just a few of the goodies which reminded me I was not a fool. I finally got really enthused about my new boat and I never questioned my decision again. I also made up my mind what to name her. *My GRL* was perfect, since this is what she is to me. I wasted no time and immediately enrolled in the sea faring classes offered by the manufacturer. After ten hour days of instruction and practice, in less than a week, I was able to begin using her on my own. The lessons were expensive but well worth it. I never would have been able to become proficient without them. I decided to work toward the captain's license and will need about three hundred and sixty days of skippering My GRL before I can qualify for a Coast Guard captain's license. The skippering days are defined as at least four hours so it really isn't a full calendar year. I started my logbook with the first cruise.

Chapter Three

I call for the bedpan after all, since Dr. Samuels is worried about the fact my pupils are showing some signs of brain swelling and won't release me. I try to explain a bump on the head is not all that serious. The end result is I have been in the hospital for two days. I don't have the courage to circumvent the rules about getting out of bed for fear of dying at the hand of the big nurse. Finally, on the second day, I am told that Samuels has authorized me to get out of bed. I am given a walker and can shuffle up and down the hall as well as visit the glorious bathroom. On the third day, I get the good news.

"You are ready to go home." Dr. Samuels has a satisfied smile.

I believe he is finally feeling pretty good about my recovery. I wish I could share his satisfaction. Since I don't want to stay in this hospital any longer than necessary, I don't tell him I still have a screaming headache and feel a little unsteady. I am convinced that it is just part of the healing process and promise myself if these symptoms don't go away soon I will call the doctor. In the meantime, he seems to think that there are no lasting effects, and that is good enough for me.

I get dressed and wait for the wheelchair which is the requisite mode of transport out of a hospital. (If you are still alive that is, if not, then it is a gurney). My mind continues to wander back to the last time I saw Gerry alive. We had just visited the boat and Gerry popped the information on me that she had another client who might be interested in buying *My GRL*. I continued to protest to Gerry that *My GRL* was not for sale since I had only had her for a month and had not really gotten my charter business off and running. I further explained I enjoyed taking her out each day and felt I was really getting the hang of how she handles.

"Oh, knock it off," she said rather roughly. "I can always find you another boat. This client seems to be in a rush which could mean a nice commission for me and a tidy profit for you."

I still maintained I would not want to part with her and I really haven't had the time to get used to her yet. I painted a verbal picture for her, of me, starting those two beautiful engines, casting off, and navigating past the jetty to the open Gulf. "How can I replace the feelings that I have for a boat which gives me so much pleasure?"

"How would you feel about a two-hundred-thousand dollar profit?" She had a look I knew, from one month's experience, meant she was not bluffing. This totally shut me up.

She and I went for drinks to the Sandbar and discussed the whole situation. I had to admit my mind could be changed with the prospect of taking the profit from *My GRL* and upgrading to another Hatteras which might be a little newer and have more appointments, if that was even possible. Who is your client?"

"I am dealing with a buying syndicate so there is not one buyer that I have met. From some of the discussions I am sure the syndicate has a person in charge buyer, but that person wants to remain anonymous."

As she talked more about the benefits of the deal I could not help thinking of the times over the last three weeks I spent on the boat. A particular memory came back to me where I was cruising along, doing about ten knots, watching the sun rise looking like a giant fireball coming out of the Gulf dead ahead of me. I remember thinking to myself, even if I never get a client for charter, I would be happy just seeing this kind of scene as often as possible. I guess it will not be that important which boat I use, just as long as I can continue to get on the water which I have grown to love. "If you are okay with the deal we can talk more, but it is sounding better and my feeling is we could go ahead and do the deal if everything falls into place."

"That really makes me happy John. I have to admit that I already told the contact that you were probably going to be okay with selling your boat."

"Well it might be nice next time to talk to me first, but you are forgiven." I raised my glass and we both smiled.

We decided to go to the Cove for pizza since we were finished drinking at the Sandbar. As we got up to leave I remember Gerry saying something about a deal she was working on that went south. I could not understand nor hear well since the Karaoke session had started, and the bar was too small for conversation once the bedlam had begun. I was thinking I would have to ask her about it once we headed outside. I never got the chance. The two guys approached us as we left the building. I had the feeling her comment was one of concern by the worried look on her face, and I think she was going to tell me something which was certainly bothering her.

As I think of it now, the discussion prior to her expression was all upbeat. She was looking forward to concluding another major purchase. She also seemed a little, but not horribly upset about the spoiled deal. She explained that it went south because the buyer was dealing in bad faith. She had concerns about the buyer's ability to pay or reason for wanting a new boat, I can't remember which. She looked like she wanted to say more, but we ran out of time. I really do not have a clue as to what was distressing her prior to leaving the Sand Bar, but seemed to hit her when the music started. It could have been the three quick beers we had got her thinking about something she was trying to forget. I doubt I will ever know, now that she is gone.

The wheelchair arrives with a smiling candy striper at the helm. She takes me to the patient discharge area. I thank her and give my name to the stern person in accounts receivable.

"Your health insurance has covered all but thirty-six dollars," she says while handing me the bill. I gave her my Master Card and am on my way.

I step outside. The day is bright and very humid. I have to blink a few times to get accustomed to the bright sun reflecting off the concrete like it was covered in Mylar. I pull out my iPhone and turn it on for the first time in five days. I notice I have twenty missed calls and fourteen voicemails. I decide to review them when I get home. I hit the YP icon and enter the word "Taxi." Coastal Cab comes up first. I hit the number and order a cab. I'm told it will be about ten minutes.

"Need a lift?" I recognize the soft voice of Ned Tranes, the Chief of Port Aransas police from behind me. I spin around in surprise.

"Hello, Chief. What are you doing here?"

"I had another person to interview about the Gerry Starnes murder."

"Is someone else in the hospital?"

"No, but someone who works here. I needed to talk to the M.E." He pauses and, thinking I probably never saw an episode of CSI, adds, "That's Medical Examiner. I am pretty sure the cause of death was a 22-caliber bullet to the brain but I need an official cause.

"Was that really the cause?"

"Sorry, that information is confidential."

We both smile at the ridiculous nature of our discussion. "I just called a cab and they will be along in ten minutes."

"They won't make it in ten minutes, and they will charge about fifty dollars to take you from Corpus to Port Aransas. Why don't you ride with me? I need to go back anyway."

I accept a ride from him and call the cab company to cancel. He directs me to his white Chevy SUV with prominent blue Port Aransas Police markings on the side and an impressive light bar on the top of the cab.

"Door's open." He nods in my direction indicating I should get in.

I am thinking Ned is a conservationist when it comes to using words. I get in the passenger side and Ned gets in behind the wheel. After much adjusting and seatbelt fastenings he starts the engine. I am immediately impressed by the tone of the exhaust. It has that low rumble which you find in your average modified high-speed racer. I make a comment about wondering what's under the hood.

Ned smiles and lets me know the city has authorized a few modifications. "Zero to sixty in 5.5 seconds." He looks at me as if I had asked about the pedigree.

"Nice." That is all I can say as we pull away from the hospital.

Between Corpus and Mustang Island there is not a speed zone any higher than sixty-five MPH, so I probably will not get to feel of the power of this machine. I find myself wishing the radio would pop to life with a request for assistance which would require Ned to punch this monster into fishtailing and high-speed dash to help. We are driving over the J.F. Kennedy Causeway about fifteen minutes from Port Aransas when Ned indicates he would like to ask a question.

"Ask me anything."

"Ms. Starnes's parents are still in town. I need to talk to her mom and dad before they leave. I want to know a little more about her. There is not much information available."

I sit looking straight ahead, anticipating when he'll ask if I know her parents.

After a long silence, Ned finally says, "Do you know if Gerry had any enemies?" This is totally off his previous statements about parents.

I want to say I think she might have one given the way she died, but I don't think Ned is the kind to take sarcasm lightly. "I really did not know Gerry well enough to have information about her private life. I do know she had concern about one of her clients that I never got to the bottom of understanding."

"Give me the details. What concern and what client?"

"She was talking about one of her clients who was giving her trouble. She never told me who it was and I didn't really get the nature of the problem."

"Damn that is too bad. This would be the kind of thing that we could follow and determine if it has anything to do with her murder. I think I will also look at her client list and see if anything is there."

We finally make it to my house. "Would you like to come in for a beer?"

"Thank you for the offer, but I am still on duty." He gives me a slight smile. "If it wouldn't be too much trouble would you come down to the station tomorrow? I have a few more questions. About ten o'clock would be great."

"Of course, no problem I will be there at ten."

I keep forgetting he does not have a lead on anyone else, and it will take a good deal of convincing for him to rule me out definitively. I thank him for the ride and walk up my front sidewalk, pull out my keys, and while inserting the front door key I turn and see Ned is still there watching me. I head inside the air-conditioned living room. I close the door and look through the peephole. Ned's truck slowly pulls away.

I haven't noticed before, but the cool temperature accentuates the fact that I am sweating profusely. I hope it is just a post trauma reaction and not a concern about Ned Tranes. If I start looking like I have something to hide, I will never get off Ned's list. I try to shake the ridiculous feeling of guilt, but for some reason I am driving myself into a state of worry. It might be I feel guilty Gerry was shot while I was lying unconscious. My rational mind tells me I'm being crazy, but now Ned has spooked me into allowing these irrational thoughts to have credibility.

I decide to lie down and see if I can chase the present headache. Suddenly, my phone rings. I look at the screen and see it is Sarah Barsonne, Gerry's best friend.

"Hi Sarah." I hope my voice has the right amount of sympathy. To make sure, I say, "I am very sorry for your loss."

The effect causes Sarah's voice to break as she thanks me for the thought. I also tell her I am sorry to have missed the burial service, but I just got out of the hospital.

"That's alright," she begins, her voice husky with grief. She does not say anymore, and I assume she is trying to regain her composure.

"You okay?"

"I really am not okay, John." She pauses again and takes a deep breath. "I am having some difficulty understanding what happened."

"I sympathize with your feelings and want to offer to meet to discuss any aspect of the situation that might help you work through this tragedy."

"Oh John that is really nice of you. I am touched." Her voice had a grateful tone.

"Would you like to meet for lunch tomorrow and we can talk more?"

"I really would welcome that. Thanks."

"We can meet at Judy's since it is one of the better places in town. Do you know where it is?"

"Yes I know it. That would be great. Noon okay with you?"

"Yes that's perfect."

"Also John, I am sorry you were hurt and I hope you are feeling better."

"I am just fine thank you." I decide not to take this time to turn the conversation to my problems. We close with looking forward to meeting tomorrow.

Once off the phone, I feel about one hundred years old. I start to regret leaving the hospital before being fully recovered. I grab a bottle of water and head to the bedroom while kicking off my shoes and dropping my pants as I am walking. I pull the covers back and sit on the bed and notice, while struggling to open the water; I still have my phone in my hand. I lay it on the end table and finally crack the stubborn seal on the cap, downing the water in several continuous swallows. I swing my legs up on the bed and slide them under the crisp cool sheet, throwing back the duvet cover since I still feel warm. I plump the big pillows and lean back and turn my attention to the phone. I pick it up and touch the phone icon, then scroll to the last missed call and start to review them one by one. There are several from various people at the law firm, a few numbers which are not in my contacts, two from Sarah, and one unknown caller.

I go to voicemail and, as I thought, the folks from the law firm want to know if I am okay given the fact that the Port Aransas killing made San Francisco news. I could never imagine this kind of story would be picked up, but one of the callers solves the mystery. She indicates on the voicemail that Gerry used to be a huge supporter of the mayor and worked on his campaigns for four or so years. The caller also said Gerry was a fairly big executive at the bank and had a high profile. Gerry's murder made the news along with the mention in the press that I was also a victim, who is expected to recover. The caller rang off with a "hope you are okay," kind of expression.

Sarah left a voicemail which was an expression of sympathy for my injuries. She also wanted me to know the service for Gerry would be two days ago. I really hope she understands why I missed it. I will have to let her know I just got the message, although I am not sure I would have been able to go if I had the message earlier.

There is a message from a person who identifies himself as Spencer Stans, representing a buyer who is interested in my boat. He asks rather clumsily if Gerry had mentioned it before her unfortunate accident. Accident my ass, I am thinking. I decide to keep his number. I have this disturbing feeling this "buy my boat thing" is connected somehow to Gerry's "unfortunate accident."

Suddenly, my doorbell rings. I get up and luckily remember to grab my robe and pull it on as I make it to the front door. Dragging the door open, I am face to face with a young guy dressed in postal blue and gray. Although I never met him personally, I recognize him as my mail delivery person.

"Hey, Mr. Cannon." He greets me with enthusiasm.

"Hey yourself." That is all I can think to say since I don't know his name. I only recognize him since I see him on the block delivering mail.

"Uh your mailbox is full and I better deliver the mail to you personally. I know you have been in the hospital." He stops talking, looks down and then as if he has found the words starts again. "I am sure you have some things that may need to be attended to, so here you are."

He pushes a stack of letters, papers, and big envelopes toward me. I grab the bundle. "Thank you," I say as we stand there for an uncomfortable moment in silence. I break the spell, "thank you again." He seems satisfied he did the right thing and turns to go. I close the door and return to the bedroom.

I am thinking I may never get to sleep. I toss the mail on the bed, throw off the robe, and climb back into bed. I open the envelope from the firm. "Crap."

The letter lets me know my leave of absence has been approved only with a six-month time limit. "Bullshit." I curse out loud to the empty room. I guess ole Peters just could not find it in his heart to give me just one thing I wanted. I knew he was vindictive, however I did not think he would go this far.

The next few envelopes are bills from the electric, phone, and gas companies. I just put them in a pile and will deal with them later. There are also several packets of shareholder meeting materials including proxies which need to be signed. I also lay them aside. I pick up one interesting envelope, which is hand addressed in a feminine style. I turn it over to see if there is a return address on the back since there is none on the front, and there is nothing there. I open the envelope and pull out a handwritten letter on blue stationary. At the bottom of the letter, Gerry's name is written in a flourish, as if she had signed the Declaration of Independence. I grab the envelope and noticed the postmark was five days ago. The postmark confirms the letter was sent prior to her murder and my hope disappears. I start reading and notice my hand is shaking so I grip the stationary with two hands.

Dear John,

I really hate to bother you with this situation. I have no one else to talk to or anyone who can help me. You see, I am concerned about one of my clients who is being very aggressive and seems to be dealing in bad faith. I was going through the motions of pretending to be accommodating but today I told his representative that maybe they should find another broker. I hope to be able to talk more about this. I am a little restricted on what I can talk about. Please don't think I am idiotic if I start talking randomly about my client the next time we see each other. I am reaching out to you with some passion and drama (sorry) since I don't know what else to do. Hopefully I will be able to explain more in person.

    Your Friend,

    Gerry

I finish reading the letter and am totally stunned. I realize now why she waited so long to mention her client concerns while we were together. She thought I had received this letter prior to our meeting. She must have put off the discussion thinking I would raise the subject, which I never did. Christ, she must have thought I'm the idiot not her. I feel guilty for not checking my mail before our meeting. That week was very busy, and mail is not something I remember all the time. We have one of those freestanding communal box setups, and I continually drive by and forget to stop. When I do remember, I usually don't have the key on me. So long story short, I can go several days without picking up the mail.

I realize I need to stop this train of thought, because not getting the mail had no effect on the outcome. Had I gotten the letter, I would have discussed it with Gerry, and the evening would have ended up pretty much the same way. I probably would have a little more information about what was bothering her and still not much of substance to have prevented her murder.

"So what's the point?" I speak to an empty room.

I lay back in the bed. My head hurts, and the prospect of trying to figure out all the ramifications of my interface with the circumstances around Gerry's situation leaves me a little weak. I close my eyes briefly and then another question pops into my head.

Should I share this letter with Ned Tranes? The question hangs there as I contemplate the alternatives.

The lawyer in me offers the argument that sharing the letter makes sense. If I don't, and it becomes a piece of important information at a later time, then I could be accused of withholding evidence. Not sharing the letter ensures there is no connection between me and Gerry's murder. This letter could look like motive and the question could be raised as to why she sent it to me. I make up my mind to take the letter with me to the meeting with Ned tomorrow.

Chapter Four

The alarm provides a blessed interlude to the nightmares which I believe visited me the whole night. Although most experts tell us dreams are intermittent I could swear I just had a full eight hours of torment.

After breakfast I take a long shower. It feels so good getting a real shower rather than a wipe down with a cold washcloth in bed. People are always joking about the desirability of a sponge bath given by a beautiful nurse. The reality is an orderly handing you a basin, a washcloth, and a fresh gown. Not much to enjoy and a lot to dislike.

In the hospital, in addition to a skimpy bath, they don't have a way to allow a person confined to bed to shampoo their hair. The hot water dropping gently from the rain showerhead is my idea of heaven. The best part is a generous amount of lather and a brisk rub of the hair. It is amazing what is taken for granted becomes a real treat when finally restored, after being denied even for a short time. I wash my hair three times and love each event.

I get dressed, turn on the US weather station on the radio, and again read Gerry's letter. My decision to give it to Ned is reinforced, as the letter definitely points to a serious concern about one of Gerry's clients prior to her murder. I can't imagine what she knew that caused her to want to drop a deal.

I suddenly remember the strange call from the guy named Spencer Stans. I reach for my iPhone. His number is the only one without a name. I touch it and the call begins. After about four rings, the call goes to one of those automated voicemails. I hang up. I don't want to leave a message when I am not even sure it is Spencer Stans who will get it.

It is about nine-thirty, and I decide to leave for downtown. As I step outside, I notice the humidity already seems high. It looks like the temperature today is going to be pretty typical for this time of year. By watching the weather forecast each day, I have learned mid-May brings highs of eighty-five or so and humidity in the seventies. Today is the same. The winds are out of the southeast and breezy with gusts up to sixteen knots. The marine forecasts call for moderate seas with waves in the two to three foot category. I'm not going out on *My GRL* today but out of a twenty day habit I still check the weather

I climb up into the Land Cruiser, and as I put the key into the ignition my phone rings. I look at the screen and the Spencer Stans number comes up with a caller unknown. I really need to add Spencer to my contacts so I know it is him, I think as I connect the call.

"Mr. Cannon, my name is Spencer Stans, and I left you a message a couple of days ago."

"Yes Mr. Stans. I did get your message and do understand that you represent a group or individual who has interest in my boat."

"Mr. Cannon, I represent a very interested party who would like to determine if you have any interest in selling your boat. The one named *My GRL.* (I guess he thinks I have a number of boats). My client has the need for a boat such as yours and is willing to pay you a fair price for what we are sure is a dear possession of yours." He pauses for a breath.

"There are a number of boats like mine on the market. Why mine?"

"Good question." Stans seems to be unfazed and then explains the logic. "My client has looked at other boats, and yours is one of the few located on the Texas side of the Gulf. The others are in very poor condition, and he believes yours has been well taken care of given the fact the craft report is very positive."

"What craft report?" I respond somewhat surprised.

"The one that Ms. Starnes sent to me." His reply has a tone

approaching condescending.

"I don't know anything about your arrangements with Gerry." I try to hide my impatience with the fact Gerry and this guy were discussing my boat in detail without my knowledge. I had only told Gerry that I might be disposed to sell the boat, not that it was for sale.

I remember what Gerry wrote in her letter to me. "Didn't Gerry tell you to find another broker?"

"No I think she was having trouble with another sale that she briefly mentioned. We always got on well and had a lot of respect for one another. I understand how this may seem to you." Stans is now picking his words carefully. "Is there any way we could get together so that I could bring you up to speed? I feel badly that Ms. Starnes apparently did not keep you advised as to the discussions we had."

I am now curious about what Stans wanted with a meeting and how much he would be willing to pay for *My GRL*. I pause for dramatic effect, and then agree to meet with him. We set up a time for tomorrow at ten o'clock on the boat to discuss the deal. We sign off with mutual lies about looking forward to the meeting tomorrow.

I pull the choke all the way out on the FJ, depress the clutch, and turn the key to the start position on the steering column. The engine kicks into life inspired by the recently installed upgraded heavy-duty starter. I arrive at police headquarters across from City Hall with about fifteen minutes to spare. I decide to pop into the library. It is a short walk away, and I want to see if they may have some interest in a few of my books. The library is cool and quiet. I wish I could stay all day, especially given the appointment I have coming up. I go to the desk and see on the wall a blackboard titled "Word of the day." Today's word is *pernicious*. I mouth the word out loud just as the librarian comes out of a room in back of the desk.

"Do you know what it means?"

"It means to cause harm. In the case of medical terminology, it means fatal."

She is very pleased. "We don't get many who know the words without some kind of prompt."

"Prior to graduate school I memorized over a thousand words that could be part of the LMAT exam for law school."

"You go to law school?"

"Yes I did and I graduated." I did not pile on by mentioning Stanford. "I also practiced law in California for twelve years." She seems impressed, but to what end. That particular past life has nothing to do with this one. "I have some books back in San Francisco that I would like to donate to the library. I don't want to sell them and they are just sitting round with no one to appreciate them."

She seems a little puzzled since I don't believe donations are something the library usually accepts. "We do accept books for our annual book sale. Since you don't want yours sold, can you give me an idea of the titles?"

"Well let's see. There is *Catch 22* by Joseph Heller, *On the Beach* by Nevil Shute Norway, *Slaughter House Five* by Kurt Vonnegut, *Jailbird* also by Kurt and *Exodus* by Leon Uris." She definitely seems interested after I say, "all the books are first printings of several classics."

"I will need to check with the library board and will have to get back to you."

"Great, I will e-mail you a complete list"

"What are you doing in Port Aransas?"

"I am trying to find a different career," I answer after a little thought.

She shakes her head in acknowledgement of the positive motivation of my answer and then offers, "We are all looking for something different, aren't we?" She smiles at me like an adoring mother. "Good luck to you." I turn and go out the door.

I leave the library with the feeling I had just been to church and just had all my sins forgiven. The librarian blessed my quest and for me that was as good a blessing one could get. A representative of an erudite institution seems to approve of my current madness.

Why seek the approval of lesser beings like my boss Peters? I think as I cross the street to the police station.

I walk into the station and a very large desk runs the full width of the reception. It is almost chest high. Behind it is a rather stern-looking young man in uniform. He has a three-stripe chevron on each sleeve, which I take to be the rank of sergeant.

"May I help you?" He has an efficient manner.

"I have an appointment with Ned Tranes."

"May I have your name?"

"John J. Cannon."

"Please sit down, Mr. Cannon, and I will tell Chief Tranes you are here." He points to a row of hard, straight-back chairs lining the wall opposite the desk.

I take a seat, not missing the subtle mention of chief and mister by the desk sergeant. I guess not all things are informal on island time. In addition to the chairs, there is a little table with a number of pamphlets loosely strewn about. One of the pamphlets warns about the dangers of drinking and driving. The item that catches my eye is the seventeen thousand dollar price tag for the first conviction. I am glad I never drink and drive. The other booklets have similar messages about underage drinking, drug possession, shoplifting, and petty theft. I can't imagine someone would be convinced to not break the law by reading these messages.

Before I really get wound up in creating a detailed and totally meaningless analysis of the prevention quotient of the pamphlets, the sergeant mercifully calls me over to the desk. He directs me through a door to the right which opens to a hallway. The chief's office is at the end of the hall. I knock and hear the muffled invitation to enter. I open the door and Ned rises behind his desk. He motions me to a chair and sits back down.

"Good morning."

"Good morning, Chief." I build in an extra measure of respect.

Ned looks at me with an expression that seems to convey suspiciousness of my obvious submissive attitude. "Yes well," he begins. "I want to talk to you some more about Ms. Starnes's murder."

"Please be assured that it is no trouble for me to talk to you anytime you need to discuss any aspect of the situation."

"Let me begin by having you go over the events of the evening again. I want to make sure we have not missed anything. After all, you were the only witness." He pauses and continues his thought with a revision, "well, at least the only witness we know about at this time."

I sigh and catch myself since I don't want him to think he is putting me out in any way. "Gerry and I met to discuss the sale of my boat. We were having drinks at the Sandbar and decided to leave to get a pizza at the Cove. Once outside we were approached by two men—"

Ned interrupts my narrative. "You mentioned yesterday that Gerry was starting to tell you something about one of her clients. This was just before you went outside, right?"

"Yes, that's right," I say. "In addition I got a letter from Gerry outlining her concerns."

He looks very surprised. "Why didn't you tell me this yesterday?" He has an accusatory tone that seems to reflect another bout of suspicion.

I need to talk fast before the cop on a chase in Ned goes out of control. "The letter was sent before Gerry and I met at the Sand Bar and I only read it last night." I try to keep my voice steady, but I am failing miserably.

"You mean Gerry . . ." He pauses and corrects himself, "that is, Ms. Starnes sent you a letter that you did not read until after she was dead?"

I have to admit Ned's question does sound reasonable. "That is exactly what happened." I respond with as much nerve as I can muster.

"What was the postmark date?"

"Here is the envelope and the letter." I hand him both. "As you can see, the postmark was almost six days ago." I add the time frame for good measure in case he can't do the math in his head.

"So you are telling me this letter was postmarked on April 29, and you and Ms. Starnes went to the Sand Bar on May 4, and you never saw the letter?"

"Yes, that's true." At least he has the timeline straight. "I just opened it last night after the mailman delivered it to the house."

"Where was the letter?" He is now trying to connect the dots.

"I have one of the free standing mailboxes in the middle of the sub-division. I just never stopped to pick it up. The mailman was concerned because the mail was building up."

"He can verify this?"

I think for a second. "Of course he can. I am not sure he will remember the letter. I think he will remember delivering my mail last night."

"I guess that will have to do. What is his name?"

I blush. "I really don't know. I have never met him before last night. I have seen him delivering mail in the neighborhood but can't tell you his name."

"Shouldn't be too hard to find out," He dials the phone. "Hello, Mary, this is Chief Tranes." He looks at me impatiently. "I have a request Mary. I need to know who delivers mail to 121 Oceanside Drive." He listens and interjects an "uh huh" and writes down a name. He signs off with a big thank you and an obvious promise to pass on hello to his wife from Mary.

He hangs up the phone. "Billy James is your mailman. If necessary I will contact him. Please don't talk to him about anything in the meantime, okay?"

I give the chief assurance I won't talk to Billy.

After he finishes reading Gerry's letter he speaks up. "This sounds like she is pretty upset. What did she tell you that night?"

"As I said before, she said something about her client dealing in bad faith or did not have any money. At the time I did not think it important so I really don't know which it is. Had I read that letter I certainly would have paid attention."

"I have to tell you, Mr. Cannon." He is looking very seriously at me, "this really doesn't feel right."

"What do you mean?" I try to keep the squeak out of my voice and do a bad imitation of base tone.

"This girl writes you this letter with the words *passion* and *drama* in there and then sees you and doesn't open up. This sounds to me like you may know more than you are letting on."

I am starting to become uneasy and fidget in my chair. If he has a video camera trained on me, he will be able to review all the body language of someone who is truly uncomfortable.

"I can only tell you what happened, chief." I am sounding more confident than I feel. "I believe she thought I had read her letter and was waiting for me to bring the subject up."

"I think I would have been a little more proactive and asked you if you got the letter if I had been as concerned as she sounded. Another thing that is strange is why she would write you the letter in the first place? According to you, Ms. Starnes and you did not know each other very well."

I have to admit Ned had me on this and was one of the things causing me to consider not telling him about the letter. I have no idea why she wrote me the letter. I feel this has something to do with selling *My GRL*, but is this something I want to conjecture about in front of the guy who seems hell bent to pin Gerry's murder on me?

"I may have a connection," I come out with this before my rational brain has a chance to stop me.

"What connection?" Ned's tone sounds like he thinks he has brought me to the brink of a confession.

"This may be a stretch." I have the hope Ned will understand I am just presenting a theory. "Gerry has been involved with a middle man who wants to buy my boat. This guy's name is Spencer Stans, and he has already called me about continuing with the deal—

"I don't get the connection." Ned cuts me off.

"Well I am not sure there is one. Gerry had a number of discussions with this guy and never told me about them." I have to admit the connection seems rather obscure. In spite of this, I continue. "It seems to me if everything was on the up-and-up, Gerry would have told me about the deal much earlier. She even sent Stans a specifications description and inspection report, and I learned it from Stans today, not Gerry. I think she wanted to bring me up to speed, so she wrote the letter in the hopes that it would grab my attention on the client who was operating in bad faith."

"I'm not sure about the stepping stone. It doesn't sound right that you find out from the potential buyer that your broker is pretty much selling your boat without your knowledge."

"Bingo." I immediately want to take my comment back.

"You talked to this Spencer Stans this morning?"

"Yes, he called me on my way over here. We set up a meeting for tomorrow at ten o'clock."

Ned rubs his chin, obviously deep in thought. "Tell you what. You meet with Mr. Spencer Stans and then I will meet with you to debrief what has been said."

"Maybe I should wear a wire. Can you get a warrant for that?" I offer to be of help.

Ned's ruddy face turns a little redder. "I won't be able to get a warrant without probable cause and right now there isn't any except for your opinion." Ned is frowning and obviously not impressed with my suggestion. "This letter connection seems really shaky, and until I am sure of who is who we'll just play it my way. You don't have a problem with that, do you?"

"I don't have a problem with anything you want to do. I just wanted to be of some help." I am very concerned Ned keeps coming back to me as the prime suspect. I think the idea of wearing a wire wasn't that outrageous. Ned's reaction causes me to feel embarrassment and I can feel sweat forming on my scalp. I decide then and there to be careful and not get myself into this mess any further. I will report the conversation with Stans to Ned and will avoid any editorials whatsoever. I get up to leave. Ned motions me to sit down again.

"Just one more thing . . ." Ned looks down at the file on his desk.

I can feel my throat start to get a catch and want to clear it without being obvious about it. I end up choking and wished I had just coughed out loud.

"You need some water?" I am sure he thinks I am a lying son of a bitch given my body language and now a nervous tickle in my throat.

"No, thank you, I am fine, just allergies," a lie that seems to work.

"You did some intern time in the San Francisco DA's office, right?" He looks up with an expectation that I will confirm.

"Yes, that's right." I answer with as much speed as I can muster so as not to appear to be contradicting obvious information turned up on a background check by Ned.

"I got a call from one of the assistant district attorney this morning. Maybe you know him . . ." Ned shuffles a few papers and continues, "Yes, here it is. James Armentrout—you know him?"

I pretend to think a little, not wanting to answer too quickly since I am sure a quick answer to this question might cause Ned to wonder if I am telling the truth. "Did he tell you how long he has been with the DA's office?"

"No, he did not, why?" Ned is irritated and getting red again.

I don't know who the guy is. "The name doesn't ring a bell, and I think he joined the DA's office after I left." I am now completely in control.

"I did not think you worked with him since that was over fifteen years ago. I thought you may have some knowledge of him since you were an attorney and he is a prosecutor." Ned has the upper hand again.

I think and then offer my counter move. "I was in litigation. I never faced anyone from the DA's office since I was involved in non-criminal cases." Score for Cannon.

Ned finally seems to accept I did not know James Armentrout. I do get the feeling acceptance of a fact is not necessarily a positive thing.

"What did Mr. Armentrout want?" I figure I can at least understand the question of knowing him.

"He wanted some information on the case since Ms. Starnes was a local in San Francisco. I think he was thinking of the voters."

He grumps a little as he tells me he has no more questions. I look down at my watch and see it is almost eleven o'clock. I still have plenty of time before I need to meet Sarah. I cannot control myself and should know better, but I stick my neck out one more time.

"Is there anything I can do to help the investigation?" I said it and can't take it back.

Ned looks at me without any expression on his face. I have no hint as to the thoughts going through his head at that moment. He continues to look at me to the point of discomfort.

He finally responds a little too loudly. "Tell the truth."

I get up and turn to leave. "Nice talking with you, Chief. Let me know when you want to meet after I talk to Spencer Stans." I had not planned to jump to the bait as if I had not been telling the truth, so I let the comment pass.

"Call me tomorrow after you and Stans meet." He lowers his gaze and looks at the file again.

I turn and walk out of Ned's office and do not close his door. I go down the hall and past the sergeant who calls after me to have a nice day. I mutter "the same to you, my friend." I am almost sure he doesn't hear me. I head outside into the bright sunshine. I get into my FJ and find I am shaking as I put the key in the ignition.

"Son of a bitch." I express a little too loudly as two old people walking by are clearly startled. "Sorry." I wave and mouth the word. They smile and I know that's not the first time they heard that curse. I sit back and try to think over what has happened.

I am as sorry as I can be for some reason Gerry was involved in events leading to her death. She was a beautiful person and did not deserve to end up lifeless in the street. If I could take back the last few days and somehow prevent her murder I would do it in a heartbeat. She and I shared a business relationship, but I felt she was more like a friend than a business associate. I will miss her and yet have not had enough time to absorb how much. It makes it so much more hurtful I am still under suspicion. The creepy feeling of guilt starts to rise again. It is not guilt as in, responsible for the murder, but guilt centered on I was not awake to prevent it from happening. I still remember the gentle touch of Gerry's hand as I led her out of the bar. She trusted me completely to take care of her. She wrote me a letter asking for my help and I feel I let her down. I don't know how I can ever get over the fact she was killed and I should have known something was wrong. It is a good thing Ned hasn't strapped on a lie detector. I'll bet in my current state I would confess to anything. I have to shake this off and go on with my life but right now I don't know how. My rational mind keeps telling me I didn't know enough to prevent the murder. My emotional mind keeps nagging at me to own up to the fact if I had gathered my mail, and if I had listened to Gerry in the bar, things would be different. Lunch with Sarah could be a nightmare if she wants to interrogate me about my actions before and on the night Gerry was killed. On the other hand, I can offer her some comfort and maybe get her view as well. In any case it will be nice seeing Sarah even if all else falls through the roof.

Chapter Five

I met Sarah the first time I took my boat out for my solo cruise after my graduation from the factory school which coincided with the celebration of my two weeks in residence in Port Aransas. *My GRL* already was safely taken care of and tied up at her end slip. I secured an end slip due to her size. The largest in line slips are only thirty-six feet and it would be impossible to use an in line since the boat's stern would be sticking out into the waterway about thirty feet.

I was lucky since a sixty-five-foot live aboard got sold and the slip became available. If my boat had been any smaller I would not have been given the chance for this berth. If the live aboard had not been sold I would have had to find a birth somewhere else. All things worked for the best.

Gerry and Sarah showed up just as I had finalized the preparations to cast off. They were dressed for the part of mates. They each were wearing comfortable-looking shorts and polo shirts. What reminded me of mates was the fact they were dressed in all white, which seemed like they were working deck hands. I yelled to them to stow their bags below and get ready to make way with the lines. They laughed and mocked me by calling me Captain Bligh.

We did not go far. I pulled *My GRL* away from the end slip. The easy maneuver was leaving the dock. The harder part would be coming back since you had to do a one hundred eighty-degree turn and back the boat to the mooring. I gently nudged the throttles and kept her below wake speed until we cleared the Jetty. Once cleared, I pushed the throttles to half speed, and *My GRL* answered the command with an efficient response. The sea was quite calm and so there was little pitch or roll. I set the autopilot for a five-mile waypoint and noticed Sarah and Gerry were already spreading towels on two deck chairs. So much for help from this crew, I thought to myself. Helping dock would be the better work so I was content to see them enjoy themselves. I called down and let them know there was lunch in the galley and drinks of all kinds. They waved and answered. I could not tell their response from up here.

After a while, they decided to join me on the bridge. They brought lunch and we chatted a little about nothing too important. Sarah told me she liked my boat, and I made a mental note to invite her back. To my surprise, Sarah was also an attorney. She graduated from UT Law School and was admitted to the Texas bar about five years ago. I made the calculation and assumed she was about twenty eight which made her ten years younger than me. I could not help noticing her smooth skin and almost perfect tan. She had her blond hair pulled back into some kind of bun so her hair looked short and tight on her head. She wore sunglasses so it was hard to see her eyes. I only caught a glimpse of them when she looked at me over the dark lenses. The glimpse told me they were deep blue and very striking. I liked the way she laughed easily and how she managed to place her hand on my arm when she was talking to me. She seemed like a guy's kind of woman. She talked fish, politics, sports, and was interesting to be around. She was practicing law in Austin working for a firm which did a lot of commercial work for big companies. She told me she was in the real estate section and did most of the contracts for acquisition of property in conjunction with the shale oil business. We had a great time talking and I committed to another trip the next time she visited Port Aransas.

I did not want the day to end, but I did not want to be coming back to port in the dark. I ordered the ersatz crew to heave to as I prepared for our return. I brought *My GRL* around to a heading which would take us back to Port A. The rest of the trip included more lawyer talk and eventually a successful approach and docking of *My GRL*. We all went to dinner at a great place named The Peche Mare. I had not eaten there before and it was Gerry's pick. The food is Italian influenced. The seafood is fresh and the pastas divine. The décor reminded me of a street in Venice. There is art on the walls and all of it for sale. The tables and chairs look like they were taken from a curbside bistro. We had a few glasses of wine, a great dinner, and a lot of laughs.

The thought of Sarah and my first meeting brings a smile to my lips. A horn behind me snaps me back to the fact I am still sitting in my FJ in front of the Police department. I turn to see a person in their car. They have obviously been waiting for the parking place which I have been sitting in for God knows how long. I am really embarrassed since one of my pet peeves is when a person takes an inordinate amount of time getting out of a parking place while I sit and wait. I always think they are slow on purpose as a manner of exercising control over me. Now I am sure this person thinks I am trying to control them as well. I start the FJ and back out of the space. I pull forward and try my best to get out of the way. The driver does not look in my direction as she pulls into the spot. Enemy for life, I think as I pull away.

It is a short drive to Judy's, and I still get there with about twenty minutes to spare. I walk into the restaurant and the owner, Judy, a tall, dirty blond, hair pulled up, well proportioned, and good looking woman, gives me a warm welcome and a hug. "It is so nice to see you, John."

She knows what will make you feel good when she greets you. During the hug, I can smell Judy's perfume. I like the way Judy smells. She wears something which has a light watermelon scent. I suppose it could be the watermelon salad but doubt it.

"Has my guest arrived?"

"No one has asked for you. Your table is ready .Would you like to sit and wait?"

"Yes I would." She takes me to a table. "Could I get a glass of water please?" I did not realize until I got here I am totally parched.

Judy delivers the water. "I will wait to order until my guest arrives."

She nods. "Your server will be Chas."

"Thank you, Judy." She walks away and I and look out the expansive window. I will be able to see Sarah as she pulls up.

I watch for several minutes, then take my eyes from the window and notice Judy's has changed a little. The dining room used to be expansive with little breaking it up, other than the serving area at the back. The ceiling is still twenty-or-so feet high and raw beamed with a pickled whitewash finish. There is now a massive horseshoe-shaped bar off to the left of the expansive room. This seems like a good idea since there is now a place to have a drink and not worry about taking a valuable dinner table. The bar is also positioned so a bank of doors can be opened onto the patio. This makes it very nice for private events as well as single gatherings.

As I was noting the other changes (mostly minor) Sarah walks up to the table. She stands over me so her slim body semi blocks out the light. I see she is wearing a pair of black slacks with a black shell top. She is not wearing any jewelry so her appearance is quite somber. I get up and give her a little hug and she puts the black clutch she is carrying on the table and sits down. I see she has her hair down and it is quite long. I am thinking that normally her deep blue eyes would be a direct contrast to her blond hair. Today her eyes seem more stormy grey than blue. Her mouth, which last time sported a carefree, glossy, luscious looking, colorful pout, is pursed up tight with little color.

Right away I can see Sarah is under a fair amount of stress. She has the appearance of not having a good night's sleep for quite a while. I take her hand. She begins to tear up and requests a glass of wine as she excuses herself, picks up her clutch, and heads to the restroom.

When she returns, the cold wine is sitting at her place. I ordered one for myself as well. She takes a sip. "The memorial service for Gerry was beautiful. The local boating club took us all out into the bay and we dropped flowers and sang some hymns. The minister was wonderful and included so many personal things in the eulogy that it was like he almost knew her."

"You don't have to tell me about the service if it upsets you."

"It doesn't upset me; in fact it seems to help. Gerry and I met in college on the first day at freshman orientation. We have been friends ever since. I guess it has been about ten years. We both joined the same sorority and pretty much did everything together."

"Did you know about her moving to Port Aransas?"

"Yes she talked to me about it, but I was still very surprised when I first heard she actually did it. I told her when we first talked that she was making a mistake. I asked her how she was going to make a living and what her social life would look like in a small town like this. She never had a good answer, but didn't seem concerned."

"As it turned out she did quite well in the boat business."

"Yes she did well. She was very unhappy working at the bank and totally happy selling boats so I guess it worked for her. Her parents were not happy. They thought Gerry was wasting her time and were very disappointed that she quit a so called good job to move into a sea town. They are real conservative and on top of that they do not show emotions."

"Did the family attend?"

"Yes the parents were there. It was very strange though."

"Strange?"

"Gerry has a brother and he did not attend."

"That does seem unusual. Any idea why?"

"No. I did not get a chance to find out since I was able to speak to the parents briefly to offer my condolences."

"It is strange that they did not reach out to you since you were Gerry's best friend."

"Her parents are still in town," Sarah offers with a sigh.

"Where are they staying?" This is the only thing I could think of asking given the revelation Gerry's parents are clearly not Sarah's favorite people.

"They have rented a condo at Surfside Towers. Why, I have no clue."

"Maybe they are trying to connect with the life Gerry had here."

"I am not sure. They don't seem too interested in meeting Gerry's friends. They mentioned that they would like to meet you, though." Sarah pauses and thinks about what she just said. "That did not come out right." She blushes slightly. She looks down at her wine. "I meant you were one person they wanted to find out if it would be possible to meet."

Sarah's blush momentarily causes me to be rendered dumb as if I had been hit on the head again. I finally find my voice. "Why me?" I know I sound like a kid accused of spilling the milk. I am thinking a very selfish thought; how attractive she is when she blushes.

"They didn't tell me. I don't think it's a bad thing. Since you were the last person on Earth to see Gerry alive, I think they might want to know about her last few hours." The words were said with a shrug of her shoulders.

"Gerry probably told them about me buying a boat so it seems to make sense." I know I am guessing and hoping now.

"Yes that is probably the reason."

"How are you coping with your loss?" I want to get the conversation back to being supportive of Sarah.

"It is very hard to spend time in Port Aransas since there are many memories of good times here with Gerry."

I know from Gerry Sarah usually stays at the Royal Cabanas condo when in town. "Are you still staying at the Royal Cabanas?"

"Yes I am. Why?" I see a strange look on Sarah's face.

"Well maybe if you change hotels it might be easier since all your memories of Gerry are connected with that hotel."

"I do not plan on returning. What is the point?" She tears up again.

I want to convince her there is life in Port Aransas beyond her friendship with Gerry. I really don't know how to begin since the only life I can think of besides Gerry is me. I am sure I will come off as a self-serving pig if I even hint that a really good reason to return to Port Aransas is so we can get to know each other better and perhaps begin a relationship. I have had a very hard time with relationships my whole life. Every time I think I am falling for someone, something happens where I get too busy, or misread the feeling of the other party. The time I proposed to Cindy Kauffman continues to haunt me to this day. There I was on one knee asking her to be my wife and she is pleading with me not to spoil our relationship with something stupid like marriage.

I don't believe I ever recovered from that experience and so I am really doubtful when I feel affection for someone. The feeling makes me want to run away which I have been able to do, up until this point, by working more and burying the feeling. Now I have feelings for Sarah and she has given me no sign it might be reciprocal. If my past experience is any gage of the present, this relationship scenario is all in my head. I sit there like a bump on a log and do not proffer my reason for Sarah returning to Port Aransas.

"We should order." This is my profound conclusion meant to break the divisional silence.

I wave to our server Chas. He comes over and we place our order. I order two more glasses of wine without checking if Sarah was ready for more. If not, I may drink them both.

I feel like such a nerd and finally come out with, "When are you planning to leave?"

"I really haven't given it much thought, but I think probably Saturday."

"That only gives us three days to get to know each other better." With those words I slip and fall on a verbal banana.

She looks very surprised and presses me without skipping a beat or releasing my eyes from the lock she has on them. "What does *get to know each other better* mean?"

I'm now in a very deep pool of yogurt and need to think quickly or die by eye contact. I'm in the position of only being with Sarah the one time on my boat and am making an assumption she wants to get to know me better. I want to convince her to stay in Port Aransas longer. Since that suggestion seems too outrageous I need to make the best of the time we will have. "I think we had a good time on the boat the last time, and I would just like to see if we would want to spend more time together." I am praying this will do it.

She lets go of my eyes with a smile and a look at her watch. "I think it would be nice to see you again, if that is what you mean." She mercifully lets me off the hook.

"How about dinner tonight?" I reply. This, then, is my demonstration of the maturity level of a high school senior.

"I really have some things to do tonight, but how about tomorrow?" She saves me again.

Our lunch arrives and we continue to talk throughout the meal. Sarah does finish her wine so there is no need for me to fill in. Chas comes back and wonders if we are finished or still working on our plates as if we are building something. We tell him we are finished and would like some coffee. We decline the dessert menu, and Chas seems a little piqued as he leaves to get the coffee.

"Lower bill, lower tip," I mention as an explanation of a possible reason Chas could be piqued. Sarah smiles and seems to appreciate the lighter moment.

Over coffee we agree I will pick Sarah up at Royal Cabanas at six o'clock. I suggest we go to The Marina View restaurant since it is on the water overlooking the marina. I test gingerly the offer to have drinks on the boat first.

"I'll get an eight o'clock reservation at The Marina View, and we can have a drink on the boat first if it is okay with you."

"I would love that," she responds. I am stunned by her affirmation.

The check arrives. I pick it up and wonder how it got so high and then remember the four glasses of wine. I immediately pull out my American Express and give it to Chas. No use looking like a cheapskate, I think as Chas runs away with the card and bill.

"I told Gerry's parents that I would have you call them." Sarah seems apologetic as she explains the commitment she made on my behalf.

I take her completely off the hook (which I consider a requisite move at this stage of our delicate relationship). "No problem, I will call them this afternoon."

"Thank you. Here is their number, and you must know you are really a good guy." This is a response which validates my instincts for good moves.

Chas returns with my card and the tab to be signed. "No mints?" I am kidding as I add twenty percent for Chas and sign the tab.

Chas pulls out Sarah's chair and we start for the door. I wave goodbye to Judy and walk Sarah across the patio to her car. We stand there awkwardly for a moment.

"See you tomorrow."

She smiles and gets into her car. I watch as she backs out of the space and does an L maneuver and heads down the driveway. She must think I'm an idiot is my thought at that moment. I can't help myself and I keep watching as she comes to a stop at 361. She lets the cars whiz by and then turns left. She gives me a little wave as she punches her accelerator in order to get to the required 60mph as soon as possible. The fact I am still standing here confirms my mental illness.

I finally signal my legs to start walking and they actually respond. My FJ is a few feet away. For some reason it is a struggle to get there. I guess my head whack is still with me. I remember the fact that I have had two glasses a wine on top of the whack, so I write my sluggishness off to wine and not the fact I am becoming attracted to Sarah, although I know I am lying to myself. I get in the FJ and take the paper Sarah gave me and call up the key pad on my iPhone. The phone rings three times and an older sounding man answers in almost a whisper.

"Hello this is John Cannon. Sarah Barsonne gave me your number and asked that I call."

"Oh yes Mr. Cannon. I'm Joe Starnes, Gerry's father and I have a favor to ask of you. I wonder if you could come by our condo at your convenience for a discussion about Gerry."

"Um why yes I would be able to stop by. What kind of discussion?"

"Well you see Gerry's mother and I are having a difficult time understanding the circumstances of our daughter's murder. We know you were with Gerry that night and would be grateful for anything you could add that would help us through this."

"I'll make myself available any time. In fact I am passing your condo on my way back to my house in ten minutes and can stop if you wish."

He seems a little hesitant, "my wife is taking a nap and I don't want to wake her. She hasn't been sleeping well."

"I perfectly understand. My cell number is 415-555-6179 Call me anytime." These are my last words to him as I end the call.

Chapter Six

I decide to take a run this afternoon. I enjoy running on the beach. I used to run with earphones plugged into my ears as I navigated San Francisco's city streets or a park. Here I enjoy hearing the sounds of the Gulf and the various seabirds that seem to follow me.

I get home and change into my running clothes. I check my watch and decide that I will run thirty minutes out and thirty back. This should shake the cobwebs from my head, is what I'm thinking going out the door toward the sea. I cross over the boardwalk which transverses the dunes and step onto the beach. I notice the wind is coming from the north, so I plan to run in that direction first since I will have more strength early on, and on the way back when my ass is busted I will have the wind to my back.

I do some stretches and then step off. The day is beautiful. The temperature is about eighty degrees and the sky is a deep blue. The Gulf water hue follows the sky and seems clear even though there are some sizable waves rolling in. I have run about a half mile, and I am lost in the beauty and sound of the sea on my right to the point that I don't notice a couple with three dogs, two of the biggest ones are off leash. I only know they were off leash after one of them grabs the back of my shorts and tries to pull me down. The woman, dressed like she was going to a Three Dog Night concert at the Marin County

JOHN W. HOWELL

California fair in the 70s, comes running, calling the dog's names. The man stays back and has the only leashed dog with him.

"These dogs are hard to control." She talks with a note of regret in her voice.

"They should be on a leash." I talk in a not-so-friendly tone.

She apologizes and attempts to secure the dogs with the two leashes tied around her waist. "I really hate to leash them." She then hooks up one and the other.

"It's the law." Again, no friendly greeting from me.

By now the guy comes up and he looks pretty upset. He is dressed only in cargo shorts and it is apparent, by the gravity effects on his chest that he is on the north side of seventy. He looks at me with a stern expression. "Really? No hello or good afternoon?"

"Excuse me; I wasn't the one with the out-of-control dogs." I think of more and continue, "What is your problem? You don't know the leash laws?"

"My problem is your mouth, sport." The old guy takes a threatening step toward me. "My dog is leashed."

"What about these other dogs?" I point to the two German Shepards barking their heads off.

"As I said, my dog is leashed; these are not my dogs." He is obviously making a fine point of possession, which is a pretty clever way to deflect the issue.

This is a classic scene where a person gets all huffy because someone calls out the fact that he is now violating the rights of others.

"Okay, chief . . ." I have made the assumption that this guy would like the flattery. "Even though you two saw me coming for a half mile and could have hooked up the dogs, and even though I was bitten in the shorts by this woman's dogs, I want to start over."

"Like how?" He is confused.

"Like this." I take off my cap and bow. I notice the dogs are leashed so I continue the farce. "Good afternoon, gentle people." I notice they are getting a little uncomfortable. "Please be so kind as to secure your dogs so that you will be in compliance with the Nueces county commission court order regarding the containment of said animals." I put my cap back on my head. "I wish you a pleasant afternoon and will now depart."

The two cannot help themselves, and they start laughing. I begin my run again and continue for a couple of miles. On my way back, I see they are still on the beach, so I wave and wish them a good day. I notice the dogs are still leashed, so mission accomplished. I still wonder why people come to the beach with the belief that only the laws which do not inconvenience them should be followed.

I get back home and check my phone before getting in the shower. Sure enough, Gerry's dad has called. I call him back. He picks up on the first ring. "This is John Cannon and I apologize for missing your call," I say.

"Ah Mr. Cannon, I wonder if you can come over tonight?"

"Yes that would be good. I can be there by six but really must leave for another engagement by seven if that's okay." I tell him this so I wouldn't be stuck there too long since I really don't know what they want to talk about. He agrees, and I am assuming he sees the benefit of not having someone hanging around at dinnertime. I have to believe he is retired and on a fixed income, so not having a third wheel hanging around for a free meal has to be a good thing. We close the conversation with the confirmation of the six o'clock meeting.

I look at my watch. I have about an hour and a half to shower and have a beer. I think quickly about which will come first. Corona wins the contest. I grab a cold bottle from the fridge along with a lime wedge from a bowl sitting on my counter. I usually have a pilsner glass in the freezer, so I take the glass out and fill it with the cold beer and take a long drought, feeling the foam mustache on my upper lip. There is no one to hear and a long "ah" comes out loud anyway. I take another sip then head for the shower.

My phone rings as I pass it on the way to the bathroom and I answer on the first ring.

"Mr. Cannon?" It is Spencer Stans. Damn, I think. I wish I had just let it go to voicemail. "This is Spencer Stans." I guess he thinks I have a hundred people interested in my boat and cannot recognize his voice.

"I recognize your voice, Mr. Stans." I can't keep the disappointment out of mine.

"You can call me Spencer. After all, if all goes well, we will become very good friends."

"How may I help you, sir?" I hope he hears the impatience, of which I have plenty.

"I really apologize, but my client is getting very impatient and I was wondering if we could meet any earlier than ten o'clock tomorrow?" He pauses, giving me the time to think about his request.

I give it some thought and really don't have anything to do after seven o'clock tonight. I am guessing getting this meeting over sooner rather than later will be a good thing. "I have some time tonight after seven."

"Wow! That sounds great." Stans almost sounds like he is jumping up and down with excitement. "Where shall we meet? My office is in Houston, so we could meet at my hotel." Stans must have a habit of answering his own questions.

"That sounds fine to me. Where are you staying?"

"I am staying at the Palm Court Inn." There is a little hint of regret in his voice. "A friend of mine told me to stay here; however, it is a little dated."

The Palm Court Inn is the oldest and quaintest hotel in town. I am wondering how you can call an antique dated. "I will be there at quarter after seven or so. See you then." I leave it at that.

Stans thanks me and ends the call. I quickly get into the shower and relax under the hot water before turning it off, rubbing myself dry with a big towel, and getting dressed. I pick up my watch and put the leather band around my wrist. I have a few minutes to burn. I get dressed slowly and finish my beer. I go back to the kitchen and toss the bottle in the recyclables and put the glass in the dishwasher. Before I forget, I put another pilsner glass in the freezer. It is now time to go.

I arrive at The Surfside Towers parking lot and it occurs to me I don't know the number of the Starnes's room. "This is great." I mumble. I hit the recent call button on my phone. I see two local numbers and choose the older. The call goes to a non-descript voicemail message. I hang up. Just in case, I call the other number and get Stans again. I apologize and tell him I butt-dialed him. He laughs and ends the call.

I am not sure if the Surfside Towers has a front desk or not. Usually these condos do not. Most have a sitting room and community center on the first floor but no way to determine any resident room numbers. I park my car in a visitor's spot and go in the front door. Sure enough, there is no front desk. There is a phone sitting on a fashionable table which can be used to dial room numbers if you know the number to dial. I check and there is no information line. I pick up the handset and I see a small instruction sheet on the cradle that indicates the need to dial nine and the room number to be connected. I dial nine, thinking maybe there is an information connection. There is not. I also try zero and there is no connection either.

I replace the handset and look around. Across from a bank of mailboxes is a bulletin board encased in glass. I walk over and notice a note written in black ink on fine beige paper embossed with Surfside Towers at the top indicating the Starnes family, Joe and Emily, are renting Suite 301 for the next two weeks. Whoever wrote the note in excellent penmanship requests the residents make them feel welcome.

I walk back to the phone and pick it up. I dial 9301 and Joe picks up. I let him know that I will be right up.

It takes several minutes for the elevator to reach the lobby floor. There is a rather elderly woman in a wheelchair being pushed by a young nurse's aide. I hold the door and the old lady thanks me and the aid smiles. I get on and wait for the door to close before hitting the button.

The trip to the third floor seems to take forever. I imagine the management has slowed down the elevators in order not to scare anyone with a too fast ascent or descent. Finally, the little ding of the elevator chime marks my destination. I get off and notice a sign pointing to the left for Suites 300 and 301 and to the right for 302 and 303. I would not have guessed there are only four suites on each floor. I am a little more impressed with the Surfside Towers with this knowledge. I walk down the hall and notice Suite 300 is on the right and 301 on the left. This means suite 301 has a Gulf view and 300 the parking lot.

I approach the door and gently rap, not wanting to ring the bell in case they have a small dog. Joe opens the door and invites me inside and then leads me down a short hall that opens to the living room. The room is quite large and has floor-to-ceiling windows on the Gulf side. The view of the deep blue Gulf is expansive and has to be worth whatever the rent is on this place. Joe invites me to have a seat on the couch and he takes an armchair to my left. On the coffee table, which is uncomfortably close to my shins, sits some cut crystal decanters with little silver signs hanging from silver chains around their necks. I notice gin, vodka, and bourbon. There is also an ice bucket and some tall tumblers and some on-the-rocks glasses. They appear to be cut crystal as well.

"Would you like a drink?" I get the feeling he offers more out of hospitality then really wanting me to accept.

"No, thank you." I would like a gin and tonic but don't think it appropriate. "I need to drive to several places and would rather not."

He seems relieved and does not offer water or anything else. "My wife and I." He begins then he stops abruptly. He continues again on a different tact, "My wife is not feeling well and she won't be joining us. She has taken Gerry's murder very hard, and I need to take care that she doesn't get upset any more than necessary."

I nod with understanding and he continues.

"Gerry called me the night before she was murdered. She was very upset about one of her clients. She did not give me much information, but she did tell me that she was going to tell you the whole story since it involved your boat."

He pauses, watching for my reaction. My body language, namely my shaking head, is giving him the message she did not tell me anymore than she told him.

He needs to confirm, so there would be no mistake. "Did she tell you anything?"

"Well, she did mention her client at the very end of the evening. We were in a noisy bar and she said something I couldn't hear. When we got outside I was hit and don't know any more."

"So you have no idea what she was trying to say?"

"No and she sent me a letter complaining about a client, but unfortunately I did not have a chance to read it before she was killed. I have to assume she was trying to tell me about what was in the letter."

"What did the letter say?"

"Just that she was worried about one of her clients acting in bad faith. She said she was restricted as to what she could say and would try to talk the next time we met."

"So the next time was at the bar. Did you talk about the letter at all?"

"No. As I said, I never saw the letter until after Gerry—"

"And she never mentioned it?"

"No and I am sure had I read the letter before we met I would know more. I am really sorry for your loss and sorry I did not read it before Gerry and I met. Maybe I could have helped more."

"I am sorry as well." He now seems distracted. I can see a glint of moisture at the outside corner of his eye. He wipes it quickly away with his index finger as if he is merely tending to an itch. I'm not sure if it was a tear or not, but I am really sorry to be here. I don't seem to be rising to this old man's expectations.

He clears his throat. "I understand from the police that you were not conscious when my little girl was shot."

"Yes, that is true. When we were approached someone hit me from behind." I sound too glad to get off the fact that I did not know too much and now want to tell more. I decide to shut up.

"The police also told me the gun was under you." He is sounding like a district attorney.

I am starting to get really uncomfortable. "I think these are discussions for the police to have and not for you and me to go over." I sound very defensive, and I can't seem to generate any corresponding sounds of confidence.

He does not react to my caution and continues very coldly, "I am trying to understand why my daughter put her faith in you when it is obvious that you couldn't or wouldn't help her."

We look at each other for what seems to me like an hour.

I break the impasse, "It appears you think what happened to Gerry is somehow my fault." I try to keep my inner rage out of my voice. "I really don't understand why you would have me come to your place just so you can accuse me of something that is not my fault."

"You seem to be wrapped up in defending the fact that you should not be blamed for what happened. Makes me wonder." He is good at maintaining his coldness.

"Wonder about what?" I am not really trying to hide my anger.

"I wonder why Gerry told me on the call if anything happened to her I should contact you with a message." His statement hits me like a hammer. "I also wonder if in fact you know more than you are telling. I wonder if you are guiltier than you think or even know you are." He finally wraps up with, "And finally, I wonder if I should give you the message." He sits back in his chair and seems like he has vented everything he brought me here to cover.

I don't really know what to tell him. I guess if my daughter had been killed in the company of someone I would expect someone to know something. I can't imagine why Gerry would think something was going to happen to her. This sounds so much like a B movie plot that I need to make sure I haven't fallen asleep somewhere. I know I am awake, but this scene seems so unreal.

With a sincere look on my face I use logic. "If Gerry wanted me to have a message I think you should let me know what it is if only because it was her wish." I see his shoulders slump and I know he agrees with me.

"Okay," he whispers. "Here is the message as clearly as I can remember. Gerry said that you should not sell your boat."

"I should not sell my boat?" I am amazed. "Gerry wanted me to sell my boat and was making arrangements." I know full well this old man won't be able to add any reasons or more information, but I had to point out the fact to him.

"That is what she said." His statement was as if I was expecting him to speak rather than giving me anymore information.

I thank him for the message and ask if there is anything else I can answer for him.

"How well did you know Gerry?"

It takes me a moment to think of what to tell him since Gerry and I had only met maybe ten times. During those times I found her to have a great sense of humor and a real dedication to serving her clients well. She was knowledgeable about boats and seemed to be respected by the male members of Premier Yachts. I know she could negotiate a good deal since that's what she did for me. I don't know if she had a boyfriend since she never talked about her personal life.

She was very good looking with brown hair and hazel eyes and a petite stature which made you feel like you were her older brother. She wore little make-up and what she did wear looked totally natural. Gerry was at home in a pair of shorts, or dressed up to go out, and always seemed to be smiling.

I only saw her look concerned one time and that was the night she was killed. I never saw her drunk although she could certainly throw back a drink with the best of them. I considered Gerry to be a friend and someone who I could trust to do a good job. I never had what would be termed a personal relationship with her. We were always glad to have an opportunity to talk.

I am sorry now I did not take more time to be with her since it seems like we just met and she was gone. I decide to tell him all those things I knew about Gerry.

"She was a very competent sales person. She made you feel like you were in really good hands. I know she was well respected by the team at Premier Yachts. She had a number of friends and I know anyone who met Gerry liked her immediately. She was very helpful to me in finding my boat and at a good price."

He thinks for a moment and then says, "I can't understand why she was not seeing anyone."

"Well I can say we all cared for her and she seemed happy." He finally seems satisfied and rises, which is my cue to get up as well. He walks me to the door. We shake hands, and I leave with the feeling that I certainly did not know any more about Gerry's parents than when I arrived.

I now have to turn my attention to Spenser Stans. I am thinking about Gerry's message as I exit the elevator and head out the front door.

She must have been thinking about Stans when she gave her father the message. While in thought I fail to register the significance of the large black SUV pulling up in front of the Towers in such a way to block my path to the parking lot.

The rear door opens and a fairly large man dressed like a banker in a too-small suit gets out, and another sizeable man dressed in the same way exits the passenger side of the machine. "Mr. Cannon." The big guy calls my name as he begins moving toward me, closing the gap between us. He is reaching inside his jacket, and I am now thinking this could be real trouble. Unfortunately, I take no evasive maneuver and remain cemented to the spot. The trouble is going to come right up and smack me in the face, and I am powerless to do anything about it.

The big man extends his arm, holding out a badge. "Mr. Cannon I am agent Jenkins FBI, may we talk to you please?" I am relieved that he did not pull out a gun. I don't know what to think about the FBI being here. The other big guy stays by the SUV, and I now see there are two others inside as well. There is the driver and another person in the back. The man in the back looks to be a little smaller than these two behemoths that have their attentive eyes on me.

My experience with the law tells me there is something really wrong when the FBI gets involved. I cannot imagine what there would be about Gerry's murder that would be under FBI jurisdiction. It must be that Gerry's murder has some multiple state aspects which have triggered an investigation. I am assuming an investigation but should probably see what these guys want before I make any conclusions. I manage a look of lawyerly bravado as I raise a question, "What is this about?"

The man closest to me, who I think said he was agent Jenkins, speaks, "This is a matter of national security and we would like to discuss how we think you can help Uncle Sam." He further explains they want to take me to a more private spot and give me the full explanation. He promises it will not take any longer than an hour.

"Agent Jenkins, right? I have a meeting with a man named Spencer Stans in fifteen minutes about buying my boat." I offer this as a matter of fact and maybe more to see if I can put off the meeting with Stans.

"Yes that is correct, Agent Jenkins, Walter Jenkins. We know about the meeting, and if you could give him a call and reschedule it would be greatly appreciated." Jenkins talks with a very refined manner which leads me to believe he has graduated from a very good school.

"I'm not sure I can come up with an excuse that sounds logical." I offer this as an opening to a suggestion from the agent. I really don't think it is a good idea to be telling obvious lies in front of the FBI.

"Tell him you have been taken into custody by an agent of the San Antonio section of the FBI."

I look at Jenkins and must have appeared very surprised as he breaks into a wide smile.

"Am I in custody?" There is a degree of shakiness in my voice.

"Makes a good story." He raises an eyebrow.

I pull out my phone and dial Stans; he picks up on one ring. I let him know I am delayed and wonder if we could keep our original appointment. To my surprise, he does not ask for reasons so there is no need to let him know anything about the FBI. Good thing, I am thinking. I will let these guys know something funny is going on, and Stans may be at the heart of it. The less he knows the better.

I shut off the phone. "All set."

Chapter Seven

Jenkins leads me over to the SUV. The guy on the passenger side nods as Jenkins opens the back door. He motions for me to get in. I climb in and move to the middle of the rear seat.

"My name is Agent Winther." The man in the backseat is talking as he extends his hand.

"I'm John Cannon." I do not catch myself in time. Of course he knows who I am and now I feel foolish. I give him a four finger grip and let go.

"Very nice to meet you." He is wearing a serious gray suit, white shirt, and conservative tie. I always notice a person's shoes, and since Winther is sitting with his legs crossed I get a good look at his shoes. Winther is wearing an immaculately shined pair of cap-toe oxfords. They look expensive.

The big guy Jenkins gets in next to me and the other one gets in the front.

Winther continues, "The agent driving is Hanson, and the one riding shotgun upfront is Weller. The big boy next to you is Jenkins and I think you two have met."

"Hello." Sounds weak, and it is all I have.

I am guessing Winther is the boss. These guys are not very talkative, so I more or less lean back and go along for the ride. I can't help but notice the SUV has some special radios and equipment. There is a rifle in a rack between the two front seats. I also notice several ammunition clips attached to the rifle with what I figure to be Velcro.

I finally decide to speak up. "Where are we going?"

"We are going to a secure spot since we need to give you some important information. We are working with the local Chief, Ned Tranes, on a very confidential matter."

"Do you know about the Gerry Starnes murder?" I interject the question at the mention of Ned's name.

"Yes," Winther responds. "We think it is a small part of some of the activity we have been observing for some time."

"Small part?" I try not to seem astonished and fail miserably. "She was killed and nobody seems to know why."

"We are aware of the situation, and although the murder of Miss Starnes is regrettable there is more going on than one person being murdered. We think many more are in danger, and that's why we need to talk. The chief will be present as well. We need to give you a complete briefing and then we have a favor we need."

"Favor? What kind of favor?"

"Why don't we wait for the briefing and then you will have the whole story. You can then decide if you want to help us or not."

"Do I have a choice?"

Winther laughs as a way to relive my tension. "We all have choices, Mr. Cannon, we all have choices."

I don't feel very good about his answer. I look ahead toward the front of the SUV and I'm beginning to become concerned about a situation which could get out of control. I am compelled to inquire and know my question is like a chicken asking the fox if there is anything to fear.

"You guys are the good guys, right?"

There is an uncomfortable silence as there is no answer from any of them.

Winther finally speaks up. "Yes, John, we are the good guys. Any more questions can wait until we get to the safe house. You okay with that?"

I nod my head, "Will I have the option to walk away if the information does not make sense to me?"

Winther tells me I can walk with no questions. His response seems pretty fair to me. But of course, riding along in a car with four guys who look like they could play on either the good or bad guy team makes fairness a moot point. These guys could do anything they wanted with me and no one would know any differently. This train of thought makes me glad we were going to meet Ned. I decide to sit back, shut up, and keep my eyes on the rifle between the two up front. No other conversation takes place until we pull up in front of what appears to be a large warehouse.

"Is this it?" I can't hide my concern. "I thought we were going to the police headquarters since you said we were going to meet Chief Tranes."

"I know it looks pretty rough, once inside I think you will feel better. Come on, we need to meet Chief Tranes inside."

Agent Jenkins opens his door and reminds me of a chauffeur as I slide over the seat and out. I fully expect him to offer his hand to assist, but he does not. Once out of the SUV we all enter the warehouse more or less in single file since the door is only big enough for one person at a time. The door is a little one which is part of a larger door on rollers so it can slide open. It is clear this building was never meant to be an office or a safe house. Winther leads us through a small anteroom with an intercom on the wall next to another door. This door seems like it is part of an office. It has a degree of quality you would not expect to find in a warehouse. There is no indication on the door as to what could be inside.

Winther pushes a button and a digital-sounding voice answers, "Yes, may I help you?"

"Agent Winther with Agent Jenkins, Agent Weller, and a guest." He waits for a response. "Did you get that?" He has an air of impatience.

"Yes, sir," the digital voice responds. "My apologies, we are just checking your clearance. Would you be kind enough to give me your date of birth and your mother's maiden name?"

Winther does not seem bothered and turns to me to indicate this inquiry is standard procedure. He provides the information, and each agent does so as well. After a few seconds, a loud buzz coming from the door indicates it has been unlocked. Winther pushes on door and holds it for the rest of us to enter.

We enter a large room which must serve as a welcome center. There are a number of upholstered chairs, two couches, and enough magazines to open a store. Winther walks to a highly polished library table on the far wall and picks up the phone. He asks whoever answers if the chief has arrived.

He frowns. "Please give him a call and see how long he will be," he orders. Winther drops the handset in the cradle.

Winther explains the chief has been delayed and tells the group someone is on their way to lead us to a room. As he finishes his explanation, a young man dressed in a similar fashion to the other agents comes through a door and requests we follow him.

We all move down the hall following the young man. There are two rooms opening to the hall. The first has a plaque with the label "Interrogation Room A." The door is closed, and no sounds can be heard. The light is on, so there could be someone in there. The next room is labeled "Interrogation Room B." The door is open and the lights are off. The young man reaches in to the right side of the door and hits the lights. The lights are fluorescent, and when they pop on, the effect is like a flashbulb in the night, only more permanent.

The walls are covered in a sound proof material and have the look of randomly patterned dark cones. There is a large mirror at one end, and anyone who has seen a cop show knows it's a one-way mirror which allows the observation of activities in the room while maintaining a cloak of secrecy. There is a massive oak table looking like it was moved in from the library, and several straight-backed gray metal chairs with gray vinyl cushions.

Winther suggests we all have a seat and make ourselves comfortable while we wait for Chief Tranes. Winther takes a seat opposite me; Jenkins and Weller sit on either side. There is a chair next to Winther that I assume it is for Ned.

It does not take long for Ned to come into the room.

"Please excuse me for the delay, but my meeting ran a little late." He picks up the chair next to Winther and moves it to the far end of the table.

He does not acknowledge me in any way, and seems a little uncomfortable. He is wearing his sunglasses, which I think is a little unusual. It could be that police officers are not comfortable without their sunglasses. When I look at him directly, he puts his head down and appears to be studying a file in his lap. Rude son of a bitch, I am thinking as Winther stands up.

Winther clears his throat. "Well, I think we can begin. Could someone get the door?"

Big guy, Jenkins, jumps up and closes the door. Winther thanks him and lays the ground rules for the discussion which will take place. He addresses everyone and cautions that nothing discussed in this room is to leave the room. He lets us know there will be no notes, recordings, or record of this meeting other than what each of us can remember. He orders Jenkins to double check the sound system to ensure that it is disabled. Jenkins gets up and goes out the door. He comes back a few minutes later and tells Winther in a low voice the recording system is off and the sound room locked. He holds up the keys for good measure. Winther seems satisfied the appropriate security matters have been accommodated.

Winther looks right at me. "I have been authorized to provide some sensitive information that will be useful should you wish to help us eliminate a risk to the US National Security."

My scalp tingles. Up until this point, I was not sure of the nature of what Winther was going to tell me. A matter of national security causes me to think of 9/11, and the possibility of a threat to US citizens in catastrophic proportions.

Winther continues, "The bureau in conjunction with the Department of Homeland Security has uncovered a plot to attack some of the principal attractions along various waterways in the US. These attractions are primarily World War II ships which have been retired. Most are aircraft carriers, and we believe the *Battleship Missouri* is at risk as well. The group of terrorists responsible has been identified as a splinter group of Al Qaeda. They believe the way to disrupt the American devil is to disrupt the revered memorials to a past glory of American military success. Al Qaeda leadership believes these guys are misguided and represent a significant risk to the movement totally. They think the effort will not deliver the desired results and will not be effective.

The Al Qaeda leadership has made it very clear to this group that they cannot count on support. We also know they have been forbidden to contact Al Qaeda and to use any of Al Qaeda's resources to claim credit for their deeds. In short, they have been shunned by the main group. This does not mean that they are any less of a threat; it's just that they are on their own and in some measure this makes them a little more desperate and dangerous. The local target, here in Texas, is the aircraft carrier *Lexington* which is moored in Corpus Christi."

I am immediately shocked to full attention. The *Lexington* is a ship which has personal meaning to me. My parents have told me the story of my grandfather's service in the Navy, since I never had a chance to meet him. When I was a kid in Indiana, my dad would pull out the old pictures and the medals and tell me about his father. He would always start with the fact his dad died when he was a ten year old boy in 1951. My dad was sure it was because of the war and I know he missed having a father since he would inevitably seem to have tears in his eyes telling me how it was growing up without a dad. My mom would always change the subject as a way to deflect the emotion which was still very strong. Today the two of them still live in Indiana and as far as I know, still revere my grandpa's service.

My grandfather, who I was named after, served on the *Lexington* as an air group navigator for the dive-bomber squadron of Carrier Air Group Nine. He was actually on the boat when it was struck by a Japanese airplane in a suicide attempt to sink the *Lexington*. He also participated in bombing activities in support of the invasion of Iwo Jima and Okinawa and strikes on the homeland of Japan as well. The *Lexington* was one of two ships to which the Carrier Air Group Nine was assigned to complete combat missions. I now had a personal link to the briefing. To destroy the *Lexington* would be to wipe out a memorial to the time my grandpa spent on it.

Winther has stopped talking for a moment to see if there are any questions so far.

I really don't have a question about what he has covered since it all sounds like a plot for a movie which has yet to be produced. I raise my hand a little timidly.

"Yes, John."

"I don't have a question about what you have covered. I just don't understand what all this has to do with me other than my grandfather served on the *Lexington*. I also want to know some information about Gerry's murder."

Winther's eyebrows drop into a frown. His answer is a non-answer. "We will get to all of that. In the meantime, are there any other questions?" No one speaks.

Winther looks at each of us and decides to continue since no one has a question. "We have been able to identify the group's objective. We have not figured out any specific member names. We believe there are about twenty- to- twenty-five members, and we also know they have a lot of money provided by an unknown financial backer. Some international voice traffic has been picked up and we have isolated the group's name. They call themselves the Desert Wolves. Some intel leads us to believe they recognize themselves as a united organization and with the added danger of being fundamentally independent operators. We don't think the individuals have a complete picture of the entire group and only are aware of their contacts and handlers. The good news is we don't believe all of them are in the US at once. We think some are still in the training phase of their operation."

Winther takes a small break and tells Jenkins he needs some water. The big guy crosses the room to a phone hanging on the wall. He barks into the handset that the team needs some sodas and water. He more or less drops the phone into the cradle while muttering about having to do everything himself.

"We do not have a very precise timetable of attack, but believe the latest communications among Desert Wolf members have pinpointed the first to be the *Lexington*. We have a general idea on how they intend to carry out the attack. We believe they intend to use an innocent-looking boat to get close to the hull of the *Lexington* and then set off some kind of explosive much like that used on the *USS Cole*. The difference between the attack on the *Lexington* and the attack on the *Cole* is the *Lexington* is a sitting duck with no defensive capabilities at all. One of our critical mission elements is to precisely pinpoint when the attack will take place. If we can get the timing right, we can staff the *Lexington* with Navy Seals and provide a warm welcome to whoever shows up in a boat which we will have already identified as the so called innocent participant."

Winther smiles at the verbal picture of getting the drop on a bunch of terrorists which he just created. He is about to continue when another member of the unit enters the room carrying a tray full of sodas and water as well a bucket of ice. He places the tray on the large table. Winther suggests we take a five-minute break so he can get some water. We all go to the tray and help ourselves.

There is very little conversation since this meeting has taken on a pretty serious tone. I can't help thinking the so called innocent-looking boat that Winther mentioned is sitting in my slip and is named *My GRL*. My mind is racing. I am wondering why Gerry wanted me to sell my boat and then send the message not to do it. I am also wondering if she somehow crossed paths with the Desert Wolves and paid with her life. Did Ned conduct an investigation and then call the FBI, or did the FBI contact him? These thoughts will need to wait until this briefing is finished. It may be the information will cover all the bases. If not, I am going to get some questions answered come hell or high water.

I notice Ned seems to be avoiding me. He stays as far as he can. I would think it my imagination had I not tried to go over and speak to him. He moves toward Winther with a contrived appearance of wanting to speak to him. I sit down and write off the fact Ned does not want me engaging in conversation. It must rankle him to know that he originally thought me guilty and now I am being prepped as if I am a member of the FBI team. I go back to my chair deciding not to try to talk to Ned again.

Winther clears his throat and indicating it is time to resume. We all turn our full attention to him.

"Now," he begins, "I would like to discuss the unfortunate matter of the Gerry Starnes' murder."

I look down at the mention of Gerry's name and have a hard time maintaining eye contact with Winther. He is definitely locked on to me, and it is hard not to look away. I look away several times and every time I look back at him he is still staring at me. I am getting very nervous.

"Mr. Cannon." He is pointing at me, "is the target of a plan to use his boat, I believe named *My GRL*, to get close to the *Lexington*." I squirm in my chair. "He has no knowledge of this plan, and until this moment he really did not know a plan was created requiring his cooperation."

Winther looks at me with some degree of sympathy in his expression. He continues, "We believe that Gerry was coerced into cooperating with the Desert Wolves. She was John's original broker. We think it was her job to get John to sell his boat to them. They are using a cover, but in the end they want complete control of *My GRL*. They believe that this beautiful boat could cruise into Corpus Christi Bay and almost dock next to the *Lexington* with no alarms being raised."

I raise my hand and without being called upon, "What makes you think she was coerced?"

Winther actually seems to appreciate the question. "Good question." He is not providing a compliment, but uses my question as an opportunity to discuss the M.E. findings. "The autopsy found some strange marks on Gerry's body. Most of the marks were post mortem. Uh, that is after death, for our non-law enforcement friend.

Our conclusion is that someone ripped what we believe to be a wire from her leaving marks resembling rope burns. The burns were marks made by the wire as it was pulled quickly across her skin."

"She also had a mark on her rib that could have been caused by a transmitter caught between her and the cement when she fell. In short, we believe the Desert Wolves controlled Gerry by hooking her up to a transmitter with specific instructions on what to say and do. The transmitter would keep her from discussing anything to anyone without their knowledge. You will recall she tried to tell something to you about her client."

I nod slowly and I am way ahead of Winther. Gerry tried to warn me about her client. These guys heard her and immediately killed her.

Winther continues, "When she said something to you, we believe these guys heard her. We are not sure if this is the reason she was killed. It seems to make sense. Of course, this one incident doesn't seem to warrant killing her. Also, we have been racking our brains with the lack of logic in killing someone who was going to deliver *My GRL*." He stops and takes a long drink from his water bottle.

I speak up. "At least we know she was not helping them of her own free will."

Winther confirms and adds a caveat. "I also think she wasn't operating with free will. We can't be certain for sure, but I believe she was under the control of the Desert Wolves. Whoever killed her felt she was a threat. I am really not sure why the Desert Wolves felt so threatened. We also have been picking up some air traffic from Al Qaeda leadership expressing concern over the antics of the Desert Wolves. So, the fact is Gerry was wearing a wire. Who put it on her is still an unanswered question."

I add one more thing. "It does look like she wanted to blow the whistle on whoever it was."

Winter agrees. "You might also want to consider this; if you had engaged in any discussion on the matter with Gerry in all likelihood you would be dead as well."

I take a deep breath. I have no response to his comment. I do add, "Her father delivered a message to me not to sell my boat."

Winther does not look surprised. "We figured he would deliver some kind of message from Gerry. The chief talked to him yesterday, and Gerry's dad told him he had a message from Gerry and could only deliver it to you. He called the chief to let him know when you were going to meet with him. This is how we knew where to find you and pick you up."

I am now making a vow to shut the hell up.

Winther decides to change the subject. "I think it is time to discuss the path forward since we have just about exhausted the information we know about Gerry's murder. The way she died was a classic professional hit—a small caliber revolver, hard to trace, and a well-placed shot. The revolver found under John Cannon was a touch of the theatrical and, in itself, serves as a warning."

"What warning would that be?"

"These guys let us know that they could have easily killed you, John, but wanted to taunt us a bit. They left the weapon behind knowing it could not be traced. They did not just drop it on the concrete; they took the time to roll you over and place it under you. This was the equivalent of tucking you in bed. You could look upon this move as a bit of professional killer humor."

"Not very funny." Everyone chuckles at my understatement.

"One thing certain is we need to somehow consummate the deal on John's boat. Without the boat it will be very difficult to track these guys. Since we know John's boat, we won't have to hunt for another one among the hundreds that could be traveling into Corpus Christi Bay on any given Saturday. So I have to put it to you directly, John, are you willing to continue the charade of pretending to sell your boat?"

They all wait for my response. "I apologize but I have a question before I answer." Winther is a man of great patience. He gives me a go-ahead signal with his fingers, a kind of "come out with it" sign indicating I should proceed.

"Let's assume the deal goes through and these guys own my boat. Let's also assume that when the day comes for the Navy Seals to go into action there are shots fired. What happens to my boat?"

"We would try to do everything to get these guys to give up peaceably. You are right in wondering what happens if shots are fired. My answer has to be that the US government will do all it can to see that your boat is returned to you in as fine a condition as possible."

"I hope you don't think of me as too petty and even though I have only had her a month, that's my pride and joy. I really don't want to sell her and I would like to help out." I have already made up my mind to cooperate and am looking for some assurance that people will try to be careful.

Winther, ever the paragon of patience, lets me know, "No one can blame you for wanting to keep your boat safe. I think it is really great that in spite of your concern you are willing to go through with the sale."

"Is it really a sale, or are we just putting together a ruse to catch these guys?" I express my other concern.

"To these guys it will look like a sale. We will create parallel documents that will be filed in court explaining the sale is really a means to stop illegal activity and therefore null and void." He also adds, "We intend to confiscate the money paid and will use these funds to repair any damage to your boat."

I am satisfied Winther will do all he can. "Sounds good. Count me in."

Ned and Winther seemed pleased I am on board. The two other guys have not changed expressions since the meeting started and continue to keep any thoughts or feelings hidden from their faces. Winther takes another hour or so to outline a rough plan where I meet with Spencer Stans and work out some kind of deal on the boat. Once finished with the deal, Stans will wire the money to my account or give me a cashier's check. Once I get the money, I will wire it to a federal account so that the chain of possession is not broken on the evidence. He gives me a three-by-five index card with the wiring instructions. Winther wonders if I would be willing to wear a transmitter so agents could monitor what was going on in case there was any trouble. I look at Ned to see if he has any advice and quickly see I am on my own.

I give it some thought and express my opinion that, if caught with a wire the consequences could be much worse than simply "caught misrepresenting the deal". Winther agrees and tells me a couple of agents will keep me under observation in case I need help. He also cautions me not to try to contact him using my home or cell phone. He explains the monitoring of conversations on those devices is really easy. He hands me a disposable cell phone and tells me not to turn it on unless I absolutely have to reach him. Winther mentions as a final thought his private number is programmed in the phone.

The meeting is finally coming to a close. It is now past ten p.m. and I have not had anything to eat since lunch and feel like I have been under undue stress. I am certainly glad I cancelled the meeting with Stans as opposed to putting it off until I was free tonight. My neck is sore from the tension. I shake Winther's hand and he indicates that the two big guys will take me back to Surfside Towers. I tell him I am grateful for the opportunity. I don't think he believes me. I turn to Ned and extend my hand, which he reluctantly takes and has a very weak grip. We shake one of those limp handshakes, which make you regret the offer to shake in the first place.

"I guess I am no longer a suspect, huh chief?" I gloat as we disconnect the limp fest.

To my surprise, Ned responds without any emotion or indication that he is attempting humor, "You never were."

With that, Winther grabs Ned and pulls him away for a private moment. Ned and Winther leave, presumably to Ned's office. I am left standing alone with the thought Ned is either pulling my leg or he has forgotten our previous encounters.

Maybe he is having an off day, is my final thought. I need to get rid of the strange feeling I have, concluding Ned is not himself for some reason. The off-day excuse will have to do.

"You ready?" Big guy Jenkins finally speaks.

"Am I ever." I reply with an element of tiredness in my voice.

Chapter Eight

The alarm blares at 8:30 a.m., pulling me from a deep sleep. I usually wake up without an alarm. I set one last night since I did not want to take any chances of oversleeping and being late for my meeting with Spencer Stans. I feel a surge of excitement at the thought of my new information and feel, in a small way, that I will be able to get some justice for Gerry using *My GRL* as bait. I am hoping Stans will be on board when the Seals repel down the deck from the hovering Black Hawks above. I have not met him yet and I already hate him. He will be the face of evil, and I will help the authorities bring him to justice. It would be nice if he tried to make a run for it and was cut down in a hail of 9mm mosquitoes.

The phone interrupts my daydream and I answer it without looking to see who is calling. It is Stans confirming our appointment today. It is really spooky that he calls when I am wishing him no good. He tells me he would like to meet me on the patio where we can talk freely. He also offers coffee and breakfast if I have not had any yet. I thank him and tell him coffee would be nice and end the call. I have no intention in breaking bread with this greasy worm.

I have a bowl of cereal after my shower and decide to wear a polo shirt and khaki slacks. I put on my boat shoes in case we need to go on board *My GRL*. I glance at the phone Winther gave me and decide I better take it as well. I put the bowl and spoon in the dishwasher and stick my iPhone and the disposable phone given to me by Winther in each pocket. At the last minute, I grab a jacket from the closet, turn on the alarm system, and close the front door. I have a two car garage and still park the FJ on the driveway which circles in front of the house. It seems like pulling in the garage is extra work, not to mention the extra steps from the garage to my bedroom. The FJ is old and does not seem to age as it sits outside.

I put the key in the ignition and turn it to start, but nothing happens. After a look under the hood, I diagnose the problem as the gear on the starter which attaches to the flywheel has somehow gotten stuck in a position that won't allow it to turn over. I go around to the driver's side and put the FJ in reverse. I gently rock the Land Cruiser in an effort to free the gear. I get back in and turn the key. I smile big as the starter gives out with the familiar sound of turning the motor over. I rush to close the hood and re-deploy the latches. I get back in and I'm ready to go.

"How long am I going to put up with this kind of shit?" The answer is all too clear: "For as long as I own this beautiful piece of junk." I smile as I head to the Palm Court Inn.

It only takes about five minutes to get to the parking lot. I park the FJ and use the emergency brake instead of just putting it in reverse. I figure this will keep the gear from getting bound up again. It will be a much cheaper fix than replacing the flywheel, which I am sure, has some kind of warp or high spot on it. Not bad mechanics for a person who used to let everyone else fix his stuff, I think.

I head into the side yard of the Palm Court Inn through a gate with a sign that reads "Guests only." I love the Palm Court Inn. It was one of the first hotels in Port Aransas and has had some notable guests in the past. Ernest Hemmingway stayed here as did President Franklin Roosevelt. The hotel has not changed much. It's only two floors and resembles a bunch of row homes since all the rooms are laid out end to end. There is no internal hallway but a nice veranda and two porch chairs for each room facing the street. When you stay overnight, you get two keys: one for the front door on the street side and one for the door on the courtyard side.

The patio has cloth-covered tables and what could pass for pretty deluxe dining room chairs. They are, in actuality, folding chairs made to be used outside. Each table has a little centerpiece of real flowers and a hurricane lamp with a candle. I am sure the romance level goes into overdrive at night with all the candles lit. There are large round terra cotta planters strategically placed throughout the space. The effect is to define separate areas and give the appearance of a large room with intimate, smaller conversation, friendly divisions. Lights are strung between the oversized palm trees, which at night would complete the illusion of a grand room. I make a mental note to come here for dinner.

I see a single diner sitting at a table far across the patio. He has the look of someone who would be named Spencer. He is wearing a white polo shirt under a white tennis sweater and has what appear to be white tennis shorts on as well. He is way too formal looking for the island and, with the heat; the sweater will kill him before noon. His hair is blond and combed in a style reminiscent of pictures of croquet players taken in the summer on Rhode Island in the twenties. His nose has a sharp angle which seems to be about forty five degrees when viewed from the side. As I get closer I notice he is wearing glasses with turtle shell rims and he seems to be interested in me so I continue to approach him. "Spencer Stans?" He gets up and puts out his hand.

"Indeed I am . . . it is very nice meeting you, Mr. Cannon."

We shake hands and I let him know he can call me John. He bids me to sit in a spot directly across from him. I move around the table, pull out the chair, and sit.

He begins the conversation with some small talk about how beautiful the hotel grounds look and makes an observation that the atmosphere must be really great at night. He invites me to order breakfast and I thank him and settle for coffee. He motions to the waiter who walks over. Stans orders two coffees and again gives me the opportunity to change my mind if I want anything else. I decline and he explains the fact he got in quite late last night and did not have any dinner.

He orders two eggs over medium, bacon, hash browns, and rye toast with butter on the side. I can't stop the feeling of a waterfall starting in my mouth. This would be the kind of breakfast I would order if I were not so stubborn. I take a big drink of water and fight the urge to renege on my principle. The waiter leaves, and Stans reaches down and pulls a file from a briefcase sitting next to his chair on the patio floor.

"Let's begin, shall we?"

"I am ready." I respond to him quickly so we can get this thing over with. I want to set the trap which will hopefully cause Stans and all his murderous cohorts to regret their actions.

"Great." He seems to be full of enthusiasm for his task. "I hope I do not appear too forward in wanting to conclude this deal."

I want to tell him he is too forward, but he continues without waiting for a response.

"So here is the offer." He hands me a folded piece of paper.

I unfold it and see his name engraved on the top. He has written the figure eight- hundred- thousand dollars in longhand and below it three points. Point one: Close within five days; Point two: Includes all equipment, fuel, and licenses currently on board or in effect; Point three: Payable in cash upon delivery of the craft.

"What would you like me to do with this?" The question is sincere since I am really not sure of the next move.

He laughs and is about to answer when the waiter arrives with his breakfast and our coffee. He gives me a look I immediately take as a warning not to talk about the deal while the waiter is near. I fold the paper and busy myself with making sure the cream and Sweet & Low are near my position. The waiter finishes and leaves. I am pouring a steaming cup of Columbian from a silver pot as Stans looks around and leans forward. He is finally comfortable that we are alone again and speaks as if no time has elapsed since my question.

"You need to let me know if the offer is acceptable or not. If it is acceptable, then we can find a notary and sign the documents. If not, then you need to let me know what would be acceptable."

I take a sip of the hot coffee and it is every bit as delicious as it smells. After swallowing the nectar, I begin my negotiation, "First of all, I don't have my broker to advise me, and so I am not sure how much *My GRL* is really worth. Secondly, I really have not made up my mind if I want to sell *My GRL*. Finally, I do not understand the rush in the process."

Stans seems a little confused and raises his eyebrow when I mention not having made the decision to sell. It is very clear now Gerry led him to believe the sale was a non-issue. He recovers very nicely indicating all my concerns are legitimate and offers to answer each in turn.

"My clients have been looking for a boat like yours for quite a while. As I indicated on the phone, they are anxious to begin enjoying your boat—"

"*My GRL*." I interject her name because I'm tired of hearing a third party label on a loved one.

"What? Oh yes, *My GRL*." He did not catch my sarcasm.

He moves to the next point without waiting to see if he has answered my objection. "As to your point about not knowing the value of your boat." He does not mention the fact my broker is dead. "I ran the blue book analysis past Gerry Starnes. She agreed that the price was a fair one."

Now I am totally pissed off. He used Gerry to vouch for his offer knowing full well she is not here to provide a contrary opinion if in fact he was taking liberties with the truth.

"Did Gerry give you anything in writing as to her belief that the eight-hundred- thousand was a fair offer?" I am now pissed but try to hide it.

He smiles and reaches into his case again, bringing a different file to the table. He pulls another piece of paper out of this file and hands it to me with two fingers. "I think you will find this helpful." I don't detect any malice in his intent.

It is a copy of an e-mail from Gerry to Stans. It is dated one day before Gerry was murdered. The e-mail details that she is in receipt of the offer from Stans and has researched it. She agrees the eight-hundred- thousand seems fair and did add she needed to discuss the offer with me before a final commitment.

I look up at Stans; he is spreading a piece of toast with strawberry jam and stops when I look at him. I try to keep the drama to a dull roar. "She never did talk to me."

Stans takes a bite of his toast. "I didn't know she did not get your authorization to accept."

Drama still under control, I put to Stans, "Are you telling me she accepted this offer?"

Stans holds his toast between his front teeth and hands me another piece of paper from the file. It is another copy of an e-mail from Gerry to Stans, and she does indeed tell him the offer is acceptable.

I am fighting to remain calm. "I don't know what to do with this," I say coolly. "There have been no papers signed, and as far as I am concerned Gerry did not have the authority to accept an offer."

Stans shakes his head in agreement. "I am totally in agreement with you. This is why I wanted to meet with you so that we could work this out. I, of course, told my clients that it was a done deal and had to go back and tell them Gerry was operating without authorization. This is also why the deal seems rushed. My clients were not happy. I am in a very bad position here, as you can imagine."

Knowing who Stan's clients are does not conjure up any sympathy inside me. "Go back and tell them that the deal can be done for nine-hundred-thousand dollars."

Stans sits back without speaking. He appears to be weighing his options and wants to think of the right thing. He finally speaks, "I think this will be agreeable." He stops talking and again seems to be thinking of the next words. He proceeds with deliberate care, "Don't take this the wrong way, but if I agree to nine-hundred-thousand you need to be okay with the sale."

"I believe *My GRL* is worth over a million and want to make certain I can replace her. I will sell at nine-hundred-thousand since I am sure I could do that. At eight- hundred-thousand I am not so sure."

Stans seems satisfied I am not acting emotionally and offers another cup of coffee while he contacts his clients. I agree and he slips away from the table to place the call on his cellphone in private. While he is gone, I think about what possessed Gerry to take it upon herself to try and do this alone. If she had come to me and explained that some guys intended to use *My GRL* for a terrorist act, she and I could have gone to the authorities and we might have ended up in the same place without her losing her life.

I finish my second cup of coffee. The waiter stops by and collects Stans' plate and asks if I would like more coffee. I assure him, I am high on Columbian and should stop. He smiles and retires to get the check. Stans comes back and instead of sitting he offers me his hand.

"My clients are very pleased to accept your offer," He has a degree of self-congratulatory tone in his voice.

I take his hand and give him a very firm handshake. He frowns slightly and I release. "Thank you, Mr. Stans." I decide to lay it on thick. "I don't think the deal would have been done without your help."

He seems very pleased about closing the deal. He suggests we go to the local real estate office named Sundown to complete the paperwork. "It is on 361 and they have a notary there. I will have the contracts drawn up, and once you receive the funds we can sign. Do you think you can find it?"

"Yeah I know where it is. When do you think the funds will be available?"

"If the price was eight-hundred-thousand, I could hand you the money right now. Since we need to add some funds it will take a day at the most."

"That sounds good. So we should probably stay in touch until you get the money. Once you have it we can meet at the Sundown real estate office and finalize."

The waiter returns with the check, and Stans pays the bill. We shake hands again, and I wish him a pleasant stay at the Palm Court Inn. He wishes me a good day as well.

I leave him on the patio and head back to the FJ through the little gate on the side. I feel pretty good about getting another hundred-thousand out of the sons of bitches. Too bad the IRS can't figure out how to give me a credit. Well, I don't know if they can, and I'm not going to bother them with it. I guess I will just chalk it up as doing my duty to God and country.

As I get into the FJ I remember Ned wanted me to contact him after the Stans meeting. Of course that was before the FBI got involved. I think he won't need to be consulted since he knows I am going to sell My GRL to the Desert Wolves. I see no need to bother Ned. Besides, he seemed to be a different person last night. "A pretty grumpy guy," I tell the FJ. No answer from the FJ other than the comforting sound of the engine turning over and firing up.

I pull out of the parking lot and decide to drive to the marina to spend some quality time with My GRL before she is conscripted into the service of Uncle Sam. I also want to make sure she is clean enough to receive Sarah for cocktails tonight. I intend to have a pleasant evening without having to explain a strange smell or a sock on the floor. I will give her a good once over.

On the way I stop at the store to pick up some essentials. I buy Boursin cheese, water crackers, and homemade crab dip. I grab a bag of white tortilla chips and a jar of chipotle corn salsa. I pick the medium heat, since I'm not sure if Sarah likes spicy food. I choose a bottle of Chardonnay and a bottle of Cabernet/Merlot blend. The Chardonnay will need to be chilled and I have almost seven hours to make sure it is the right temperature. I congratulate my advanced thinking.

I arrive at the marina and park in front of my slip. One of the nice things about my slip is it has a view of the channel which runs from the Gulf to the Port of Corpus Christi. Every day scores of ships move in and out, bringing in and carrying out the lifeblood of commerce. A special experience is watching the large freighters move slowly up the channel and witnessing three or four dolphins racing in the bow swell staying ahead of the monster. You can almost see them laughing at the sport. I glance toward the channel and I'm disappointed there is not a big ship in sight. I turn to the gate which protects my slip from any unwelcome intruders. It remains locked at all times, and the only way in is to enter the code on the keypad. I do so and push the gate open with my upper arm as I hold the wine and snacks by the handle of the plastic bag in my other hand.

I walk the full length of the dock and up the stepladder to get on *My GRL* at the lowest part, near the stern. I always get a thrill upon coming aboard. There is so much to love about this baby. She has beautiful decking, and all her appointments are first class. The ladder railings are a lot of work and give me a particular good feeling since they are of little significance, but shine like new money. This also includes light housings, horns, and cleat covers. I can see myself as I pass them and although it seems a little crazy I enjoy knowing they look so good as a result of my labor. This makes me wonder if turning her over to the likes of the Desert Wolves is really a good idea. I dismiss doubt with the picture of justice painted by Winther.

I enter the galley, open the refrigerator, and put in the cheese. I place the Chardonnay in the lower section and the red in the warmer top section of the wine cooler. The chips, salsa, and crackers go into the pantry. I plan to lay everything out before I leave with the exception of the cheese. I will put the cheese on a plate and leave it in the refrigerator until we return from Sarah's.

I need to empty the dishwasher and put in the dishes that are in the sink. I sigh and begin the process. I am almost finished when my phone rings. I answer, and it is Stans. He tells me with excitement a miracle happened the money came through right away. He wants to meet now at the real estate office. I look at my watch and see I can meet him and wire the money to the Feds and still make it back in time to straighten up the boat. I tell him I can be there in ten minutes. He seems very happy as we end the call. I grab my file which contains information about the boat as well as the title.

The drive to the real estate office takes the full ten minutes. There are some workers spreading tar and gravel on the road, and everyone is confused about how to pass the work crews. The tie-up only lasts a couple of minutes, but in a small town like this a couple of minutes of infrequent delay feels like an eternity.

I walk into the office and see Stans sitting at a desk in a conference room in the middle of the Sundown real estate agent's office space. I wonder how these people do any private discussions. This office resembles an old English money changing house where there are no secrets allowed. I sit across from Stans. We are joined by a pleasant-looking middle aged woman who is introduced as the Notary. Stans has a bunch of papers which need to be addressed.

We sign a number of documents, including the bill of sale. Once the signing is finished Stans hands me a cashier's check for nine-hundred-thousand dollars and my copy of the paperwork.

"Thank you, Spencer." I am as gracious as possible under the circumstances. "When would your clients like to take possession?"

"They would like to come over tonight and take a close look at what they have bought."

"Is there any way to make possession tomorrow?" I hope I won't have to beg.

"Gee, I don't know." He hesitates a minute. "Did you have plans?"

"I was just going to have a small cocktail hour for a goodbye, just me and a friend."

"I think we can accommodate that," It sounds like it might cost me something. "When is your function scheduled to end?"

"We should be out of there by eight."

"Oh, that won't be a problem then. I know my clients won't even get into the airport until about ten."

I am relieved and hand him the spare keys and tell him the other set will be in a small cupboard on the bridge. I assure him he can't miss it. "It is the only little door on the boat."

Stans smiles and thanks me for the keys and information. We shake hands, and I leave the real estate office after I thank the notary for her help.

I get in the FJ and fire her up and drive over to the bank. I step up to an unoccupied teller, and she is very pleasant as I fill out the paperwork. She does not even blink at handling a check for close to one million and processing my request for a wire transfer. She seems a little embarrassed wanting to see my ID, which I happily supply. She looks me up in the computer and sees that my balance is in excess of the amount of the check. She processes the transfer without further comment. She hands me a receipt and lets me know the money will be in the account by five today. I thank her and go back to the FJ and head for *My GRL*.

I have about three hours to get *My GRL* in shipshape for Sarah's visit. Now that I am no longer the owner, I do not feel the imperative to appear as neat and orderly as I once did. I think I will just pack my stuff into a bag and take everything else which seems out of place or junk and either find a spot for it or throw it out. I grab a plastic bag out of the cupboard and begin picking up beer cans and plastic cups. I work forward to the master bedroom and believe I have everything of no value collected. I reach into the closet and pull out my sea bag from the floor. I really do not have much on board. I go through the drawers and pull out some spare underwear, t-shirts, sweatshirt, and a pull-over sweater. I pick up the spare pair of deck shoes off the closet floor. I push all the stuff into the sea bag and look around the room, grab my alarm clock on the table next to the bed, and drop it into the bag. I am satisfied all my personal effects have been removed. I move down the hall and check each stateroom, and as I suspect there is nothing in them I need to take off the boat.

I decide to go home to shower. I throw the two bags into the FJ. I go back aboard *My GRL* for one last look around to make sure nothing is left. I think I have it all, but if I have left anything I am sure when Sarah and I come aboard later I can pick up whatever it is. I feel a little sad and tell *My GRL* that it will only be a temporary separation. I am not sure if I think temporary for her sake or mine, but it does not matter. I have to believe it is true.

Chapter Nine

I am actually happy heading to Royal Cabanas to pick up Sarah. While taking a shower I came to the realization *My GRL* is a possession and can be replaced. I should concentrate on thinking she will be put in service for a greater good. This realization allows me to feel better and kind of let go and enjoy the moment. The night temperature is projected to be delightful in the mid-seventies with a light breeze. Now, at quarter after six, it is in the eighties, and with the top and doors gone, the FJ allows for a refreshing drive. The trip to Royal Cabanas will take about ten minutes so I decide to enjoy it to the max. I am quite content to drive and listen to a pleasant album by a new group The Jaiy Randy Band. The melodies are very catchy, and some of the songs describe what it is like to live in a place like Mustang Island since the songs were written by a resident. The group has not been fully discovered yet. I bought the CD after hearing them play at a concert in Robert's Park, which is the local venue. I sing along with the seventh song named "Crazy Fun" after I hear the chorus a couple of times. The song holds my attention since it describes actual places on the island.

> *Lazy, lazy sun; crazy, crazy fun*
> *Down on ol' mustang three sixty-one*

Lazy, lazy sun; crazy, crazy Fun
Down on the Island, marker forty one"

The ten minutes go quickly. I reach Royal Cabanas and pull up the long drive to the circular driveway which leads to the front door. I am about five minutes early so I pull up in front. The valet immediately approaches the FJ and wants to determine if I am checking in. I turn the music down.

"I am picking up a guest." He takes a step back and allows me to open my own door. "Can I keep her here for about five minutes?" I am hoping it is okay.

"Yes Sir, "he answers quickly. "If you want me to park it just let me know. In the meantime, please leave the keys if you are going inside so I can move it if I need to."

I nod that I understand and head for the front door. "Keys are in the ignition," I call back. I pull open the big door to the Royal Cabanas.

I go inside the rather substantial lobby. There is a desk at the far end of the room with two clerks dressed in bright green blazers. The outside colors of the building are green and white and I notice the color scheme has been carried to the inside as well. The floor is travertine and has an area rug in a conversation area. It shares the space with rattan furniture and is woven to appear to be flowing water only colored in white and green. The casual pillows on the furniture are green and the cushions on the back, the seat of the chairs, and couch are white. The net effect is a feeling of very casual coordination.

There is a small bar in the lobby as well with three patrons at separate tables. I am thinking they are waiting to pick someone up as I am, so I decide not to join them and slowly walk to the opposite side of the room. There is a restaurant through two french doors which I do not open. I take my time looking at the menu which is in a display case on the wall by the doors and think this may be worth a try. I like the fact the menu is dated today and features entrees which seem to change, maybe not daily but often. Under today's special is a mouthwatering description of grilled, fresh line caught, yellow fin tuna served with oven browned red potatoes, haricot verts and spinach salad. My mouth reminds me that dinner time is coming up.

"See anything good?" Sarah breaks my reverie.

"I think everything and everyone looks good including the person who just interrupted my fantasy meal."

Sarah laughs out loud at my attempt at a pick up line. I give my best shy imitation and admit that the line was not the best.

"Oh I think it was cute." I can't help feel a little warm as I blush at her compliment.

Sarah is dressed in dark slacks with a light colored long sleeved blouse. She has a lovely silver John Hardy necklace with a large aquamarine pendant suspended on a rope chain worn so the pendent is a beautiful accent to her blue eyes. "You really do look nice and I'm not telling you that to curry any favor."

"Why thank you John. You look pretty nice as well."

I am thinking we have stretched this dialog about as far as it will go so I thank her for the compliment. "You ready to go?" I offer my arm and escort her out of the Royal Cabanas.

The valet is giving me what could be the Mustang Island version of the New York stare and doesn't move from his place. I walk Sarah to the FJ and open the door. She climbs in and I am very glad she is wearing slacks since the FJ is not the easiest vehicle to gracefully get into or out. I should have warned her, but I forgot. I go back and press two dollars into the valet's hand and thank him for allowing the FJ to stay where it is. He smiles slightly although I am sure he might have been expecting a five. I smile as I walk back to the FJ and Sarah.

We cover the distance to *My GRL*, trading stories of the day. Sarah is very surprised to hear I sold *My GRL*. I don't give her any particulars; just I sold it to a guy name Spencer Stans. I tell her the market for boats is such that I sold *My Girl* at a profit and will be able to buy another. She seems to understand and repeatedly shakes her head as if she thinks I am crazy.

We pull into the marina and make our way to the parking place near the gate. I immediately see *My GRL* is not tied up to her mooring.

"What the hell," I mutter. I get out and walk over to the key pad. I punch in the code and push against the gate and then remember I left Sarah in the FJ. I let the gate slam shut and walk back.

"You look pale," she says I open her door.

"I expected *My GRL* to be here for you and I to enjoy one last time." Even as I give the explanation, I can see that Sarah is not buying the simplicity of my story.

I change my response. "The son of a bitch knew we were going to use her for cocktails and be off by eight o'clock. I do not understand why she is not here."

Sarah gives me a sympathetic look and suggests I give Stans a call to see what happened. This is why I like Sarah—she has many facets. She has the ability to turn chaos into a meaningful action item. I pull out my phone and call Stans.

His phone rings three times and he answers with a curt, "Stans here."

"Hey, Spencer, this is John Cannon." I pause so he can register who I am.

"Yes John, I saw that it was you when you called. I'll bet you are wondering what happened to your boat."

"I sure am Spencer. You and I discussed the fact that I would need her for a couple of hours tonight. What happened?"

There is a pause on the other end. I detect a short sigh before Stans starts talking again. "John my clients got in early and went over to see the boat. They stopped by my hotel for the keys and paperwork. I was going to go with them but they insisted that it would be okay for me to stay at the hotel and arrange a dinner since they would be back shortly. When they got to the boat they loved her and wanted to take her out. They called really excited and I told them you would be using the boat for a while and then they were welcome to take her. The next thing I know I get another call from the ship to shore radio and they are underway. I questioned when they would be back and was told that they would not be back." Stans takes a deep breath and then tries to offer some consolation, "I hope you can make other plans for cocktails."

"Other plans for cocktails?" I speak way too loud into the phone. Sarah looks at me with concern. "You have got to admit Spencer that this is not the way to make friends and influence people. I thought we had a deal and that possession would take place sometime after ten." I am so indignant at the audacity of these people I just want someone to hear me out. "What if I still had some of my personal things onboard?"

I am starting to think Stans is a little embarrassed by his client's actions. He offers to call them with a list of personal items if I give it to him.

"I am sure we can get them back." He has some empathy in his voice.

I finally begin to realize it is useless venting on Stans. It is clear his clients do what they wish and he has no control over them. I throw him a bone now that I am cooled off. "That's okay; I think I took all my stuff off this afternoon."

I am fully exhausted of dealing with Stans. I bid him good-bye. Sarah would like the details, so I fill her in. She seems to be in my corner in that taking *My GRL* ahead of time seems very rude.

"Is anything illegal about what they have done?"

"The possession of *My GRL* was to be at the close of the deal and delivery of the check. Stans obviously did not have his client's agreement, so long story short, there is nothing illegal about his butthead clients taking off with *My GRL*." I finalize the subject, sarcastically, "I am surprised they untied *My GRL* before taking off." The thought of the boat and pilings heading out to sea has us laughing. We decide to have a cocktail at the restaurant and head for a short trip to The Marina View.

I feel lucky to get an upfront parking place and take it immediately. I ask Sarah to hang tight so I can go around and open her door. She smiles at my obvious attempt to explain away what could appear as a maneuver demonstrating male dominance.

"I really know about this door. I tried to get out back at the marina. I think you have some kind of scam going on here." She laughs at her own joke. I smile as well and get out, go around, and open her side.

We walk into The Marina View, and I go to the maître'd and explain we are early for our eight o'clock reservation and would like to have a drink on the patio. The waiter takes us outside, seats us next to the water and will let us know when our table is available. He also lets us know that our drinks can be transferred to the dinner tab.

"Just let your server Michelle know. Have a lovely cocktail."

Michelle shows up with the menu for other drinks and appetizers. I tell her we want to order both, but will need a minute.

As I look over the appetizers, I am thinking besides being rude, Stans' clients really have hastened up their demise. I really should not be disappointed in grabbing my boat out from under me. After all, she will be the conduit to justice and I should really feel good.

"I think I am over the grab of *My GRL*. After all, it is a compliment to her and me that Stans' clients loved her at first sight." I need to get off the downer track and back to cheerful.

JOHN W. HOWELL

I suggest we order Calamari and some steamers and then we can have some of each. She agrees.

Michelle comes back and we order two margaritas, on the rocks not frozen, no salt, and the appetizers. Michelle leads us to believe we just ordered the best thing in the restaurant. Although the rational self knows she tells all her patrons the same thing, it still feels good to hear you have made a good choice.

"I think your assessment of the situation regarding the taking of *My GRL* is the right way to think about it." Sarah says. "It appears to be a compliment to the quality of your boat."

I am thinking about what Sarah would think if she knew the truth. I'm not sure she would continue to describe it as the better road that I have taken.

"Don't you think so?"

I had been deep in thought when she spoke so her words cause me to come back to full attention. I tell her I appreciate her thoughts on the matter. I can't tell if she knows I wasn't really listening while she was talking. I was listening enough to be able to respond, so I don't think she suspects me. In any case, Michelle arrives with two of the biggest margaritas I have ever laid eyes on, let alone drink.

"Enjoy. Your appetizers will be coming out shortly."

"Boy, there is no risk in finishing this drink before the food arrives." I raise my glass. "Here is to friendship."

Sarah raises her glass and I touch hers with mine. "To friendship."

We both take a sip and smack our lips. "I think this is the best Margarita I have ever tasted," I say.

"I agree. It reminds me of when I went to Aguas Calientes in Mexico on business. I was drinking an authentic margarita, but I swear it was not this good."

I had to add my story. "When you check into the Hotel Cabo San Lucas, they hand you a giant margarita, which is very good but not this delicious." As we praise our drinks, Michelle comes back with the appetizers.

We tell Michelle we would like to know the secret to these margaritas and she leans in close and tells us in a low voice, "Fresh key lime juice and agave nectar."

We eat the appetizers and marvel at their goodness as well. "So how did you happen to find yourself in Aguas Calientes?"

"I needed to take a deposition from a pretty high-level member of a US company who had a manufacturing plant in Aguas Calientes. In order to understand what was going on, my boss decided I needed to travel there and visit the plant so when I took the deposition back in the US I would be able to ask some pretty tough questions."

"Wow that is a pretty bold move."

"I had a cover story of posing as a member of the procurement group of one of my client's companies and that I was looking to buy products produced at the plant."

"Did it work?"

"Yes it worked well. No one suspected anything and I was able to gather a lot of information. It was rather tense work but the city itself is delightful. The guys at the plant took me everywhere and what was really nice is I stayed in a five star hotel for the price of a Fairfield Inn.

"So you really enjoyed the intrigue and the travel."

"I found I really loved it."

"Which did you enjoy more, the intrigue or the travel?"

"I think I liked the intrigue better. You know it was really interesting to pretend to be one person but really be someone totally different. I liked fooling the people at the facility. Also when I got back to the States, the deposition was a home run since I had enough inside information, the other side learned early not to try and mislead me."

"I am surprised you liked the intrigue. You in no way resemble an undercover expert."

"Oh I found that all you really have to do is be yourself and everything else falls into place."

I am now looking at Sarah in a different light. I had assumed she was a capable lawyer but now I learn she also enjoys pretending to be someone else. Not sure what this means, but it is different. We spend the rest of the evening involved in conversation about various travel locations. I believe Sarah has traveled to about every place on Earth. In what seems like minutes the meal is over, we decline dessert, and have finished at The Marina View.

We head into the parking lot and Sarah wonders if I am okay to drive. I assure her the margarita has worn off. Since I did not have wine at dinner, I feel pretty comfortable driving. I fire up the FJ, and as I'm about to back out of the parking space, a familiar SUV with Port Aransas police markings pulls up and blocks my exit.

I get out of the FJ and walk to the driver's side of the

police car. "Evening, Chief." I greet him in the friendliest way I know how.

Ned rolls down his window and a rush of cool air hits my face. This is a reminder the temperature and humidity are still quite high even though it is after nine.

"Did you talk to Stans about your boat?" I hear some peevishness in his voice.

"Yes, he and I met this afternoon and I sold the boat as agreed."

"What do you mean as agreed? Who agreed? I thought you and I left it that you would call me after your conversation with Stans."

I suddenly get a very strange feeling in my stomach. It's the feeling you get when you wonder if you have turned off the stove after you leave the house. You are sure you did turn it off and then you get this nagging feeling you are really not sure you did.

I clear my throat, "We had the meeting with Winther and decided to sell my boat to Stans."

"Who the hell is Winther?" He then grunts as he gets out of his car. He faces me, and then lets me know in no uncertain terms that he considers it a breach of trust I did not call him. I am now getting concerned, since Ned does not remember being in the room when the strategy was laid out.

"I need a direct answer, chief . . . do you know Special Agent Winther of the FBI?"

"Never heard of him." He takes a step forward. "You had better explain what you think is going on because in another minute I am going to take you to the station and book you on suspicion of murder."

He places his hands on his hips and I can see his large gun. I'm not sure he meant to intimidate me with it. If he did, it worked.

I don't know where to begin, so I just plunge in and tell him about the agents meeting me at Gerry's parents' place and taking me to a safe house. I tell him he was there or at least someone who looked like him. I relay the fact it was agreed that I would sell the boat and wire the money to the FBI. Ned finally holds up his hand, indicating I should stop talking.

"We need to go to the station. I can't follow all this right here. I need to take some notes and we need to really get under this."

"Do you think there is a problem?" This may be the most naïve question of the year.

"Let's see. You sell your boat because someone tells you to, and you send the money to the same person. A problem? I think you have either been scammed or are trying a scam yourself. I don't know which. I can tell you I have never been in a meeting with you and these so-called agents to discuss selling your boat. I am sure of that much. What the hell else is going on, I have no clue so we need to talk more and not here." He turns and gets back in his car. "Take the girl home and get down to the station. I'll give you thirty minutes before I call the state troopers with a warrant for your arrest."

I cannot believe Ned was not at the meeting. The person there was the same height, build, and had an identical appearance to Ned right down to the mole on the right side of his nose. Now that I think about Ned not being there, the impersonation was good but there were some big holes in credibility. I am starting to feel like the biggest fool on earth. When I shook Ned's hand in the meeting I should have known. When he said I was not a suspect I should have known. The fact he would not talk to me, I should have known. Should a, would a, could a, and it is way too late, I think to myself

"Chief, I am telling you the truth." I talk to him, feeling a panic rising.

"Then you will be there in thirty minutes." He slams his door and starts his SUV and pulls away, leaving a little rubber on the parking lot.

I return to the FJ and get in. I explain to Sarah the chief wants to talk to me and he has given me thirty minutes to drive her home and return.

"I'll come with you," she offers obviously concerned. "You may need a good lawyer if the chief's tone is any indication of the due diligence that he will go through. It sounds like he thinks you are pulling a fast one."

"I appreciate your concern; I think I can handle it." I do not really believe what I just said. "Besides," I continue, "I really don't want you to be my lawyer."

Sarah looks at me with a frown on her face. "Why not? You afraid of having a female lawyer?"

I smile and tell her which in retrospect, has to be the most presumptuous thing possible, "I would rather have you as a female friend."

She blushes (a good thing) and tells me she understands if she were my lawyer a relationship other than professional would be impossible.

"Okay. I guess you need to get started and take me home so you can make it back before you are handcuffed over the hood of a state trooper patrol car." She smiles and I feel real warm inside again.

We make it to Royal Cabanas, and on the way Sarah makes me promise that I will call if there is trouble. She also wants me to call after I leave the station, and I argue that it will be way too late given the complexity of the situation. She makes me promise to call first thing in the morning or tonight if it is not too late. We give each other a hug goodbye and I head back to town.

I walk into the police station. "John Cannon to see Chief Tranes." I talk directly to the guy behind the desk. He tells me to go right in and that the chief is expecting me.

Ned's door is open. I stand in the doorway until he motions me in. I sit in one of two chairs in front of his desk. He leans back in his chair, which gives a low squeak in response to his large frame.

He looks at me for what seems like forever and finally speaks, "I am glad you showed up."

"As I think of what has transpired, I think I need your help."

"We can get to help later; first I need to trust you are telling me the truth as you know it."

I notice the "as you know it" allows for the disillusioned beliefs of the truly crazy. Right now I do feel I am either crazy or the biggest fool on earth. I guess time will tell.

I respond, "What can I do to get this trust?"

He seems pleased with the response. He picks up his pen and asks me to begin at the beginning.

"What made you think these guys were FBI agents, and when and where did they pick you up?"

I explain how they were there when I left the Surfside Towers at about seven last night. "They showed me their IDs and badges and I thought they looked legit."

"Did you get a number to call or really look closely at their credentials?"

I look at Ned and try to sense if he is kidding me or not. "Who would question two big guys with badges?"

Of course he said he would. I admitted I had not, nor did I have any reason to suspect that they were not real agents.

"What kind of car did they drive?"

"A Chevrolet Suburban," I answer with certainty.

"What color and what size?"

"It was black, and I don't know the size."

"You sit in the back?"

"Yes."

"How many were in back with you?"

"Two."

"Were there any seats behind you?"

"No. Why?"

"Sounds like they were in a Tahoe and not a Suburban. The feds never use Tahoe's to transport. They like to put an agent behind and one beside. That takes three sets of seats. What you describe is only two."

"So you are thinking these were not real agents?"

After thinking he speaks in a slow way, "Well, I am not sure. This is only one piece of information other than you seem to believe I was in cahoots with them."

"I don't think you were in cahoots. In fact I thought you . . . uh; the person imitating you was acting very strangely."

"How is that?"

"He looked down a lot, avoiding eye contact and was clear across the room. When we shook hands after the meeting, his handshake was weak. I posed the question around if he still thought I was guilty and he seemed not to understand what I was talking about."

Ned places his hand on his chin, which is the universal body language statement of doubt. "You did not think that strange at the time?"

"Well, yes, not so strange that I would make some kind of connection and put a halt to the proceedings. I have to tell you that the impersonator had all your movements down pat. His face looked identical to yours, right up to the tan and silver mustache." I decided not to mention the mole.

"Yeah, it makes sense that you wouldn't connect that this was an imposter." He puts his hand down on the desk. "Who is this Winther character?"

"He said he was the lead out of San Antonio."

"You checked his ID?"

I look down and almost whisper, "No."

"Doesn't matter anyway. He would have a phony ID had you checked. Did you get any other names?"

"Yes, there was a big guy named Jenkins, and another big guy named Weller, and the driver was Hanson."

"You have some memory; I am impressed."

"I have a trick in remembering names."

"Someday maybe we can trade mnemonic stories. For now I need to know where they took you." He is sounding impatient, and I realize he is putting me on with the compliment about the memory. I think he believes I have a good memory and no brains.

"It was a building on Avenue A. It looked like a warehouse on the outside and was an office on the inside."

"Avenue A is nothing but warehouses and storage facilities. Do you have an address?"

"I don't, however, I think I can remember the building. It had a parking lot out front with a nasty chip out of the concrete barrier. The space was marked for visitors, which led me to believe there was company parking places somewhere else."

"Did they take you in the front?"

"Yes."

"Did you wonder why they took you in the front way?"

"I never thought about it. We went through a door into a reception area. Seemed very logical to me."

"What about the reception area? Any personnel there?"

"No. There was an electronic communication device and a door that opened remotely. I was very impressed by the security. We actually had to wait for clearance."

Ned rolls his eyes. I can tell he believes what impressed me is pretty simple stuff. I describe to him how the party proceeded to the interrogation room for the briefing. He is very interested in hearing the briefing in detail. I told him as much as I could remember. He is also very interested in the so called M.E. report about Gerry wearing a wire which was removed after her murder. He pummels me with a number of questions about the terrorist plot on the public monuments. When I mentioned the *Lexington*, he gives off visible cues which tell me he is really surprised.

"So." He pauses slightly and I can tell there will be another round of questions. "They suggested that you go ahead and sell your boat and you didn't put up any objections?"

I was right about another round. I will try and not appear too stupid. "I did object and was told that my boat would be returned to me and Winther would make sure papers would be filed which would negate the sale. He also assured me that the government would underwrite any damage."

"Did you speak up and try to understand why you were to wire the money to the Feds?"

"I was told it would be used to fix the boat and then go into government coffers to maintain the integrity of the evidence. Since I would be getting my boat back good as new and the balance could be used by the government to fight terrorism, I did not question. In fact, I sold the boat for a hundred-thousand more than the terrorists wanted to pay. I figured this would be my way of contributing to the mission."

"I guess you were pretty proud of yourself for that trick. When did you wire the money?"

I now see Ned has come to the conclusion that I am an idiot. I try to keep some semblance of confidence in my voice. "I wired it about twenty minutes after I got it this afternoon."

"Did they tell you to wire it right away?"

"No, I just thought it would be best not to have a check for nine-hundred-thousand dollars sitting around."

"Okay, I can see that. Let me go over this again. What time did these guys meet you last night?" He is looking at his notes.

"I guess around seven p.m. because I had an appointment with Stans at about seven fifteen and was leaving the Surfside Towers to go to the Palm Court Inn to talk to him. They wanted me to cancel the appointment which I did and rescheduled it for this morning. They also mentioned you had talked to Gerry's parents and that is how they knew I would be at the Towers."

Ned makes a note on his tablet. "I suppose we could check the security camera at the Towers to see if it picked up your visitors. Also, I better check my phones since I did talk to the parents and confirmed with Gerry's dad that you had a six o'clock appointment. The only way they could have known is if my phone is tapped."

He picks up his cell phone and punches in a number. He waits for a moment and then wants to be connected to the security officer on duty. After another moment he is connected. He wants to know if the video from last night is still on the hard drive. He smiles as the answer is obviously yes. He tells the officer to secure the disk in a safe spot, as it may be evidence in a murder. It is also obvious by Ned's expression that the officer wants more detail. Ned rings off with an explanation that the situation is highly confidential and no more information will be forthcoming.

He ends the call. "The disk is available. I will go over and pick it up. Not sure what will be on it, but it could be helpful. I'm gonna place a call to the manager of the security company and make sure nothing happens to the disk. Also, I am not making any more calls from my office phone until I have it checked out."

I feel a sense of relief there could be evidence of the meeting with the guys who posed as FBI agents and the information I gave Ned is believable enough for him to take precautions. This feeling is only temporary.

"By the way John, there is still something not right about your story."

"W-what do you mean?"

"Until I clear you as a suspect I have three ways to look at what you have told me. One, someone defrauded you out of your boat. Two, you sold your boat and for some reason you lost the money or it was taken from you. Three, you owed someone the money and you were forced to give up your boat. All three give me reason to believe you are trying to get me involved."

"For what reason?"

"Yeah, I have not figured that one out yet. Could be for insurance I don't know. Let me tell you though, the person who killed Ms. Starnes did rip something off her body, which left post mortem marks. Your explanation fits the finding of the M.E. Now, either you ripped the wire off her yourself or your story has some truth connected with it."

"Which is it?"

"Let me just add this." He pauses and seems to be thinking, then continues talking. "You are the only one who has articulated the wire theory, and I doubt that you are dumb enough to put yourself under suspicion."

He is carefully choosing his words. "If I can get some proof that you were abducted by parties unknown, then I would tend to believe you were told this information rather than experiencing it yourself. This would lead me to believe these were the guys who killed Ms. Starnes and I would feel good about opening an investigation."

I am very relieved. "I can tell you, chief, if the video was working and the camera was aimed at the driveway and front entrance, you will be able to see these guys take me away. Their car was never hidden."

"Let's hope so. In the meantime, I think we should go to Avenue A to see if you can find the warehouse which is supposed to be a safe house for the FBI."

"I am more than happy to do that." I try to be enthusiastic but feel totally exhausted.

"I think it can wait until tomorrow. I will pick you up at your place at eight a.m. I will have the disk, and we can go to the station to maybe take a look after we visit the safe house." He then looks to me for confirmation.

"I think that will work." I sigh. "You said maybe take a look. You trust me enough to let me see the disk? Why do you think going to Avenue A can wait until tomorrow?"

"I don't think there is going to be anything on it. I will look at it tonight; so yes I trust you to see it with me. By the way, you look whipped, so I don't think you will be the best tracker tonight. Get some sleep if you can after losing nine-hundred-thousand dollars." I detect an element of sarcasm in his voice.

I think a moment before speaking. "You know, chief, I have no concern about the nine-hundred-thousand. I will beat myself up for being naïve, but not for wanting to do the right thing for my country. If this turns out to be a pure scam to get my boat then so be it. I happen to think there is some element of truth in the story these guys used. I think they are going to use my boat for some statement which will horrify people. The effect will be to put these criminals on the map and give press to their twisted objectives." I have to stop talking, as I am sure I am now sounding like a fanatical anti-terrorist nut job.

Ned looks thoughtful. He finally gets up from his desk. "Let me walk you out."

We leave his office and go down the hall to the reception area. He extends his hand and I take his.

"Goodnight, Mr. Cannon." He places his hand on my shoulder as he gives me a firm handshake. "I'll see you at eight o'clock tomorrow."

I mumble something about tomorrow and turn and walk out the front door. It does occur to me his firm handshake is totally different from his imposter and the hand on the shoulder is an act of kindness. I also come to the conclusion Ned is slowly beginning to believe me in spite of the weirdness of my story. I remember I did not mention the prepaid cell phone to Ned. I simply forgot about it and have an instantaneous feeling of remorse. I hope this doesn't come back to bite me in the ass now that I am making progress. I will correct this tomorrow, is the thought that lets me go to sleep.

Chapter Ten

I wake up with a start. I know I have forgotten to set the alarm before falling into bed. I grab the clock, dreading the bad news. With some relief, I see it is only six-fifty. I place the clock on the end table and notice my hand is shaking. "You need to relax," is the message I send to my whole body. In answer, my body seems to be telling me, "Get this crap settled and we will stop the shaking, the noises, the rumbles in the stomach, and the noxious fumes."

I sigh, thankful that the night passed in relative peace. I remember I had better call Sarah and grab my phone on the way to the bathroom. I hit her contact number and listen to the rings.

A very sleepy voice answers on the fourth ring.

"Sorry to wake you but wanted you to know that Ned and I had a very nice conversation. I cleared up the little misunderstanding from yesterday and he and I will be looking into some things this morning."

"Things? What things?" Sarah sounds like she is still half asleep.

"Aw, just some evidence that he thinks we should go over. You go back to sleep. Nothing to do with me. I will call you later." I keep the details to a minimum since I don't want Sarah to get involved, as I do not know what I am dealing with.

"Sounds good John. Goodbye."

"Goodbye." I end the call.

I jump into the shower. As I am coming out of the shower and drying my hair vigorously my phone rings. I look at the caller ID and see it is Ned. "Hello, chief." I have some concern in my voice.

"I am calling to tell you I have the disk and I'm on my way. I wanted to give you a heads up in case you were still in bed."

"No problem," I answer as if I appreciate the wake-up service. "I am pretty much ready to go. Would you like some coffee?"

"I have had mine, so I'll pass. See you in ten minutes." The phone goes dead.

I finish dressing and punch the coffee maker. I hit the extra strong button and plan to use extra half and half. The strong hot coffee is ready in a minute. I dump it in a to-go cup and fill it with half and half along with two Splenda packets. As I take my first sip, I hear Ned's SUV pull up. I look around and do a mental check. I have my wallet, keys, and my cell phone. I see my glasses in their case on the other side of the room. I consider leaving them, but cross the room to pick them up and then see the pre-paid phone sitting on the counter. I decide to take it with me. I lock the front door and head toward the car.

"Good morning, you ready?" Ned sounds real chipper.

I respond with the classic "More than ready. Let's go."

Ned smiles at my smart ass attitude this morning. I think he is pleased I seem well rested. Not out of concern for my welfare. He knows that if I am rested I will make a better bloodhound. He explains that we will go to Avenue A to see if we can find the safe house and then go back to his office to look at the disk. I want to know from him if he trusts that the security people kept the disk in a safe place. Ned explains he has known the officer since he was in diapers and trusts he will do whatever Ned wants. I express concern that the people who got my boat obviously have enough resource to eliminate a video if necessary. Ned does acknowledge my concern, and believes that the boat thieves are long gone.

"Do you think Spencer Stans has any information?"

"Naw. I checked him out after you told me he was handling the sale. He is a legitimate boat broker. I truly believe if his clients are not on the up and up he doesn't know a thing. As a precaution, I requested the Houston police run a check and keep an eye on him."

I decide to wrap up every loose end. "Did Gerry's parents shed any light?"

Ned looks at me as if I just asked his age. I guess being quizzed by a suspect doesn't happen every day. "They had nothing. They did tell me Gerry, uh, Miss Starnes, has a brother who lives in the DC area. We also checked our phones and the lines are clear. This does not mean there wasn't a tap yesterday. Right now there isn't."

"Interesting about the tap. Have you talked to him? Gerry's brother, I mean."

Another look of encroachment. "Not yet."

Ned pulls the SUV to the curb at the beginning of Avenue A. We get out and decide to walk from the beginning to the end since it is only two blocks. We start on the right side even though I said the warehouse would be on the left. We cover the two blocks in about five minutes and cross the street to the other side. While we are walking, many people passing in cars wave at Ned. He waves back and seems pleased that he appears to be so well liked.

About the middle of block I stop in front of a warehouse that has about six concrete curbs and parking places marked "Visitor" on the front. I notice the second curb from the right is chipped. "This is it," I declare.

"Are you sure?"

I don't think Ned doubts me; I just think he is being careful. "Yes, I am sure."

We go to the door and try the handle. It is locked. Ned knocks on the door. We wait and he knocks again. There is no sign that anyone will answer. Ned pulls out his cell and makes a call. He stipulates that he needs a warrant with probable cause to be listed as illegal trafficking in controlled substances. He ends his call and before I speak he updates the results, "The DA on the other end. The warrant will be here in about thirty minutes. Let's go to the Cove for some coffee."

We walk to the Cove, which is around the corner on Gulf Street. The Cove has the décor of an amusement park pirate ride. There are Jolly Roger flags hanging from the ceiling and treasure chest beer coolers behind the bar. There are a number of signs on the walls reminding buccaneers to check their pistols and the prohibition of swash buckling. The bartender has a wide sash over his rotund belly and wears an open collar puffed sleeve shirt. He actually looks like he would take your gold.

The bar regulars are all present, since alcohol is legal after seven in the morning. There is a collection of oil workers and various others who keep a twelve-on, twelve-off schedule. To the average person a shot of whiskey and a beer at seven in the morning might seem disgusting. I know, to me it is. To these folks, this is an after work ritual that helps them hang on in a grueling life. Most everyone waves and shouts at Ned. He graciously acknowledges them. He calls to the bartender for two coffees and wonders if there are any donuts left. The bartender laughs since there has never been a donut served at the Cove.

The two coffees arrive and I am quite impressed that they are served with half-and-half and a jar of various artificial and natural sweeteners. Ned sees my surprise and comments about all the city folk who find their way to Cove, and at last Cove is accommodating them. While I am preparing my coffee with the right amount of half-and-half and a Splenda he tells me a story of a couple from San Antonio, actually Olmos Park (a toney suburb) who came into the Cove to pick up a pizza. While the guy was paying the bill the regular pirates decided to make fun of the outsiders. They were boisterous and said that they would like a piece of pizza, and as Ned tells the story, they weren't talking about pizza.

The wife who stood about five feet tall with blonde hair and was wearing a smart sundress and a pair of high heels, immediately asked them if they were talking to her, acting like she was Robert De Nero in Taxi. He relates she said something like, "Excuse me, you talking to me?" The boys did not know what to do. The husband walked up and said, "Is she bothering you boys?" He good naturedly told his wife to leave them alone and both walked out. All the jaws that had dropped came back to a full and upright position, and everyone had a good laugh. After that, the Cove was changed forever and the city folk with their need for good coffee and artificial sweeteners were welcome.

We finish our coffee about the time a uniformed officer comes through the door with a paper in his hand. "Here is the warrant, chief." He hands it to Ned.

"Let's go." Ned gets up after he looks at the warrant. He waves to the assemblage and we go out the door.

Outside, Ned tells the officer to come with us and to remain outside as backup. "Anything funny and you call for help, you understand, Leroy?"

Leroy gives his best "yes, sir" and we go to the door of the factory. Ned grabs the handle of the door and twists it hard; pushing on the door just to make sure it is locked.

"Deadbolt," he whispers.

He takes a tool out of his pocket and inserts it in the lock. He turns the tool carefully and the sound of the bolt being thrown open is very loud. "That should do it." He looks at me with an expression of satisfaction.

He turns the doorknob and the door opens. He looks inside briefly and tells us all to hold position. He goes to his SUV and comes back with a small mag flashlight.

Ned starts through the door and warns over his shoulder, "Stay back until I check this out. I'll let you know when it is clear."

I stop and hold the door open as Ned disappears to a very dark interior. I see that he has switched on his flashlight and the beam moves side to side very rapidly. It stops and the interior space is suddenly flooded with light. Ned calls from inside indicating I can come in.

I take in the huge space of the fully lighted warehouse. There are no rooms or doors, just a massive space with nothing in it.

Ned is clear across the room. "There is nothing here but space." He is almost shouting and his voice seems to bounce all over the massive area.

I cross the room and when I am closer I tell him, "I can see this is an empty building. I am sure it is the right one. I can only imagine that the guys moved everything."

Ned gives me a look, broadcasting his frustration without having to mutter a word. "You said there was a remote-controlled door. Show me where you think it was in relation to the front door."

We move back to the front door. I back up and take the number of steps that I think put me in front of the remote-controlled door.

"Right here." I point to the floor. "This is where I think the door was placed."

"Did it open in, or did it have to be pulled open?" He is now sounding like he believes that he needs to be very precise in checking out the story.

"I remember Winther pushing against the door like it was heavy, so I think it opened in." I am now thrilled that Ned has not simply given up by walking away.

He goes to the spot and drops to one knee and looks carefully at the concrete floor. "Was the floor concrete or another material?" I hear some impatience in his voice.

My spirits now takes a quick drop. I can't remember the composition of the floor. No wait—I remember the furniture in the reception looked like it belonged in an office. I now remember that there was a table on the wall, and I was fascinated as to how the table was reflected in the floor. That's it.

"The floor was made of tile. I'll bet it was travertine or some kind of high-quality tile because it reflected the table which was on the wall over there." I am now excited I can remember such detail and pointing to the wall to our right.

Ned looks closer at the floor. "I can see some kind of dust here that looks like it might have been grout. We will need to gather a sample and run it past the lab in Corpus."

"Wouldn't grout indicate that there had been some kind of tile down there?" I am grasping for straws.

Ned smiles. "It could, but it could also be any number of things, like bags of grout stored here. Let's look around and see if there is more."

We search the warehouse and find what appears to be grout dust is in no other location. It is just in the area which could have been the reception room. Ned also discovers some patched holes in the floor.

"A nail driver could have made these marks, which would be used to put in the base two-by-fours for a wall. It looks like the wall is about the same size as the reception area."

He continues to walk around and comes back to me. "I believe the hallway and room where the briefing took place were here as well. I want to take some of this patch material. I think it is quite new and want to confirm."

"So you think there used to be rooms here?" I have the sound of hope in my voice.

Ned, not being one to hand out hope too easily, lets me know there could have been rooms here a long time ago. He wants to test the patch material for freshness before committing to any idea that I might have been telling him the truth.

He has a long history of investigation and he explains, "Things are not always as they seem." He finishes taking samples with his penknife and places them in plastic baggies.

"I don't think we can do any more here." This as a summary statement in preparation for leaving. He looks around one last time. "I think we should call the landlord and see if there has been any construction in the building that he knows about." We head outside.

Ned calls to the officer over the SUV roof and tells the officer to tape off this area as a crime scene.

I get into the SUV. "Does the area being marked as a crime scene mean what I think it means?"

"What do you think it means?"

"I think you are starting to believe my story and want to preserve evidence in case it is true."

He almost laughs. "I will need the scene preserved in case the story about you being fool enough to sell your boat to complete strangers and then sending the money back is true. Nine-hundred-thousand dollars is grand theft and I may be forced to open an investigation."

"What about the blowing up of the *Lexington*?"

He continues to project he is being patient with me. "Do you have any recordings of the conversations or documentation that someone wants your boat for anything but resale?"

I have to admit I don't have a shred of evidence and finally get his point, which as a lawyer I should have gotten long ago. Being close to the situation, I am all wrapped up in the terrorist story. If he is convinced I have been defrauded out of my boat he will investigate. He has no interest in determining why the boat was taken. He is assuming it will be sold and the thieves will pocket the money. Of course, what a small town police department will turn up on an investigation is anybody's guess. I believe the operation was much too sophisticated to be a simple for profit venture. These guys built several rooms in that warehouse and then tore them down within hours of completing their intended function.

They had a federal-looking SUV and documentation that sure looked real. I guess the best I can hope is the videotape shows me getting into the SUV and Ned finally believes something happened and will try to get to the bottom of it. I just hope he knows what he is getting into. I have met these people and I am convinced they know their stuff. They were very convincing, and I am sure that when push comes to shove they will not hesitate to take out anyone who gets in their way.

"What happens if the tape shows me getting into their SUV?"

He gives me that patient look again. "It will prove you went along with some people and decided to sell your boat to them. The piece that leads me to believe that I need to get involved is if what you're telling me is true about them, giving you the M.E. findings, these people are also responsible for a murder."

"Why, then, is the story about blowing up the *Lexington* not believable?"

"Why would they tell you a story that is true and then let you spread the story all over the place? They would risk someone believing you, and then there is a possibility the authorities stop the terrorists before they can pull off their caper."

He has a ton of logic in his argument. I can't think of any reason, other than the fact in my experience as a lawyer, a really good lie has some elements of truth to make it believable.

"So you think these guys stole my boat, and in the process Gerry was in the way, got killed, and that's the end of it?"

"I need to get more information before I come to a conclusion like that. You will need to look at the disk."

Ned starts his SUV and backs away from the parking space. We pull away from the warehouse and it is clear we are heading to the police station, which is on Harper Street and only three blocks away. We cross Station Street, which is a main thoroughfare, and then another block at Alister Street. A couple in a golf cart runs the red light in front of us causing Ned to slam on his brakes. The couple have looks of fear on their faces and Ned wags his finger at them. The driver mouths that he is sorry. Ned nods and we all go our own way.

"Tourists." Ned shakes his head.

I'm sure the couple feels they are very lucky. I think it would have been a different outcome if Ned did not have a disk to review.

We pull up to the police station and Ned pulls in to his designated parking space. I get out and follow him into the building. I feel like a kid following his dad into a workshop with a broken bicycle. The kid knows his dad will fix the bike and all will be well again. I have the feeling Ned will look at the disk and figure out the next step. He may even know the people on the video, which would be even better. Best of all, it will show some truth about my story

We go past the desk sergeant and straight to Ned's office. He motions me to the same chair as always and sits down heavily in his own chair. He opens the laptop sitting on his desk and takes the disk out of its case. After his laptop boots up, he pushes a button on the side of his laptop and a DVD tray slides out. He puts the disk in and shoves it back into the laptop.

"I looked at this disk last night and I want you to verify that it is you on the screen. You want to come around to this side of the desk so you can see it? It is very interesting and I am sure you will be surprised at what you see."

I jump up and go around the desk. I get behind him just as the video comes to life. There are six different views on the screen. Each has an electronic label. The lobby, backdoor, side entrance, front entrance, and two elevators have separate views. The time and date are in the lower right hand corner of the screen.

"This is the master view," Ned explains. "We can go to any one of these views if we see something."

He also tells me since this is a twenty-four hour disk he will speed it up to the point where it is closer to the time I was at the Towers.

"What time was your appointment with Mr. Starnes?"

"The appointment was at six. I think I got there a few minutes early."

Ned is quiet as he fast forwards the disk. "Ah, here it is five-forty-five. We will let it run from here."

We both watch as the minutes crawl by real time. At about five-forty-nine the front entrance view shows my FJ coming up the drive. I pull into the parking lot and get out and go toward the entrance. I drop off the entrance view and in a moment I am picked up in the lobby view.

The lobby view shows me wandering around like a lost person. It seems like an embarrassingly long time for me to finally get my bearings and proceed to the elevator view. As I watch the video, I am quite surprised by the bald spot on the top of my head that shows on camera as a bright spot. I make a mental note to see if Rogaine is in my future. I exit the elevator at five-fifty-nine. Ned forwards the video and stops a little too late. He rewinds and we can see I return to the elevator at six-forty-five.

After a brief ride down on camera, I emerge from the elevator into the lobby view. I cross the lobby to the front door and push through. I immediately look to the front entrance view, expecting to see the backside of me going down the driveway.

There is nothing. The front entrance view is completely black. Ned fast forwards the video for at least an hour of video time and it is all black. He continues until the picture is restored.

"Looks like the blinders came off at seven-forty-three." He

stops the recording. Ned pushes back from his desk, almost running over my toes. I get out of the way in time.

He looks up at me, "I am thinking someone either doctored this disk or got to the camera. My guess is they got to the camera since I am not sure how they would be able to pull the disk and then return it in time."

I am now wondering why Ned has not thrown up his hands and put the cuffs on me. "Why aren't you putting me in cuffs?"

He laughs, "This came to me last night when I first saw the disk. The blanked out segments proves your story. Someone went to the trouble of not wanting to be seen. If you were telling a lie, the recording would show you walking out because there would be no reason to cover the camera. The fact that the camera was covered shows someone had something to hide. I know you did not cover the camera because your time at the Towers was fully documented. This blackout speaks loudly to the fact that you were set up to lose your boat. Don't know why, or care. I do know that I need to get to the bottom of this. There is a dead girl involved in all this, and I think the situation is connected."

"Can we tell when the camera was covered?" I am trying to be helpful.

"I will back it up to that point. I am sure it will be sometime between six and six-forty-five. My question will be for the security guy on duty. Where was he while one of his six views went black?"

Ned turns back to his laptop and rewinds the recording to a point where the black appears. "There it is, six-twenty-one. So here is an hour and twenty minutes of a blackened camera and the security person on duty at the time does not know or if he knows he does not care. We need to talk to those guys."

I am grateful for Ned's passion and still have an uneasy feeling that this little town investigation is not going to turn up all the clues necessary to solve this crime. I may be wrong, but there ought to be some big guns pulled in on this. I am going to try a suggestion.

"Do you think the state troopers or Texas rangers should be brought in?"

Ned looks at me like he is a robot with lasers for eyes. "Where the hell do these ideas of yours originate?" He has a disappointed look on his ruddy face. "For your information, I am a graduate of Ohio State University with a degree in criminology, and Michigan State University with a master's in law enforcement. I went through the FBI academy and served in the Agency for twenty-five years. I am a retired agent with contacts. I have been police chief here for five years and, let me tell you, I have not lost one bit of skill." He stops and sighs deeply.

"I am not questioning your abilities. I just think this may be a bigger case then you have resources to handle. That is all I meant to convey."

I am now feeling guilty for questioning Ned's ability to handle the case, which I surely did.

"Yeah sure." He sounds like he has read my mind. "You can do whatever it is that you want, but this is my case and I will handle it. If I need resources I know where to go."

"I would like to help."

"I have no problem with you. You need to understand that I need to work this case without interference."

"I understand. Will you keep me in the loop?"

"I will need to talk to you from time to time. Anything I can tell you I will. I would appreciate it if you would keep me informed of any contacts with Stans or any of your phony agency characters."

His mention of the agency characters reminds me I need to tell him about the prepaid cell phone that Winther gave me. I feel it in my pocket and I need to get it out of there. I decide since there is a little bad blood between us right now not to let Ned know I have it. I am not sure what I will do with it, but it might be interesting to give a call on the phone to see what happens. I am already feeling guilty for keeping this information from Ned.

"Chief?" I am now meek.

"Yes, Mr. Cannon." He sounds like he is expecting an apology.

"I have more evidence I did not tell you about."

"Tell me about it now." His voice has a sound kind of like he is willing to offer absolution

I tell him about Winther giving me a prepaid cell phone in spite of deciding not to do so. I tell him I have not used it and I pull it out of my pocket and hand it to him. I also can't stand it, so I tell him I was thinking of not telling him and making a call. He sits in silence while I talk.

He finally speaks. "Thank you for trusting me with this phone. We need to dust it and then give it to a forensic engineer to see if it can be traced. I doubt it, but it's worth the try. You did good telling me about this."

For what it's worth, I am grateful for the compliment. I suddenly realize I am really very dependent on praise. I think it must be as a result of the trauma to my head in the attack. In any case, I think I am back in Ned's good graces. I decide I will try to tag along on some of the investigations until Ned tells me to get lost.

I take a chance. "Why don't we go and talk to the security guys at the Towers."

Ned smiles broadly. "You are unofficial. I'll let you be involved until you screw up. I understand you are an officer of the court, so raise your right hand."

I think he is kidding. "Raise my right hand? What for?"

"I need to swear you in as a deputy investigator and consultant."

My hand shoots up and he makes me swear to uphold the Constitution and to follow all directions issued by any uniformed member of the force. After I swear he lets me know I am an unpaid consultant. I tell him it is fine with me.

"I'll need you to sign an agreement that will formalize your status." He rifles through his drawer while muttering about the location of the form. "Ah, here it is." He hands me a paper that is an agreement to pretty much uphold what I just swore.

"I have no problem signing this, chief. I think it needs to be filled out with name and consultant title though." I hand the form back to him.

"Yeah, thanks. I will do it now. By the way, you can call me Ned since we will be working together." He takes a pen and fills out the form and passes it to me. I review it and it looks okay so I sign. I hand it back.

"Chief, er, Ned, are we going over to the Towers to talk with the security guys?" I want to make sure he doesn't leave me out of that discussion since I am very interested on how a camera could be blacked out without anyone's knowledge.

"We need to do two things first. One: we need to call the owner of the warehouse and see if there has been any recent construction. Two: we need to call the manager of the security company and find out when his guys will be on duty. I don't want to go to their house. I would rather quiz them while they are at the workplace. While I am thinking about it, I want to send the samples of the concrete patch to the lab to see how old the components are."

Ned is looking at me to see if I understand why we are not going to question the security guys right now. I nod in agreement and Ned takes the plastic baggies and puts them in a box along with the prepaid phone and some instructions which he wrote down while we were talking.

"I will have a uniformed officer run these over. The lab is in Corpus and I don't want to wait for the mail."

He picks up his phone and tells the other end to have someone named James step into his office.

"As soon as the officer picks up the package I will place a call to the warehouse owner first and then the security company." He finishes just as there is a gentle knock at the door. "Come right in."

The door opens and a young officer gingerly enters the office. He starts an excuse for the interruption and Ned cuts him off. "I have this package that needs to get over to the CCPD crime lab right away."

He hands it to the officer and the officer wants to know if he should wait or bring anything back. Ned tells him to get a receipt so there will be a chain of possession, should the material become significant evidence. The officer acknowledges the direction given by Ned and leaves with the box.

Ned seems satisfied the officer will see to the handling of the package and picks up the phone. He dials and whoever answers gets his request for Randy Stovall. He listens as the person on the other end is giving him some information.

He finally speaks. "Tell him Chief Tranes of the Port Aransas Police department would like him to call." The other person obviously is a little flustered.

"Yes, that's right." He then gives his cell phone number. He acknowledges the other person's promise to deliver the message. "Tell him it is urgent." He has the last word and hangs up.

"I hate to leave heavy handed messages. Most of the people return the call and are really anxious. This guy will be on guard, and I am not sure he will be able to give us the information about construction since he will be cautious about my reason to know. On the other side, if I just leave my name they never call back." He shrugs at the damned if I do or don't conundrum.

"People aren't good at returning calls." I relate this in support of at least trying to get messages returned.

"Might as well move on to the security guys."

JOHN W. HOWELL

Ned picks up the phone and dials again. He explains he needs some information from the crew working security on the night that I visited the Towers.

"Yes, go ahead." Ned rolls his eyes while looking at me. He covers the mouthpiece of the phone with his hand and whispers to me, "He is looking at the schedule."

The security guy gives Ned two names of his team who were working that night which Ned writes down and shows me. He obviously asks the nature of the problem as Ned assures him if there is a problem he will be advised. Ned tells him it is just a normal inquiry. He further explains as part of the normal routine he needs the officers on duty to verify that the videos fairly represent what was actually going on. Ned checks if it will be okay to talk to these two tonight and the answer is obviously positive since Ned thanks him and hangs up the phone.

"No use getting him upset." Ned tells me in explanation of the white lie about routine.

"Looks like we may be finished until tonight." I am still attempting to stay connected.

"I hope the warehouse guy calls back, but in essence you are right. I think we can run you home and then meet tonight to go to the Towers."

"Can I buy you lunch?" I offer.

"I will need to pass. I must go to the gym and work out. I have been gaining a little weight lately and need to pay attention to my exercise routine. I lost five pounds and need about five more to disappear."

His reason for skipping lunch sounded sincere, so I did not read anything into his refusal. Just a day ago I would have thought he still considered me a suspect. I think that is all over now.

"How about a rain check?" Ned is smiling.

"You got it." We both get up and leave his office. When we reach the reception area, his phone rings.

"Chief Tranes." Ned is listening patiently. "Thank you, Mr. Stovall, for returning my call." Ned points back to his office and I turn around and go back. He follows while talking to Randy Stovall. I could not hear the entire conversation. The gist was there was major construction on the warehouse and Randy was aware of it taking place.

After Ned hangs up he tells me that Randy had rented the

warehouse to a movie company located in New York. They rented the warehouse for thirty days for the purpose of shooting a movie. They built temporary offices inside the warehouse. Randy saw the work and told Ned that it was very attractive. They tiled the floor and built walls. According to Randy it was very realistic. He also told Ned that the company promised to return the warehouse to its former condition. He said he inspected it after they were gone and returned the security deposit.

"We are going over to Randy's office to pick up some information." We start to move through the office.

"What kind of information?"

"Names, addresses, a rental contract, and anything else these guys left."

Chapter Eleven

We get into Ned's SUV and quickly head over to Stovall Holdings Inc. office on Alister Street. It's a one-story building with a raised covered porch and has the architecture of a house on the beach. We walk up the five steps and see there are rocking chairs placed along the porch like an old southern plantation house. A man is sitting on one of the rockers and stands as we take the last step. He looks like he just stepped out of a high fashion store. He is wearing a pale salmon-colored polo shirt and a pair of khaki shorts that hit him just above the knees. He has a pair of sandals on his feet and is wearing wired-rimmed glasses.

"Hello, chief. Randy Stovall. I don't believe we have ever met." Randy extends his hand.

"Nice to meet you. This is John Cannon; he is working as a consultant." Ned and I shake hands with Randy.

"What can I do for you, chief?" He pauses. "Before I forget my manners, would y'all like a cold drink? It is really getting warm this time of year."

"No, thank you. John and I just came from the office and we are good." Ned speaks for both of us. I take the cue and nod in agreement.

"You mentioned on the phone that you are interested in looking at some of the documents that were executed between my company and the film group."

"Yes, that's right. We need to gather some information about whoever rented your warehouse."

"Did they do something wrong?" Randy sounds concerned.

"We are not sure. It could be that these guys are running some kind of fraudulent operation."

"Well, I can tell you they were up-and-up with me. I received the money agreed to and they kept their word on every turn."

"How did they pay the rent and how much was it?"

"In cash, and it was ten thousand for the month with a five thousand dollar security deposit which they also gave me in cash."

"Did you think there was something unusual about a cash deal?"

"No. I have a few clients that pay in cash."

"Are they regulars or one-month-stands like these guys?"

Randy is starting to get nervous. He becomes a little defensive on the questions about the cash payment. He is fidgeting with the paper which he was reading when we came up. "They are regulars. What difference would it make for a temporary rental? Is there a law against accepting cash?" His question came with a little edge in his voice.

"Nothing illegal, however, I would think a cash transaction would raise a question in your mind."

"Well, I can tell you there was no question in my mind. I Googled MFM Studios and they seemed legitimate. They also paid in advance."

Ned's eyebrows shoot north. "In advance you say?"

"Yes, that's right."

"And still no question?"

Randy is now turning a slight shade of red. "Look, chief, I already told you I had no question. If you think I did something wrong I would like you to simply tell me what it is and knock off the insinuations."

Ned smiles his kindly grandfather smile. "You've done nothing wrong. Please excuse my questions, but we are trying to get to the bottom of an ugly murder and we do not have a lot of information about who is responsible."

Randy looks truly shocked and seems a little embarrassed at his outburst. He apologizes to Ned and assures him that there is no question that he won't answer. Ned smooths the situation with nice words about cooperation and clears his throat, "Do you still have the money?"

Randy answers, "Well, I put it in the bank. It is in my account."

"Understood. I was wondering if any of the bills were still available."

"I don't think so. As I said, I went to the bank and made a deposit. I would not want that much money sitting around."

"Quite right.." Ned wants to move off the subject. "You said that you returned the security deposit."

"Yes, after I looked the place over."

"How did you pay them the security deposit?"

"By check."

Ned smiles like a person whose car is stuck in the mud and is starting to gain traction. "Can we see the canceled check?"

"I bank online, so I will have to pull the check from my account and you can look at it on my computer."

"Sounds difficult." Ned is losing patience.

"Not really. I'll go and get my computer. Why don't you have a seat and I will be right back."

He disappears through the door before Ned can answer. Ned turns to me and wants to know if online banking is safe. I tell him it is and he rolls his eyes at the thought.

Ned speaks what he is thinking. "All cash is a little suspect."

Randy returns with his laptop. "Here I am. Are you sure you don't want something to drink? The humidity must be eighty-five percent."

Ned again declines and I shake my head.

Randy sits back in his chair and opens the laptop which he has placed on his thighs. He makes a couple of key strokes and then invites Ned to come look over his shoulder.

"See here." He is pointing at a spot on the screen. "This is the check that I wrote to MFM Studios. The front view shows that it is made out to MFM. The back view shows that it was endorsed and placed in deposit at JP Morgan Chase."

"I see that there is an endorsement stamped with 'for deposit only' and MFM's name," Ned observes.

"That's right," Randy agrees.

"Can I get a copy of this?"

Randy makes another couple of key strokes and then tells Ned the best he can do is give him a screen print since he is not really in a file online that is printable. He does offer to contact the bank and get a copy of the check. Ned tells him a copy would be great and in the meantime if it would not be too much trouble he would appreciate a screen print as well. Randy goes inside to print the materials.

Ned seems a little frustrated. "I thought we would be able to get a name on the check. We will need to check out MFM Studios. I suspect it is a legitimate company and that the guys taking your boat hired them to create the illusion that they were federal agents."

"Makes you wonder if they shot any film." I wonder aloud to Ned as an afterthought.

"Good point. We will need to call MFM and get a little more information. If they shot film maybe they have it. If not, maybe they have some thoughts on why they were hired to do a film and never did. This is a great point John."

I turn a little red I'm sure, "I have another thought that I would like to share."

"Go for it."

"Shouldn't we notify the authorities that *My GRL* was acquired under suspicious circumstances?"

Ned seems deep in thought and then gives me his honest read. "You have no proof that you did not sell your boat in a legal transaction to a recognized broker acting on behalf of his clients. You and I would be laughed out of any agency at this point. We need to do more leg work on this before we alert anyone."

I concede. "Just a thought," I mumble.

"No, I appreciate your thoughts." Ned sounds sincere. "Keep them coming." He nods in the direction of the door and signals the time to be quiet. "Here comes Randy."

We both turn and look at Randy as he approaches from the door. He has the screen print which he gives to Ned. Ned looks at it and squints and mentions it is a bit fuzzy. Randy explains that screen prints are not very good. Ned shakes his head in agreement.

"At least we can make out the endorsement and the fact that it was deposited with JP Morgan Chase." Ned offers this in recognition of Randy's attempt to be useful.

We tell Randy we appreciate his help. Ned tells him to give him a call when the copy of the check comes in. Randy also shows Ned the rental agreement. Ned looks at it quickly and wants a copy of it as well. Randy tells Ned he can keep this one since he made a copy of the original. We turn to go and Randy enthusiastically agrees to call

Ned first thing on arrival of the copy of the check. We all shake hands, and Ned and I step off the porch and cross the lot to Ned's SUV.

"Something's not right." Ned speaks as I shut the door.

"What?" I have no idea what is bothering him.

"I think having someone pay the rent with ten thousand dollars in cash, without so much as a question being raised by the landlord, sounds fishy."

He starts the SUV. "He collected in advance, not only the ten Gs, but also the security deposit of five grand. What would you do if you were running a business and someone offered you payment in advance like that?"

"I guess it would depend on how much I needed the money."

"Exactly. If I did not need the money, I would have a ton of questions about what the renter was planning to do with the property. I would want to make sure there was no funny business going on like drugs, sex, or rock and roll. I would be concerned with the liabilities as well. I will look at this agreement closer and since you are a lawyer why don't you look it over and give me an idea if old Randy has protection or did he just need the money so badly he signed off."

He hands the agreement to me. I quickly look it over. "Looks pretty standard. In fact, I think it was generated by Randy since the filename here at the bottom has his initials and the date."

"Well, that blows the sign-off-too-quickly theory."

"But not the Randy-needs-money-badly theory."

Ned laughs. "As if that means anything either."

"How can we find out if Randy is in financial straits or not?"

Ned thinks for a moment. "I know a forensic accountant. I will give him a call and maybe we can get some information on Mr. Stovall. By the way, I have changed my mind about the lunch if you are still buying."

I smile. "You name the place."

Chapter Twelve

After lunch, Ned drops me off at my place. We make an appointment to meet at the police station at six-thirty to go to Surfside Towers and have a discussion with the security guys. I take a nice long nap and get up about four-thirty. I put on my swimming trunks, grab a towel, and leave my house from the back door. I cross the raised deck and descend the two weathered steps to the base of the sand dune which separates my house from the Gulf of Mexico. The sand dune has a beach walk raised enough to go over the top of the dune to the beach. It has a gradual grade up, goes over the dune, and then a significant slant down to the beach. I grab the handrail to keep from falling on my butt and sliding down.

The tide is out at this hour and the beach is wide. I wade into the water and reach the first of three sandbars in front of my house. I walk up the gentle grade until the water is about six inches deep. I continue down the sandbar until the water is waist deep. The gentle waves keep hitting me and send a chill through my body. I duck under to eliminate the shock of the cool water hitting my warm skin. I keep wading and reach another sandbar. I go up the slope until the water is no higher than my knees. Now that I am no longer sensitive to the water temperature it seems warm and inviting. I dive headfirst and swim toward the third sandbar. The water between the second and third sandbar is over my head. It is only about a fifty yard swim, which I have no problem doing, and when I think I can stand up again I find I am in water up to my waist. I stand on the sandbar and look back toward the beach. I see it is almost deserted. There are a couple of families on vacation and that is about it. Looking back toward the sea, I notice a flock of pelicans in a single file formation passing overhead undulating with the currents of the light sea breeze.

The sky is bright blue, which has the effect of influencing a deep blue hue in the water. It is an almost cloudless sky overhead. The few substantial clouds that are present are way out to sea and as white as snow. I am thinking there will be no rain for a while. Two trainers from the Naval Air Station cross the sky heading north practicing close formation flying as they seem to be separated by inches. In contrast to the easygoing pelicans that tend to more or less follow each other, the aviators seem locked together as a single machine.

The swim in the Gulf is, to me, one of the best reasons to live on the Island. A few short minutes in the salty water seems to put back energy and stamina. Floating in the water eases my muscles, which have been stressed by worry. I totally relax.

Soon it is time to go back and get ready to meet Ned. I cross the boardwalk and head toward my house. I take a shower under the outdoor showerhead, wrap a dry towel around me, and go inside.

I decide it would be a good idea to check in with Sarah. I give her a call, but she doesn't pick up. I leave a message. "Yeah Sarah It's me John. I guess you recognize my voice, but just in case. . . A hum, I will be with Ned this evening since we are real buds. Funny huh? We are going over to the Towers to talk with the security guys there. I'll give you the details when I call later. No need to call since I will be heading to the police station in a few minutes."

As usual, my message sounds stupid when I replay it in my head. I wonder why I don't just hang up when the person I am calling doesn't answer. I tend to give too much information and can imagine the person on the other end wishing I would simply go away.

I finish dressing and check the time. It is about time to leave for the police station. I grab an apple on the way out. If the questioning of these two guys gets hot and heavy there is no telling when the session will be over. I look around to see if I have forgotten or left anything on. I do this even though I know I did not use the stove or coffee maker. I think I must have a small case of Obsessive Compulsive Disorder, but I hate to get in the car and have to turn back because I forgot to check something. When I close the garage door, I always tell myself, "door going down," so I remember I have checked the door.

The late afternoon sun is hanging at about four o'clock in the western sky. Since I am heading south I do not need sunglasses, so I leave them on the dash open with the lenses firmly implanted in the defroster channel by the windshield. I have found that even a fifty-knot wind won't dislodge them. I start the FJ and head onto Oceanside Drive. The police station is about two miles from my house. I pull onto Eleventh from Oceanside, turn north, and head downtown. Eleventh Street runs from the outskirts of town to the very center. It runs into Avenue G, which leads to Harper Street where the police station is located. No one really likes to take Eleventh because it has long needed repair and is as rough as the proverbial washboard. Speeds above 15 MPH tend to render the occupants of a vehicle as candidates for tooth or kidney replacement.

The road is deserted this evening. I can see a car heading south about a mile away. By the looks of it the driver is trying to go fast as they are having trouble maintaining a straight line as a result of being buffeted back and forth by the rough road. I am wondering why they are in such a hurry. As our two vehicles close the distance, I can see two people in the front seat of what appears to be an SUV. They are swaying back and forth in reaction to the vehicle virtually bouncing from one side of the road to the other. I am afraid they are going to lose control and smash into me. I am getting ready to pull off the side of the road when I see the person on the passenger side stand on the seat with his head and shoulders sticking up out of the moon roof. These tourists are really behaving poorly.

The guy pulls a huge rifle up through the moon roof. He brings it up to his shoulder then aims it at me. Three red flashes indicate he has an infrared scope. My heart is pounding as I realized the guy surfing the roof of the SUV is going to start shooting. As if my thought caused the action, I hear the dull thud of a bullet passing somewhere through the FJ. I don't wait for the next shot; I yank the steering wheel to the right as hard as I can and stomp on the accelerator.

I hear another thud as another slug finds its mark. I am now bouncing over the sandy soil that is the heart of Mustang Island. I have pulled onto a field and decide to throw the FJ into four-wheel drive. The four-wheel lever requires leaning way over near the passenger side. I lean over just as the windshield blows out toward the front of the FJ. Another slug meant for me. With the four wheels engaged, I take a direct route perpendicular to Eleventh Street. I look in the rearview mirror to see my assassin's progress. I can barely see them as my FJ is throwing up a dust cloud, wearing deep groves in the soft sand and weed field. I can certainly tell they are still coming but can't make out how fast. They have a more powerful machine and I am uncertain if they have four-wheel drive.

My only chance is to make it to the beach, which is about three blocks away. If I can get on the beach I will be able to get some help from the beach patrol. Maybe these guys won't want to kill me in front of a bunch of tourists. I am not sure, but I think they have stopped shooting. Whoops, another thud means I am wrong. They still want me dead. I quickly scan the fuel, oil, and temperature gauges to see if anything vital has been hit. All seem normal as I hear another shot hit. I give a thought to a serpentine maneuver to make hitting me much more difficult and then weigh the benefit versus the speed cost. I decide to keep going ahead.

As another bullet crashes through my windshield on the passenger side, a substantial trench looms ahead. I am not sure I can make it up and over and see I have no choice but to try. I grip the steering wheel as tight as I can and pray I am not thrown out since I did not check my seatbelt to see if it was fastened. I can feel the shoulder strap against my body and since I can't check I can't be sure. I am amazed that my OCD haunts me even in this dire situation.

As the front of the FJ drops into the trench, I hold her steady and keep the pressure on the accelerator. The front wheels spin until they catch the earth on the other side of the trench. The rear wheels go over the edge and spin until they also catch earth. The front wheels pulling and the rear wheel pushing are enough to carry me up and out of the trench. I can barely keep the wheel in my hands as the FJ gives a violent pitch up and then another down as all four wheels finally grab earth on the same level.

The dust cloud is so large it has totally covered the FJ in a fine grit. I manage to wipe the dust off my face and can see the dunes that are the last barrier to the beach straight ahead. A funny thought comes over me as I contemplate going up and over the dune. I can imagine the startled look on the faces of those who would never expect a vehicle to come out of nowhere and onto the beach. I also hope the beach patrol is there and will be happy to pay the ticket for such an illegal move. I glance in the rearview mirror in time to see the SUV hit the trench. The four-wheel drive question is answered, as the trench does not even slow them down. They go through it like it was designed for them.

I now feel I may not be able to avoid getting killed. I reach the dune and go up to the top and over. I quickly determine there is no one in the way. I half slide down the dune and turn the front wheels to the left. I hit the beach and immediately snap to the left. This is the direction to downtown. The speed limit on the beach is 15 MPH. I floor the FJ again. I turn on the hazard flashers and begin laying on the horn. People look up in panic, and I manage to avoid them or they manage to get out of the way. I am reluctant to look in the rearview since I don't want to take my eyes off the beach ahead. I decide to take Avenue G, which is a beach access since it is heavily traveled and I am betting these guys do their best work in private.

I manage to make it to Avenue G. I pull a hard left turn and race up the beach entrance. I look in the side view mirror on my left as I make the turn and cannot see the SUV. I continue ahead and glance in the mirror and again no SUV. I am thinking my strategy worked. I continue to check and do not see them behind me. I keep looking all the way up Avenue G. When I come to Sixth Street, which is my right turn, I look right and left and behind me. They are not there. I make the right turn on Sixth and then a left into the police parking lot. I turn off the FJ and sit. For the first time I feel like I am going to throw up. My hands are shaking, and I am sure if I get out of the car I will fall to the ground. I decide to call Ned from where I am. I pull out my cell and shakily hit his auto dial number. He answers on the first ring. I tell him what happened and he tells me to stay put. I end the call and put my head on the back of my hands, which are supported by the steering wheel.

"What the hell?" Ned surprises me and I jump.

"Two guys tried to kill me." It is the best I can do.

"Have you looked at your FJ?"

"I have not had the strength to get out of it let alone look at it." I finally hit the seatbelt release and slump forward. I did not realize it before, I have been hit. There is not much blood however I definitely feel weak. I tell Ned, "I think I've been shot." He grabs his phone and places a quick call. The police station is right next to the EMS, so a crew arrives in less than a minute. Ned hovers like a mother. He keeps pressing for an update. The medic tells him that there is no danger of me dying and I will need some stiches. I think he makes Ned feel better when he tells him that the bullet did not hit anything vital passing through soft tissue. At least Ned is not hovering as much. I make a joke that since the bullet hit nothing vital it must have passed through my head. No one laughs.

"What soft tissue?" Ned is serious.

"The hip." The medic answers Ned with no elaboration.

Ned smiles. "You mean he was shot in the ass?"

"You could say that, sir." The medic is not amused. "We need to get this man to Corpus for treatment, so if you will excuse us we will be on our way."

"You are dismissed." He is still smiling which makes me feel a little better.

While the EMS crew prepares me for the trip to Corpus, Ned explains that he will question the guys at the Towers and then see me at the hospital. He quizzes the medics to see if they think I will need to spend the night. They believe I will be treated and released. They warn Ned that it will be up to the doctor to make the overnight call. Ned tells me to keep my cell close. He will see me at the hospital and drive me home.

"If they are going to release you and I am not there yet, call me and I will be there in twenty minutes."

"Thanks Ned." I sound a little weak.

I have to admit I really don't want to stay at the hospital, but I am definitely not in the pink so to speak. I think I will let the professionals make the call. I tell Ned goodbye and I'm lifted into the ambulance. I verify with the EMS that he was telling the truth about the flesh wound. He confirms it again. He wants to know if I would like anything for the pain. I joke about a margarita and decline anything else.

He tells me it would be good to start a drip which will help prevent symptoms of shock. I give him permission and he hooks me up to a plastic envelope on a metal rod with a needle and plastic tube. He is very good. I do not feel the needle going in. I do, however, feel the difference in temperature of the stuff going into my veins. It seems oddly cooler. Since the trip will take over a half hour, I give in to a small nap. I close my eyes and feel a warm, peaceful sensation and the gentle rock of the vehicle.

I dream quick sequences of events, none of them very

memorable. I pass through bright lights and deep blackness. I have dreams of voices, commands, and whispers. The dreams have a vague familiarity of having been in the same place before yet still seem unreal. There are no nightmares and the dreams seem to be the exact opposite. There are calming effects of cool breezes and warm winds. The dreams seem to go on forever, and I do not want to wake up. I would like to stay in this ambulance forever.

Chapter Thirteen

"Mr. Cannon, you need to wake up." A voice I think I've never heard before comes out of a bright light and jars me to wake up.

"Who is that?" I can hear my voice is hoarse.

"I am a medic who has closed your wound. My name is Jason, not that it means anything."

"Where am I?" I am getting really tired of this question.

"I think you will get all your questions answered in a while. For now you need to rest." Jason gets up and moves across a very small room. The room has a small workspace on the opposite wall and a set of bunk beds right beside it. I look up and see I am in the lower bed of a set of bunk beds on this side of the room as well. I try to rise up off the bed but feel tightness across my chest. I also have a feeling of pressure across my thighs. Both tell me I am being restrained. I move my right hand in preparation of feeling what is holding me to the bed and realize my arms are restrained at the wrist.

"Hey, Jason, what the fuck? Why am I tied down?"

He answers very calmly, "So you won't hurt yourself. You had some pretty wild dreams." Jason then takes a chart and steps toward a door. The door opens into the room, and it is clear this room is on a boat as he steps over the twelve-inch threshold. He turns and grabs the door on the other side and pulls the door shut. The handle clasps shut with a loud metallic click.

I am alone and pull against the restraints. I quickly see that it is useless to try and move beyond the slack in the bindings. The slack is almost nonexistent. I cannot bring my hands anywhere near my body or face. My legs are immobilized, and even a small turn of my body is impossible. I get a very close feeling, like I am trapped in a small space. I fight the urge to panic and scream out for help. Whoever put me in this straight jacket-like position means for me to be here, and I don't think pleading for help will have any effect.

I look around and see the room has no windows. From the smell and white decor it seems to be some kind of medical quarters. I can also feel a constant vibration that is low level yet noticeable. The last time I experienced this kind of movement was when I had a very cheap ticket on a cruise to St. Thomas. The source of the St. Thomas vibration was the huge diesel engines that ground away continually while the boat was underway. I only felt the vibrations when all was quiet and in bed. I am now thinking given I am on some kind of boat. From the looks of this stateroom with its four births, it must be a very large boat.

I am trying to piece together how I could have possibly been put on a boat and under complete restraint. The last thing I remember is telling the EMS person that it would be okay to attach a shock pack. I remember he attached it and the needle did not hurt. That is the last thing I remember. They must have knocked me out with a drug. I have no idea how I got here or how long I was unconscious. I cannot feel the gunshot wound, so it must have been taken care of by that Jason guy as he said.

The light in the room is painfully bright. I close my eyes to escape the glare for a moment. I think I am still under the influence of the drug since my eyes seem quite sensitive. When I close my eyes big tears flow down my cheeks. I am not crying and the tears flow anyway. It must be the irritation caused by the drug. As I contemplate the tears, I hear the door click. I open my eyes to see who is coming in, only all is a blur.

"Hello, John, nice to see you again."

I can't see who it is and yet I would never forget the voice of Winther. I wonder if it would be better to just ignore him and not respond. I guess my curiosity and the desire to get some answers take priority.

"Agent Winther, you old dog." I toss in some bravado I didn't feel.

"I am glad you are doing okay." He actually sounds like he means it.

"I would be better if you let me get up out of this bed and then tell me what the hell is going on." I decide to keep up the front of bravery.

"Well, John, that is going to be very difficult given the fact that you broke your promise to us."

I was taken aback. "What promise did I break?"

"We requested that you call on the cell should you have any questions or concerns. We find that you did not and went to the Chief of Police."

"What was I supposed to do when I find my boat gone and your so-called agency disappears?"

"You should have called. We would have been able to give you assurance that everything was proceeding according to plan."

"What about that fake Chief of Police you guys put in the room?"

"We needed absolute security on this operation. We needed to have one of our own impersonate the chief so that the information would be held to only those who needed to know."

"And what was I supposed to do when the chief comes a calling wondering why I haven't called."

"You should have gotten on the phone and let us know."

"Why did you need a chief impersonator in the first place?"

"We didn't think you would believe us if there was no one you knew who was involved as well."

I am thinking Winther is starting to make sense, and I am beginning to worry I have in fact made a big mistake by not calling. I would not have bought in without Ned being there and once I thought something was up I should have called. Of course had I called I would be safe and an accomplice to whatever these guys are attempting to pull off.

"So what is next?"

Winther smiles and sits in a chair next to my bed. He crosses his legs and folds his hands in his lap. "That really depends on you."

"What do you mean?"

Winther does not move. My eyes have cleared and I can see Winther very well now. He is dressed in casual clothes appropriate for the weekend. He has on a short sleeve sport shirt like one worn by Tom Hanks in the movie *Forrest Gump* and khaki slacks. For some reason he looks older than he did when he was an FBI agent. I think the combination of lighting and his weekend clothes have taken a little of the power look that he had then. His hair is salt and pepper with more salt than pepper and tells me he is older than I thought. He continues to smile, yet his expression turns slightly darker. There is a subtle move of the eyebrow and a quiver of the lip that signals displeasure.

"We could have killed you on the Island. We could have done it twice. The first time was when we took out the girl with the big mouth. The second was when we wanted to capture you. We didn't either time, and do you know why?"

I take a deep breath and hold it when Winther admits to the murder of Gerry. Winther is what he appears to be. He is a career criminal and everything he told me was a lie. I decide to answer his question anyway.

"Why didn't you kill me?"

"Since you went to the chief of police of that podunk town, your story would carry enough validly to force him to call in the feds, especially if we had killed you."

"You don't think he will go to the feds, given the fact that I am now missing?"

Winther chuckles like a kid with a secret. He is enjoying laying out his little plot one piece at a time. He suppresses more chuckles as he informs me Ned will not be concerned about me missing since Ned fully believes I am dead.

For the second time I hold my breath. I finally let it out, "Why does he think I am dead?"

Winther is beside himself. "The ambulance unfortunately was involved in a huge accident. It rolled over on the causeway, caught fire, and all three occupants were burned beyond recognition. The resultant explosion destroyed what was left of the forensic evidence. The South Padre Island Drive was closed for a whole day, and the heat of the fire nearly destroyed the causeway itself. It will be years until they figure out who was who in that accident. In the meantime, a very nice service is being planned for you and the two EMS workers in Port Aransas. You all will be buried in a common grave."

I strain against my bindings. I call Winther a few names, and he continues to sit in his chair totally unaffected by my tirade. He allows me to vent and when I am finally spent he continues.

"We plan to take you with us when we strike at the heart of American pride. Of course if you become a pain we will put you in a fifty-gallon barrel and drop you into a nice deep trench somewhere in the ocean, suitably weighed down with concrete of course."

A chill goes through my body as it is very clear Winther is totally insane. I need to be less combative and try to find out as much as I can. I make a mental note to try and stay alive as long as I can.

"Why do you want to take me with you?"

"Ah, a good question—not an easy answer. You see, we all have clients that we need to serve. The client who is funding this expedition is especially interested for you to witness our moment of glory."

"And who would that be?"

"As they would advise in any good mystery—all in good time, my man, all in good time."

Winther gets up and turns to leave. He tells me if I behave I will be given some freedom since we are now steaming in the Atlantic and there is really nowhere to go. He does crack himself up by suggesting I could jump overboard if I wanted to be free. He offers to give me the run of the ship provided I wear handcuffs and ankle bracelets. I, of course, accept and he tells me someone will be back to fit me. He also lets me know he would enjoy having my company at dinner tonight. I figure I best play along and accept. In a warped way he seems pleased.

He tells me as he leaves, "Dinner will be at seven. You will be given a cabin and your clothes are there. Dress is informal. See you then."

Chapter Fourteen

I lay there, my mind racing. I wonder who the poor person was who took my place in the ambulance. I wonder where this vessel is going. I am hoping there will be an opportunity to contact Ned to let him know what is going on. I am also thinking despite the "accident," Ned will continue to look into the real fact I was shot at and wounded. He must think it an unusual coincidence that I died on the way to the hospital. He also has talked to the security guys and must have some questions about what went on there. I have faith he will continue down the path of getting to the bottom of the situation. Another thought pops into my head. What if these guys go after Ned? That would be the simple way to keep the situation under control.

I really can't figure out why they think I am the only one who needs to be stopped. They had no hesitation when they silenced Gerry. I cannot figure out my connection. They got my boat and I can't see any other reason to keep me around. Of course, Winther mentioned his client. I have to wonder who that could be. I can't believe there is anyone on this Earth who hates me enough to want me to see what these guys have planned.

The metal click signals the door being opened again.

"Knock, knock. I have come to accessorize your wardrobe."

"Very funny, Jason."

Jason steps over the threshold carrying some impressive irons. He has some handcuffs which look brand new. They catch the light as if they are made of silver. I am thinking they must be polished nickel or brass covered with a coat of nickel and pretty tough to cut through. The leg irons are made of the same material.

"I am going to loosen your restraints and then you just sit on the edge of the bed." He adds, "I don't want any trouble from you, okay?"

I laugh inside at the idea of me giving Jason trouble. I am in no position to make trouble. What would I do? Take out poor Jason here and then jump over the side? I think I will take my time to see where opportunities might be to either make an escape, or disrupt this operation. I'm sure I don't have a great chance to subvert the whole deal or escape given the fact that the degree of difficulty is eleven on a scale of ten. I count up the odds; One: I am outnumbered by who knows how many. Two: I will be shackled and handcuffed. Three: I have no idea where I am, and think probably in the middle of the Gulf of Mexico. Four: I have learned limited survival skills. All in all it does not look good. Rather than let Jason know I am feeling pretty helpless, I'll give him a good answer.

"You'll get no trouble from me."

Jason does not respond and we seem to have a deal. I will give him no trouble and he will truss me up like a felon on death row. He unloosens the restraint around my right wrist. He then attaches one handcuff. He questions if it is too tight. I tell him it feels fine. He then does my left wrist and loosens the band across my chest. He seems satisfied I will not try to bolt notwithstanding the band across my thighs. He snaps the ankle irons on my legs and then unfastens the band across my thighs. He helps me up to a sitting position, since not having the use of my hands makes getting into a sitting position very difficult.

Once up in a sitting position I feel light headed. "How long I have been lying down?"

"I'm not authorized to tell you anything."

I drop the issue. I am thinking it must be for quite a while since I now feel like throwing up. "I feel like I am going to be sick." Jason quickly moves to the cupboard on the other side of the room and out a plastic container which is suited to the purpose, walks back, and hands it to me. The net effect is I don't think I will be sick. "Can I hold onto it?"

"Yes, it will be okay."

While Jason is affixing a chain from the handcuffs to the chain he has placed around my waist, I wonder why I wanted to keep this container. I am guessing it is the first thing I have been able to acquire that might be useful later. It is very comforting to have a physical object in my hand that might help an escape and right now, for the life of me, I have no idea how. Jason finally finishes by attaching a chain from the ankle bracelets to the chain around my waist.

Jason holds my upper arm with one hand and tells me to step down from the bed; I sort of slide off the edge of the bed into a standing position. Jason tells me I will not be able to take independent steps and must shuffle; otherwise I will fall on my face. I have seen criminals on TV similarly restrained. I have never wondered how it felt and now know the whole idea is to keep movement to a minimum. Jason has done a good job. My first few steps are very shaky. Jason has me shuffle around the small room until I get the hang of it. He finally declares me ready to navigate on my own and shows me how to step over the threshold without falling.

We proceed down a narrow hallway past several closed doors. The boat has a slight motion which throws me off. Several times I have to bend my knees to stay on my feet like I would if I was on a surf board. It is amazing how much help the arms are in keeping balance. They are useless balance aids when attached together at the wrists. We come to a stairway which leads up. Jason lets me know that I am to go in front of him and advises me to take one step at a time. He tells me he will be behind me in case I fall.

After a few stairs, I can see his point. I am forced to grab the handrail on my left with both hands and kind of jump up on each stair. There must be ten or more stairs. By the halfway point I am out of breath yet keep going, since I don't want Jason to think I don't do this every day as part of my exercise routine. We reach the top and I pause to let Jason up as well. The stair leads to another hallway, which we slowly navigate.

After passing about five others, Jason stops at a door. He rotates the handle and pushes the door in. He motions me to enter the room. I step over the threshold and enter the room. The lighting is quite dim. There is a porthole across the room which adds some light. I can also see I am above the water line, which means I can at least look out and see more than just four walls. Having a room above the water line makes my options a little better as well.

Jason tells me the room will not be locked and I am free to move around the boat. He suggests that I take it easy since I am not too steady on my feet. He also tells me dinner is at seven and he will come for me to show me where the dining facilities are located. He nods toward the bunk and lets me know there are clothes and underwear there for me to use. He steps over the threshold and is gone.

I look around the room. The furnishings are pure freighter. There is a double bunk against one wall and metal desk bolted to the other. The only chair is a metal, straight back relic which hasn't had a change of looks since those installed on the *Titanic*. There is a small sink with a mirror above it on the same wall as the door. I make note that the head and shower must be a communal affair. I walk (or hop) to the porthole. Looking out, I see only the Gulf. I half expected to see land, but there is only deep blue water meeting a lighter blue sky on the horizon. The seas seem calm with swells about two feet. The boat is relatively stable as it makes its way to wherever it is going.

I really don't know how I am going to be able take a shower, as for now, I need to find the head. I go out the door, avoiding tripping over the threshold, and hop-walk down the hall. About two doors away is a door marked "head and shower." I open it and step up and in. The door is outfitted to close automatically if released. The room is totally dark, and since I can't hold the door open and hunt for a switch to turn on the light I am forced to let the door go. It swooshes shut and I might as well be blind since there is absolutely no light at all. I run my hands up and down the wall next to the door until I feel a switch. I activate the lights and see I am in a room with two metal commodes, a single shower stall with a fabric curtain pulled across the opening, and a small metal sink like the one in my room.

I use one of the commodes and then wash both hands with some difficulty. The faucets are the kinds which turn off automatically. The sink has a stopper so there is a way to draw a basin of water. I then hold the hot first and then the cold to fill the sink. I put both hands in the sink to get them wet and then pump the soap dispenser. I build up lather and then thrust my hands back into the sink. After all this I see there is no way to dry them. This simple process takes ten minutes.

If someone doesn't let me out of these handcuffs I can't see how I will accomplish defecating and necessary clean up. For the first time in my life I give some thought to those who have lost an arm, or hand, or gods forbid, both. To go through life needing others to help with the accomplishment of natural functions has to be hell on earth. I am particularly thinking of our military casualties and the adjustment they and their families have to make. Makes me wonder why I haven't recognized their sacrifice until now.

Deep in thought I open the door. I am quite surprised to see what appears to be an armed solder standing in the hall. He is heading to use the bathroom. He is dressed in olive drab combat clothes. An equipment belt is wrapped around his waist on which rides a side arm as well as an assortment of pouches. He also has a substantial sheath with knife or bayonet and several hand grenades attached to what appear to be suspenders on either side of his broad chest. He is carrying an AK47, and he is wearing a beret and his face is wrapped with a patterned cloth. The only feature subject to observation is his eyes. His eyes show surprise at my appearance. I am not sure if it is a surprise to him I am out of my room or that I look like I am walking the last mile in the big house.

His eyes soften, and I can see crinkles in the corners indicating he is smiling. He raises his AK in what I imagine is a Middle East good old boy salute hello. His surprised look would be no different if we were in the same situation and a different venue. If I had just walked out of a bathroom at Brooks Brothers and this guy was coming in he would register the same surprise of encountering someone when you do not expect to do so. I wave meekly and continue to move out of the way. He waits until I am clear before giving me one last look and pushing through the door.

I get back to my room. I think about the fact armed men are also on this boat. Seeing the soldier does not change anything; it only shows these guys are serious about whatever they have planned.

For the first time I finally notice I am wearing scrubs. The small mirror gives me a view of a pretty desperate character. I haven't shaved since I was taken, and since I have never grown a beard I am not sure how many days my current growth represents. I am thinking about four but have no way to get a more accurate estimate. When I get close to the mirror, I see I do indeed look like a convicted felon. The scrubs are green and might as well be prison orange. I have large bags under my eyes and attribute them to many days of being immobile. I hope moving around will see them gone.

Not to be too vain at a time like this, but I really look a lot older with the hair on my face and the dark baggy circles under my eyes. Why I care is beyond me, but I do. It's not like this boat has a bunch of beautiful women all dying to meet me or anything. This concern for self-image may separate those who have something to live for verses those who have given up. Pure ass vanity. Anyway it is good for me I care, because I intend to give these guys a run for their money.

My thoughts are very brave and then I contemplate changing clothes or taking a shower. Right now it is totally impossible to do anything unless I can get out of this hardware. I need to go find Jason and request he unhook me for a shower and a change of clothes. I turn from the sink and mirror and walk (sort of) to the door. I use both hands and pull the door in. I avoid the cursed threshold one more time and enter the hallway. I look right and left, trying to decide which way to go. There is no clue as to where people might be on this thing so I shrug and go to the right. I pass a few doors and since they look like cabins I decide not to try them and keep my shuffle moving forward.

After a couple more doors I come to an open area where there are several doors on kind of a quadrangle. One is marked "crew only" and I don't think I want to go there. The one that is interesting has a window and "observation" stenciled above the window. I go to it and look out. All I can see is a gray wall which is part of the structure. The structure is definitely on the outside of the ship, so I grab the handle and push against the door. The door opens out and I can feel the wet, hot, fresh salt air hit me in the face. I go through the door and let the wind slam it shut behind me.

The structure seems to be part of another section of the ship. I walk to the right and come to a narrow passageway which has the structure on the left and a low chain fence between regularly spaced posts on the right. The path does not seem wide enough for me to walk facing forward so I turn facing the sea, which seems to be going by at a hundred miles per hour. I look out and feel my reproductive parts react to the very narrow walkway. I instinctively press my back against the structure. The wind is whipping at my scrubs and seems to be intent in seeing me double over the low chain and fall head first the fifty or so feet to the water below.

I make my way along the walkway, like a crab would if faced with the same circumstances in his life. I move my butt and then follow with my feet. I am hoping my butt has the best chance of gripping the structure because I have no limbs capable. I move very slowly and see I am making some progress. At least I have not been swept into the sea, which given my current extra weight and lack of mobility would be a short cut to immortality.

I finally reach a wider part of the ship. I can tell I am covered with sweat inside the scrubs since I am now kind of sliding along the structure. I actually look back to see if I am leaving a smear where my back has been. I can't really tell. I continue along the walkway and look up to see another deck above the one I am on. The bow of the ship is directly ahead given the wind blowing in my face. Once there, maybe I can find a deckhand who can get a message to Jason or Winther.

As I am gaining confidence on the walkway I come to a screeching halt. A camouflaged soldier very much like the one I met at the head, steps out of an open hatch and looks like he wants me to stop. He is yelling something and between the wind, his covered mouth, and his non-English, I do not understand what he is trying to communicate. He is holding his AK in the port arms position and before I can react he pulls the trigger. It seems like a rainstorm of copper casings bounce off the metal deck. I immediately do a poor imitation of a squat thrust and hit the same metal deck. I actually land on some of the casings and am surprised to feel how hot they are. I let out a yelp as one of the casings burns my left cheek.

The guy doing the shooting is also yelling something over and over. I cannot understand what he is yelling. I assume it is something like "get the fuck down," but I don't even know what language he is screaming in. I can't get any lower on the deck, so whatever he is going to do will be a matter of his choosing. I am now being pelted with casings from his AK. He suddenly stops firing, and the echo of his last round floats away on the wind. It is so quiet I can hear my heart beating. If not, I certainly can feel it in my ears. I am thinking that the shooter is taking his time to reload. I don't hear any sounds of clips being taken out or being put in. I hear nothing outside my head.

Chapter Fifteen

As I lay on the deck it occurs to me the sun is very hot on the left side of my face and I am not sure I should move to switch sides. Before I can make a decision, the sun seems to disappear and a cooling shadow passes over my face. I decide to engage the person who is standing over me.

"Hello there." I give my greeting as best I can with one half of my face pressing on the deck and the spent shell casings.

"Hello yourself." Jason has some kind of warped humor sound in his voice. "Are you okay?"

"If you mean do I have any bullet holes in me, the answer is no. I have no bullet holes, so yes I must be okay."

"You sure take things literally don't you?"

"Jason, in case you haven't noticed I am lying on a bunch of spent cartridges, which came from a very active AK47, which was in the hands of a very angry looking person in full combat gear, who was yelling at me in a language I don't understand; so yes, I take it literally the person doing the shooting wanted me to do something that I still don't understand."

"He wanted you to turn around and go back to your quarters." Jason tells me this as if any fool would know that.

"Why the gunfire?" I ask while rolling over in preparation to sit up and get back on my feet.

"Not sure," Jason answers. "These guys shoot their weapons all the time; maybe it is a way to let off steam."

"Is it safe to get up?"

"Oh yes." Jason answers cheerfully as if I didn't even need to be concerned. "The guy is gone. He left when he saw me arrive."

With some effort I finish rolling over and struggle to sit upright. I need to get up since there are still some casings causing discomfort, sort of like sitting on what feels like ball bearings. I kind of roll to one hip, and then use my hands to push me into a position where I can pop a small jump to my feet. I accomplish the feat and hear a couple of casings which were stuck to my backside hit the deck. I am now glad I kept up with a vigorous workout program since I use quite a bit of strength on the maneuver, and in any less shape I would not have been able to get to my feet.

"Nicely done." A compliment from Jason, the smart ass.

"Thanks." My reply is tinged with sarcasm. "I wonder if you could let me out of these restraints so I can shower and change clothes. I was actually looking for you when I ran into Mr. Trigger Happy Man."

Not to be outdone he says, "I was looking for you for the same purpose. I have been authorized to give you one half hour without the restraints. The only caveat is the door to your cabin needs to be locked and a guard posted outside."

"That is fine and I don't expect that I will go anywhere."

We head back to my cabin and this time take a stairway down and then one up to avoid the narrow walkway. Jason becomes chatty. "I would never have tried going on that walkway let alone with the added degree of difficulty of being in restraints."

"Why thank you Jason. That's a compliment, but want you to know I was scared stiff the whole time." I don't want him to think I have any daring do at all.

We get to the head and shower. There is another nasty-looking guard standing in the hall. Jason takes off the ankle and wrist cuffs. He tells me there is a robe and towel in the head. He asks me if I need anything else. I tell him no, and he lets me know he will be back in one half hour.

"Once you finish your shower the guard will take you back to your cabin. I will lock this room and leave the key with the guard. If you find you need anything just have the guard call me."

"I will, Jason."

He turns to go and I am sensing Jason may be doing this work for some reason other than his loyalty to the cause. I think it might be helpful to try and get on his good side. He could have some vulnerability I could use to help me escape or to disrupt whatever these guys plan to do.

"Jason?"

He stops and turns back to facing me.

"Thanks for this."

I can see he has a brief flush. The fact that I gave him credit for the kindness had its effect. He was pleased I thought he was in charge of the largess. I am sure Winther tells him what to do or not to do, but I think we just made a connection. He mumbles something like "no problem," then goes out the door. I hear the bolt hit the strike indicating the door being locked from the outside.

Since I don't have a lot of time, I decide to hit the head and take a shower. When I get back to it, I plan to look my cabin over very carefully for two things. The first is any eavesdropping equipment. The second is for anything I can use to unlock the cuffs, which would be easier than cutting them off.

I read somewhere that cuffs like mine are steel coated with nickel. They can be cut with bolt cutters. The problem is I won't be able to use a bolt cutter on my hands since they require some distance away from the object to be cut. I would be able to cut the ankle bracelets and that would be all. I might be able to use a drill press if there is some kind of automatic function that would let me start the press and then put the cuff chain under the drill to separate my hands. I would have to get to the metal shop assuming there is one on board. I would not be able to get the cuffs off, but would have the use of my hands.

I jump into the shower and continue to make plans. I will try to find the metal shop. I will look for bolt cutters and a drill press. If there are none then I will look for a hacksaw. My plan would be to use the bolt cutters to free my feet and to cut the waist chain. I would use the drill press or hacksaw to cut the chain between my hands. The hacksaw will have to be put in a vise, and I would have to pull the chain link back and forth over the blade. I feel pretty good about what will be my secondary plan. My primary plan involves finding a way to unlock the cuffs.

This would be the easiest way to conceal the fact that I have an avenue of escape since I would be able to unlock them at will when the time was right. To find a drill press, bolt cutter, or hacksaw means once I am free I will need to take quick action since I don't believe these guys will let me walk around without being restrained. I would have to time everything perfectly and not be detected until the job is finished. A tall order, I surmise.

I finish the shower and grab a towel. While drying myself off I carefully look the room over to see if there is anything available that could be used to pick a lock. Jason has left a toilet kit which contains some soap, shampoo, a comb, a toothbrush, and toothpaste. I see nothing useful for escape. I assume they think a razor might be a little risky so they did not include one.

I pick up the toothbrush and tube of toothpaste. I open the cap and see a small covering over the end of the tube. I pull it off and see the tube is plastic. If the tube was metal maybe something could be done, but plastic offers no way. I squeeze some paste on the toothbrush and put it in my mouth. Nice mint flavor. I brush very hard and count to sixty on each of the four quadrants of my mouth. Now that I think of it, I haven't brushed my teeth for a while. The last time I remember was the morning Ned and I went to the warehouse. I spit into the sink. I notice the handle that controls the stopper in the sink is in the down position with the stopper open. I pull the handle up and the stopper closes. I hold my breath because sometimes the apparatus has a connection below the sink which has a pin or a wire holding the moving parts together.

I do not want to be obvious about looking below the sink. I keep brushing and turn on the water. I push the handle on the stopper down, and the stopper opens and allows the toothpaste foam and water to leave the sink. I pull the brush out of my mouth and cup my hand under the faucet. I lean over and suck some water into my mouth, then spit. I tap the toothbrush against the sink and purposely drop it so it lands under the sink. "Shit." I remark loud enough to be convincing if being listened to from a remote location.

I lean down to retrieve the brush and catch a look at the stopper connection to the handle. Sure enough there is a cotter pin at the end of the stopper rod holding the rod where it is inserted through one of several holes in a thin ribbon of metal connected to the handle. I pick up the toothbrush and rinse it off under the faucet. I need to plan carefully. The cotter pin could be used as a makeshift key. It is going take some work and is certainly better than a hairpin, which I had hoped to find on the floor of the shower.

I contemplate taking the pin right away. If I take it now the next person using the sink will discover it gone, and then I will be searched and will never have a chance to get another. They would probably throw me in a bare room, and I will never see another cotter pin, let alone bathroom, again. No, this will take planning. I feel real excitement at the thought of getting free and surprising the hell out of everyone.

I put on the robe and grab the towel and toilet kit. I knock on the door and hear the bolt clunk into the open position. I pull the door in and I'm standing face to face with the same soldier I saw the last time I was in the head. His face is still covered and I can tell by his eye crinkles that he is smiling. He allows me to step over the threshold and start down the hall. I get to my cabin and open the door. I step in and give a goodbye to my escort. I think he answers goodbye, but it was not in English so I am not sure.

I wait for the bolt to hit the strike and then start getting dressed. I dress slowly and start an examination of the cabin. I make every excuse to look under and over everything. I drop shoes and a shirt for the under the furniture examination, and stretch while standing on tiptoes for the over. After a thorough look, I can't find any obvious listening devices or cameras. In the course of my cabin check, I look under the small sink. This one has a cotter pin as well. This will make life easier since I can take this pin and do a makeshift temporary fix on the stopper. I don't have to use the stopper, so anything I rig won't need to be too sturdy.

I am now ready for Jason to come back. I sit on the bunk and continue my planning. I will need to refine the cotter pin to suit my purpose as a lock-picking device. The first thing which will need to be done is the pin will need to be straightened. I am not sure how difficult this will be and I am sure I won't be able to do it with just my fingers. I will need at least a pair of pliers, and if I had them and a vise, I would be in business. The next thing will be to adjust the cotter pin so it can get into the heart of the locking mechanism to release the lock. I am assuming the cuffs are the twenty-dollar variety and are more of a release rather than a tumbler kind of lock. A tumbler lock would need a key specifically grooved to trip each segment of the tumbler. The release type just needs a key which can bypass the internal gate to depress the release. The theory of hand cuffs is that the person being restrained is in the company of an officer and not necessarily the locks can never be opened. Of course I could be wrong and the cuffs could be very expensive and designed for no escape. I will only know what I have when I try to pick the locks.

The door noise alerts me to the fact that Jason has come back. He actually knocks on the door before opening it. I call out for him to come in. He smiles as he enters the door. I see the guard has left. The door closes and Jason goes about his duty of putting me back into the shackles and cuffs.

"How long have you worked for the Desert Wolves?"

Jason's head jerks up at the mention of Desert Wolves. "I am not supposed to talk about anything like that."

"Who is in charge? Winther?"

Jason again reacts by looking somewhat nervous and accidentally drops his handcuffs, causing a loud chains-hit-the-floor kind of noise.

"I can't confirm anything. You need to stop the questions."

"You sure don't look like a terrorist."

"Mr. Cannon, if you don't stop I will need to report you and the result will be less than pleasurable."

"Are you part of this operation willingly or doing this against your will?"

Jason looks around as if he is checking to see if anybody is in the room with us. I think he is going to tell me something one way or another. He leans very close to my left ear while he is attaching the handcuffs and whispers, "We all do things against our will, Mr. Cannon. Now please quit talking or I will call the guard and you will find yourself in a very dark room below the lowest place in this boat."

I figured it was worth a try. His answer leads me to believe he is being forced to serve these guys. His statement about the dark room was for external consumption, and I am sure he passed, especially with those who don't speak English as their first language. I don't speak again. He continues his work and when finished he advises he will be back shortly to accompany me to dinner with Winther. I would have asked Jason for Winther's first name, but his threat about the lowest room sounded like someone could follow through and I don't need that kind of aggravation.

He gets up and is about to leave. I look at him and he mouths what I take to be the word "wire" while making circular motions around his midsection. The poor sap is wired for sound. No wonder he can't speak freely. All of our conversation is recorded. I nod and he turns and leaves.

Now I have another plan that needs to be developed. I need to figure out how to get the wire off Jason so we can have a substantial talk. This might take priority over the need to pick my locks. If Jason and I can agree on a way out, he will be able to let me go. The objective will be to get control of the wire so the people listening won't know it has been compromised. I start thinking of places a wire would not go. The shower comes to mind immediately. I am sure Jason is allowed time to shower without wearing the wire. Well, I am not sure and need to find out.

This raises another thought which will need to be figured out to determine if Jason is without his wire anytime. I need to be able to communicate with Jason without vocal sounds. Pencil and paper comes to mind immediately. I could write to Jason about a plan while we are talking about something else. I wonder how hard it will be to get pencil and paper. I could approach Winther for the materials under the guise of needing to write a goodbye to my family. I am assuming Winther will at some time tell me I am curtains. He has already hinted that a person wants me to witness whatever carnage these guys have planned. I am sure this person, whoever it is, does not intend to allow me to leave after they accomplish their goal.

I feel comforted in having a number of avenues to pursue. When I woke up earlier, I did not have a clue on how to control this situation. I now have a number of possibilities. I am completing my thoughts when I hear a knock at the door. I shuffle over and pull the door in. It is Jason. It is obvious he is not coming in and expects me to go with him.

"You ready, Mr. Cannon?" He is playing it straight.

"I am ready." I step over the cursed threshold one foot at a time.

"We will be having dinner in the captain's quarters." Jason takes the lead and I follow.

I make it a point to pay attention to the route to the captain's quarters. I want to be able to come back at the appropriate time. I figure the quarters can't be too far from the bridge, where the good stuff like a radio and navigational gear is located.

Jason leads us down the hall to the same opening I encountered earlier. Instead of going out on the deck we take the unmarked door in the center. The door actually conceals an elevator. Jason hits the button for up and we wait until we hear the arrival of the elevator. Jason slides open the elevator door and gets in. He motions me in as well. Once on board he slides the door shut and punches the middle of six buttons. The elevator makes a jerky ascent to what I presume to be the third deck of this ship.

Once the elevator stops Jason slides the door open again and pushes against the outer door. He holds the door for me, and I make my way out of the elevator to another hallway. He lets the door close and takes the lead again. We pass another two doors and then come to one with the title "Captain's Quarters." "This must be it." I make this a joke, given the name on the door.

Jason does not appear amused and opens the door and holds it. He indicates that I should go in, so I step over the threshold and enter what appears to be a small anteroom. Jason closes the door, takes my arm, and guides me through two double doors that are directly ahead. We enter a surprisingly large room. There is a large table preset for dinner and a number of chairs.

A quick count confirms room for ten. There are four on each side of the table and one at each end. The table has been covered in white linen and is set with silver flatware and crystal stemware. Each place has a charger where the first plate will go. The chargers look to be custom made. It is hard to verify but appears to be pewter with a wolf's head in relief. It looks like there are at least three flights of wine given the number of glasses at each place setting. The flatware setting indicates at least three courses, which seems to confirm the wine estimate.

The centerpiece is fresh flowers arranged in a low profile to allow the participants to see each other. The room itself is in stark contrast to the elegance of the table. It is gray and has a number of ugly conduit pipes running along the walls and has a ceiling that I estimate to be no more than seven feet. There is a door on the far end and by its slightly opened appearance it swings both ways. I am thinking the kitchen must be beyond the door and service staff will use it for the dinner.

"So where would you like me to sit?" I poke Jason with the question knowing he won't appreciate the joke. I half expect him to tell me to sit anywhere I want and he replies we should wait for Winther before sitting down, and as if on cue Winther enters the room through the double doors.

"Ah, Mr. Cannon," He extends his hand. "You are enjoying your stay, yes?"

I take his hand with my two, "Mr. Winther I cannot remember when I have enjoyed a stay as much."

He laughs heartily and tells Jason to take me to the end of the table on the far side of the room. I will have a lovely view of the double doors. While we are maneuvering to the far end Winther mentions loudly that he expects a few more for dinner.

"I will introduce you when everyone gets here. In the meantime, Jason please take the cuffs off of Mr. Cannon's wrists and attach him to his chair."

Jason nods and directs me to sit in the chair. I sit down hard since the chair is a little lower than I thought. Jason wonders if I am okay and I tell him yes. He takes off the wrist cuffs and threads the chain connected to my waist chain around the rear of the chair and locks the cuff on one of the slats in the back. This will not hold me should I decide to run. My connection to the chair would make movement out a door very difficult.

"Would you like a cocktail?" Winther directs the question to me and leaves Jason out of the invitation.

He motions to Jason that he should leave the room. Jason turns and goes out the service door. He passes what appears to be a waiter in white coat and gloves. I have never seen a waiter who looks like this guy. He resembles a pirate who has been pressed into service. He doesn't look too pleased about it either. He scowls at my response. "As a matter of fact I would enjoy a Tanqueray Gin on the rocks with two olives."

I did want to add, "And hold the spit" I fight the urge.

"I'll have the same," Winther says then takes a place next to me.

The waiter nods and uncurls his lip and disappears. I mentally name him Quasimodo since he reminds me of the character in *The Hunchback of Notre Dame.*

"I think you will find tonight's guests very interesting." Winther leans a little closer. "They are a collection of some of the finest specialists in their respective fields. I needed a team who could come together and execute a master plan with flawless precision. Each of these people has proven themselves in various operations and now is working for me. The plan has been designed and each of these leaders knows his role and is prepared to complete the individual contribution necessary for total success."

"So what is the plan?" I interject my question as the waiter comes back with our drinks.

Winther laughs. "I have to admire your nerve. If I tell you the plan I will have to kill you. Is that what you want?"

"I figure I am toast anyway, so like the cat I am very curious."

"I would try to control your curiosity." He then lifts his glass in a toast. "Here is to my mission and your satisfaction."

Chapter Sixteen

I would have normally touched glasses with a person offering a toast to my *satisfaction* but in this case I merely tilt my glass in Winther's direction. I have no idea what he means by my satisfaction and thinking back to the rhyme "curiosity killed the cat, satisfaction brought it back," I am wondering if maybe he has not planned to do away with me. Of course I may be reading into his toast something that is not there. Winther seems very calculating, and I don't think he does anything without purpose. Like this dinner. There is something he wants to prove with a dinner like this. I'll just have to wait to see what it is.

I look at my drink to see if there is anything floating or not dissolved. There is not. I take a sip of the cold gin. It is delicious so I take one more.

"To your satisfaction?" Winther wants to know as if we are sharing a secret.

"Very much so." I answer his question truthfully, deciding to play along.

The double doors open and the rest of the dinner guests enter and make their way to a place at the table. Winther is welcoming everyone and explaining that each should take a seat and he will do the introductions, after all have ordered a cocktail. There is little conversation among the guests as they are used to keeping their mouths shut in front of strangers. It appears to me these folks don't really know each other well.

Quasimodo moves down the table taking drink orders and I have to admit he seems to know what he is doing. If he was the one mixing my drink I would like to hire him. Once he is finished Winther stands and begins the introductions with a statement that he is pleased all could make the dinner. There are ten at the table and Winther goes around the room introducing each in turn.

"On my left is the beautiful Helen Daubery who is an expert in linguistics. Next to her is Alfred Quay who has his ear on communications." He points to the person next to Alfred, "say hello to Fred McDonald. He is the best electronics person on this earth." Fred lights up at the compliment. Winther then nods at the pretty girl sitting next to me. "I am not sure you have had an opportunity to talk with Cynthia Tulane yet. I encourage you to please do so before the night is over. She can explain one hundred different ways to kill a person." Winther pauses while the tittering about Cynthia dies down.

"I am going to skip our guest for a moment and move to the person sitting next to him. Rory Grunter has been with me from the beginning and is the brains behind the strategic planning for each mission. He is also a good one to talk to since he has a lot of information." Winther takes a sip of his drink. "Next is Jerry Arêtes who comes to us from Columbia and has the experience in armament as a result of his activities in support of Castro." Jerry also beams at the praise. "Next to Jerry is the lovely Jane Winston who was the first female to penetrate the security system of the Pentagon. She is not only easy on the eyes but can hack the hell out of any computer system." Jane wags her finger at Winther in mock scolding of his obviously chauvinistic comment.

It looks like she enjoys compliments on her beauty as she is smiling widely as she scolds. "Finally on my right is Morse Shipman who is the navigation genius on this trip. He can tell you where you are within three inches of accuracy." Morse nods politely and smiles broadly.

After the introductions, Winther also thanks them for taking time from their busy schedules to be personally involved in the mission. He hopes spending the next few days on the boat won't be a hardship. He then lays the ground rules for the evening. He assures them all that they can relax and enjoy the time together because, until the mission is complete, no information will leave the boat.

I take another long pull at my drink. I am getting a little anxious about being in the presence of this group. The room seems to be getting warmer or at least more humid. I don't think the room was designed to accommodate ten people. Looking around the table my first impression is that each of these individuals runs some piece of business which is totally illegal.

As I look at each I detect a line of hardness that in spite of a smile or laugh seems to be on each of their faces. I think each of them is a little wary of the others in the room as well. There is a tension which is difficult to pinpoint, but certainly can be felt. It is in the quick glance of the eyes when a noise is made in the kitchen and the way each seems to be preoccupied in a thought rather than truly listening to the person talking to them. None of these people look like they have any weakness nor would have empathy for others who are weak. If necessary I think they would not have a problem cutting the throat of anyone else in the room.

Winther goes on about how important the mission is and that each of the people in the room will look forward to sharing the point of history that is being written through their actions. I have to believe all these people are paid mercenaries since in the limited time I have had to listen to them talk together. I never heard one mention the so called cause. I really don't know for sure but this may be why all of them are being patient with Winther's rambling. Of course Winther is an engaging speaker so maybe that is as simple as it is.

The drinks arrive and Winther stops talking while they are being served. Once each has a drink Winther turns to me.

"I now want you to meet John Cannon. John is a special guest of our benefactor and I have given him the designation as guest of honor." The room titters at the suggestion so I know Winther is joking at my expense. He continues, "It is his boat which will be used to carry the explosives to the target. We think the entire mission will be a success because of John's boat."

I almost choke on the word explosives. It did not occur to me until this moment that the story Winther told me while impersonating an FBI agent is *totally* true. These nuts intend to blow up a national treasure. I believed it was just a story to trick me into giving them my boat. Now I know *My GRL* is going to be used for a horrific explosion. I am wondering where she is right now and pretty much block out what is said for the next few minutes.

The dinner takes on a new life. By the time the appetizer arrives there is animated talk going on between the participants. They are inquiring of each other if they were involved in this or that horror. As the wine passes more freely, the conversation covers more subjects. A momentary unnatural silence drifts over the room when one of the guests quizzes another, a little too loudly, if he had ever been stalked by drones. Winther breaks in and makes a joke about the comment to the effect that being stalked is better than the alternative. Most laugh and return to previous conversations.

Winther spends a lot of time talking to Morse Shipman beside him. Most of what they talk about is general observations on the weather and the prospects for success. My interest is raised when Winther queries Shipman if he will be able to verify the ship's location when the time comes. I assume he is talking about *My GRL*. To my surprise Shipman explains that he intends to home-in on the telecommunications of the midshipmen to their families. He further describes how the midshipmen cruise has time set aside for the midshipmen to call home to assure their families that all is well.

I can't believe my ears. What does the midshipmen cruise have to do with any of this?

Almost like he can read my mind Winther turns to me and observes without hesitation, "We believe one of America's treasures is the midshipmen class of Annapolis Naval Academy and we intend to take your little boat out to meet them while they are enjoying the midshipmen summer cruise. Your boat will be loaded with enough explosives to turn their ship into a fireball. It may not sink but still there will be severe causalities."

I am speechless. I look at Winther and finally my mouth catches up to my brain. "You think the government is going to stand by while you casually drift up to a Navy warship with the intent to blow it up?"

"What about the *Cole*?" Winther looks at me coldly.

I am momentarily at a loss for words. All I can think to do is to keep Winther talking. I noticed he had a couple of drinks before dinner started, so maybe he is loose enough to let me in on the complete plan. I decide to work in more questions. I figure the worst case is he tells me to shut up.

"The *Cole* was pre 9/11, when the military had to check and double check before engaging in hostile actions. They did not blow the terrorists out of the water because they did not have time to get permission. That was a different time than now. Why do you believe a US Navy warship will allow a sixty-five-foot boat to get close enough to cause major damage?"

Winther looks at me with an expression I have seen before on the face of a poker player just before laying down four aces. "John, John, John." He is shaking his head. "Let me help you understand."

He pauses and turns to Shipman on his other side who, as I remember, was introduced as the navigation genius and requests to be excused for a moment. Winther turns back to me and leans in a little.

"You see, John, it is really quite simple. Imagine a beautiful boat like your Hatteras on a warm day cruising in the same harbor as the Navy ship. Imagine the Navy ship getting ready to dock next to the aircraft carrier *Intrepid* for a public relations visit to the port of New York for fleet week. All hands will be involved in preparation for the delicate maneuver. Most of the midshipmen will be on deck in their dress whites so the docking and photo op will have the proper flair for the occasion. Do you think the Navy warship will be on alert at a time like this? The captain will be most concerned about how not to screw up the docking.

This is a friendly port in the home country. Who would think anything could happen? I doubt anyone on the ship will be on lookout for a huge bomb heading their way. Most of the heads will be turned toward the dock and not outward looking for trouble. Even if your boat is spotted in the harbor, so what? There will be a couple hundred boats of various sizes. I doubt yours will stand out. We will be able to get within one hundred feet and that is about all we will need. I have calculated the force of the explosion and can assure you not only will the Navy warship sustain significant damage, but that old bucket of bolts *Intrepid* will as well. Think of all the people standing on these ships when this thing goes up. They will not know what hit them. The carnage will be humongous."

Winther stops and takes a sip of his wine. The waiter removes his main course plate. He waits until the waiter moves down the table.

"Any questions so far?"

"I really don't have any questions that you will want to answer."

"Oh, give me a try."

"Are you absolutely out of your mind?"

I thought my question was very clever and would probably get me thrown back into the cuffs and to the dark place mentioned by Jason earlier. To my surprise, Winther smiles and takes the question like a professor. He actually gives me an answer.

"I would be out of my mind if I contemplated this act without a reasonable cause. You see, John, my Muslim brothers need to make a statement to your countrymen and our own as well. You have probably not paid attention to the history of the ageless struggle that has been going on between my faith and the followers of the Christian/Judaic traditions. I take it you are either a Christian or a Jew, am I correct?"

"I am a Christian."

"Of course you are. The Christian/Judaic tradition has, over the course of history, been responsible for the useless slaughter and enslavement of members of my Muslim faith for no other reason than my faith does not recognize the Jewish God, the Christian God, or son of God, Jesus as the true God or son of God. We embrace Allah as the one and only true God. Under the sign of the Star of David or the cross, so-called crusaders have worked to eliminate the right of my people to exist in peace. We have been denied a homeland in Palestine where Israel now has confiscated our property and continue to struggle for recognition of the basic right to worship the way we choose and to live on the lands taken from us."

I have to interrupt, "Is it right to live by the sword simply because past generations did so as well?"

"That is a very good question, John. Let me answer this way—now not only are we at war with the Christians and Jews, my people are also engaged in a struggle with those of the same faith as well. The caliph, who represents the political unity of Sunni Islam worldwide, has condemned our methods of seeking justice as 'too radical.' The caliph's view reflects those of some local Imams who we believe have become soft and have given up the tenant of an eye for an eye. My people have been warned eternal fires await us if martyred in the course of what they consider an unorthodox war against the west. Even Al-Qaeda, the militant organization of Islam has given us fair warning that we are on our own. So this 'life by the sword', as you call it, is the only course left to us if we are to achieve a just resolution for centuries of injustice. We have no voice other than that of the terror that we intend to inflict. We also believe that members of our faith will join us once they see how effective our methods will be. I envision sitting down with western governments for the purpose of drawing out the terms of lasting peace."

He stops and takes another sip of wine. His face is flushed and he seems slightly out of breath. It occurs to me he is highly impassioned to achieve what he considers a successful conclusion to not just this operation, but his whole strategy as well. I am thinking he envisions himself as the savior of his faith and world leader to boot. He waves the waiter away when the waiter presents the dessert. He is staring at me, waiting for my reaction to his grand plan. I decide not to disappoint.

"You are right. I have not been paying enough attention to understand it all. Am I right in that you see yourself as the potential savior of your faith?"

"By golly, John, you have hit the nail on the head. I don't think there is anyone who has the vision and courage to win this war except me."

I am thinking that this same conversation probably took place back in the 1930s between Adolf Hitler and some guy during dinner. The hair on the back of my neck is standing straight up. I look into Winther's deep brown eyes and see his passion blazing deep within. I am sure this man will have to die to be stopped. I need to get some more information about how this operation is funded and try again to find out why I am here with these people. Winther is clearly nuts, however maybe he can give me information which will be useful.

"So Winther . . . by the way, can I use your first name?"

"Certainly, it is Ralph."

I thought he was going to have a more eastern name. I guess the Ralph goes with the Winther. "So, Ralph, who is funding this operation?"

"You have met him. He is the brains behind Taft. You know the company that lost the litigation to Avery and you were the counsel to Avery. You were responsible for putting him on the stand and were also responsible for making a complete fool of him. He did not forget what you did to him. Do you remember the incident I am talking about?"

Boy do I remember. I never had the chance to go back and review the case after the incident in the elevator at the accountant's office and yet I remember the CEO of Taft. His name was Jacobs, and he was the most arrogant person I ever faced in litigation. He was sure he was going to prevail to the point where the judge finally threatened him with contempt of court if he did not stop his disparaging comments about Avery and me. I recall, he turned beet red after the dressing down by the judge.

I went on to further embarrass him with some copies of letters he had written threatening the Avery CEO. The language was coarse and I pointed out several misspellings to ensure that the words meant what they were supposed to mean if spelled correctly. I did this on purpose to humble him. Taft, a major manufacturer of telecommunication equipment, was accused of encroaching on Avery patents, and Avery sought relief from the federal court.

Avery made similar products to Taft and had been in the marketplace years before Taft. It was also well known that several of Avery employees were recruited by Taft. Taft was making competitive inroads in traditional Avery markets, so Avery brought suit. The court found that Taft had to pay damages of one hundred million dollars and pay Avery license fees of ten percent on every Taft product sold in competition to Avery. I think the reason the opposing council was so rude on the elevator was that he probably got fired. I remember he did not do a very good job.

Now I have a bigger worry than the opposing council. The CEO of Taft is funding an operation of pretty large scale. I know he is pretty wealthy yet did not know he was this wealthy. Time for more questions to Ralph.

"I did not realize Jacobs had so much money."

Ralph laughs and takes a long drink of water. "Oh yeah, let me assure you he has the money."

"Where did it come from?"

"He is one of us. His father has enough oil to float the Earth."

"So he wants to help you in your quest?"

"He was singularly the most influential person in getting me to finally step up and do my duty."

"You knew him before you started to put this plan together?"

"He is my father's brother."

"Your father is helping as well?"

"No, he has disowned me. He believes my mission is without merit."

"Why does Jacobs want me here?"

"You caused him to lose face in front of his peers and, more importantly, you humiliated him by pointing out his weakness with written English."

"I did not know English was not his first language."

"Yeah well—that will not help you now."

"Does he intend to kill me?"

"I really don't know. He only told me to make sure you don't escape. I think he will visit the ship before we reach our destination. Maybe you can find out from him yourself."

I think for a brief moment, "Don't you think he is going a little overboard about a little humiliation and the loss of the case?"

"I don't question his motives. I can tell you this—in our culture, had you been one of our countrymen, he would have the right to vengeance for his humiliation. The money he owed was not recoverable from a vengeance standpoint. He used the patents. This means he was actually in the wrong so this is something he has to live with, without seeking revenge. Your actions, on the other hand, cry out for vengeance."

"Doesn't make me feel any better." I decide to change the subject, "What is the destination?"

"As I said; the harbor of New York."

"Where are we now?"

"We are cruising north of Florida in the Atlantic and, in case no one told you, we are in a Bay Class container ship. We went around Florida, between it and Cuba, and will continue up the coast to New York. There now, you have the plan. I hope your curiosity is satisfied."

Winther turns back to the table and announces that if everyone is finished he will be hosting a friendly game of bridge in the next room. He also offers cigars and brandy for those interested. He then turns back to me.

"Please don't be offended Mr. guest of honor, but I need you to return to your cabin. I hope you understand we have some company business to discuss before playing cards."

I do not relish being put back in the handcuffs, but still I am ready to go back. All these guys make me more than a little nauseous. I see them in a new light, like looking at a gathering of monsters. What would have been a normal smile I am now seeing as a leer; a laugh before I knew what they were up to has become a taunt with derision. I decide to go for one more question.

"I am not offended. By the way, how long until we reach New York?"

Winther smiles, "You have no more than three days to figure

out a plan of escape."

Geez, he does read minds. Oh well, I have my answer. The sad part is he will probably put a tighter constraint on Jason knowing I will be working on a plan. It is very logical for him to think that somehow Jason and I will figure out a way to communicate. Winther interrupts my train of thought.

"Your valet is here to take you back to your cabin."

I look around expecting to see Jason standing behind me. Instead I'm surprised to see Quasimodo smiling at me in a sinister way. He does not speak and continues to look at me with the scary smile on his lips. I turn back to Winther as Quasimodo removes the locked handcuff from the back of my chair.

My surprise was obvious, and Winther seems to believe an explanation is necessary. "Jason will not be looking after you anymore. I have put a new person in his place."

Chapter Seventeen

Winther seems to be ahead of every move. He has replaced Jason because somehow he does not trust him. Whatever method Winther has used to intimidate Jason seems to have worn off since he no longer wants Jason and me to communicate. It does make sense Winther replaces Jason since it is probable that he and I are the only ones on this boat who have nothing to gain by blowing up the midshipmen cruise. I am very glad I was polite to Quasimodo. I even said "thank you" for the drink. Maybe he and I can form a bond.

I continue to sit in my chair. Winther nods to Quasimodo, who steps forward and turns my chair one-eighty degrees, which leaves my back to the table and Winther. Quasimodo is holding the cuffs by the chain which will connect to my waist. They are swinging slightly, and he and the cuffs remind me of a hypnotist in action. I half expect him to tell me I am getting sleepy, yet he still remains silent. I also notice he doesn't blink. Quasimodo bends down and places the cuffs on my hands and reattaches the chain leading from the cuffs to the waist chain. When he is finished and satisfied the cuffs are reattached securely, he grabs the arms on the chair and rotates it another one-eighty until I am again facing the table and Winther.

"I wish you a good night." These are his final words to me tonight.

On a signal from Winther, Quasimodo rips me out of the chair and it falls over backward to the floor. He shoves me roughly toward the double doors. It is obvious that the rest of the party will wait until I am through the doors before getting up and adjourning to the drawing room for smokes and brandy. We reach the doors and Quasimodo almost tosses me through them. I am complaining about the treatment and he shows no sign that he hears or understands.

We reach the anteroom door and he pulls it in while holding on to my cuffs. He holds the door and kind of slings me through. My feet catch on the threshold, and I hit the deck hard. I land on my right shoulder and think I hear a pop. Pop or not, it hurts like hell. I see red for a minute as the pain roars through my neurons and reaches the center of my brain which sends the message I have an injury. I scream out involuntarily. Quasimodo steps over the threshold and grabs my left bicep, yanking me to my feet. He then holds me up and runs his hand along my right shoulder. I am indicating "ow" a lot with each touch. Quasimodo seems to understand the problem. He has an almost sympathetic look as he slams me against the bulkhead. I pass out immediately.

I resist the urge to inquire where I am when I wake up. Quasimodo is sitting in the chair across the room. He gets up and comes over to the bed. I notice I am wearing scrubs again. He must have undressed me while I was out.

"I have reset your shoulder. It was dislocated when you fell. It will feel much better tomorrow."

"Wow that was some kind of procedure." I lift my left arm and although very sore it does work. "Where did you learn that technique?"

"My people live on a remote island. We have no doctors and the only treatments available are those we can do ourselves."

As Quasimodo speaks, I am picking up a far eastern accent. I try to engage him on the nature of his island. "I cannot give you any information."

"Can you tell me the time?"

"You have been asleep for three hours.

That would make it about one or two in the morning. I am not sure, but I get the feeling old Quasi doesn't have a watch. He speaks very good English, so I know he doesn't have trouble telling time. I can feel the cuffs and ankle bracelets in place so I know he has not been given the authority to release my bindings.

Quasi gets up and looks like he is going to leave. He moves toward the door and says, "You are free to use the head down the hall. You should not wander around the ship tonight."

I doubt seriously I have the strength to do much wandering. I need him to help me get up since I would normally lean on my left forearm to raise myself into a position to get off the bed. He comes back to the bed and gently helps me to my feet. I am beginning to believe he thought I was much tougher than I really am when he threw me through the door.

"Thank you for the help." He seems embarrassed since even he must realize that it was his fault I needed help in the first place. My thanks must have sounded like a barb. I really did not intend it to be so. "My falling was not your fault. I have the biggest feet in town." I am not sure I have any affect and at least he knows I am not about to purposely criticize my captors.

He lets me go and surprisingly I can stand on my own. He is satisfied I do not need any more assistance, so he tells me he will be back tomorrow to let me shower and then goes through the door. I wait until I am sure he is gone before I venture toward the door myself. I struggle to open it. My shoulder seems to be in the way with every movement. The pain is not like it was, however it still causes me to wince and curse.

I finally get the door open through a combination of pulling it a little and wedging my butt into the opening as a place holder. I step over the threshold and let the door slam shut behind me. I walk with some difficulty, and with clumsiness due to ankle restraints. Each step seems to jar my right side so I have to take it easy. I reach the head and have to work out a system which will allow me to go through the door, step over the threshold, and not hurt myself too much in the process. All comes together and I find myself standing over the toilet. I finish and go to the sink.

Another look in the mirror confirms the horrific appearance, so I decide to avoid eye contact with the Cro-Magnon opposite me. I turn the faucet on and quickly put the closest hand under it and catch a few drops before it stops. These faucets must save a lot of water but are hell to use when you only have the use of one hand. I wipe my face with the moisture I was able to capture.

I struggle with the door for what seems like the one hundredth time and manage to step over the threshold before the door slams shut. I get back to my cabin and repeat the process with threshold and door again. I decide to have another look around the cabin even though I looked it over pretty carefully before dinner. I believe one cannot be too careful when dealing with these kinds of people.

I move slowly and try to look natural as I have a look around. I am trying to make as little noise as possible in case they are listening. Of course when you try to be quiet it seems you make more noise than you would otherwise make. So it is with me. The cabin seems clean at first inspection. I am about to go to the sink for the cotter pin when I spot the camera. I would have noticed it earlier if it were there. It is positioned to be able to see the whole cabin. It is no more than a small shiny hole looking somewhat like one of the bolts in the corner of the wall. The big difference is the bolts are flat gray and the camera looks like it is black and wet. I may not have recognized it had it not looked very much like the backup camera on my car back in San Francisco.

If there is a camera there must be a microphone as well. I tell myself not to look at the camera, which would be a tip off that I have found it. I continue to look around for the microphone. I have to fight the urge to overact at being casual since I know I am being watched. I decide the best way will be to lie in the bunk and find out if I can see the mic. If not, then I will assume there is one and let it go at that. No use alerting these guys I know the camera is in place. I go to the bunk and sit down. I painfully recline since the only way to see the room is to lie on my left side. My pillow is not very puffy so when I fold it in half it provides a little more support. Once I lay down I look around. I see nothing unusual. I decide to give up and just accept the idea I can be seen and heard.

I painfully get back into a sitting position. It is time to get some sleep. I get up and shuffle over to the light switch. I turn it off and I'm amazed to see how completely dark the room has become. I imagine whatever kind it is the camera is not night vision type, so I'll wager I am now in a blackout. The only way these guys can track me is through sound. I stand perfectly still.

I need to think about a plan to get the cotter pin without being discovered. It is clear with Jason out of the picture my comfortable plan including him needs to be revised. I am back to the cotter pin as a hopeful solution. Since these guys can hear me and can't (I hope) see me, I decide to create a little play. The first thing I do is yawn loudly. The second is to shuffle over to the bed. I push on the mattress as if I have gotten into bed. I push several more times to simulate turning over.

I am not sure how I sound when asleep but start breathing heavier. I continue to breathe like I am asleep and begin to slowly move toward the sink. Since I don't know where the microphone is located, I vary my breathing pattern so when there's a change in my position in the room won't be detectable. My biggest worry is making any kind of chain noise while I am moving toward the sink. As I think about it, if I were in the bed I would make a chain noise by moving my arms or legs. I decide to limit the noise by making sure each move is done carefully. I actually move about two inches at a time. I have to first move my right foot and then follow with my left. There is an occasional sound of metal hitting metal and nothing more out of the ordinary.

I reach the sink after a half hour of movement. I ease myself to the floor. I cannot see a thing in the blackness so I reach out and carefully try to find the pin. I hit the rod with my handcuff, which sounds to me like a pipe wrench clanging on pipe in a ten story building. I snort and pretend to stop breathing and then start again to simulate a bad dream. Hopefully they will think my cuff hit the bed. I feel the pin and need to pull it off the rod without a corresponding noisy reaction by the rod. I hold both and pull the pin with the force I think will separate the pin from the rod. I also pull on the rod to balance the force so eventually when the pin lets go there will not be noise.

It works. The pin is in my hand and there was no sound. I need to hold on to it while I stand up, because the last thing I need is to drop it and then try to find it again. I wiggle backward so when I stand I won't hit the sink. The prospect of another half hour of creeping across the floor is too much for me to bear. I stand up and then cough and move quickly to the bed. I push the mattress again to simulate getting up. I go to the wall with the light switch and finally grope enough space to find it. I turn it on.

I struggle out the door and down the hall to the head. I finish and I'm back in my darkened room. I certainly hope I pulled off my little play. I lie down again and have the cotter pin, which is a good thing. I feel the pin, and it is clear since it is so thick I will not be able to bend it without a tool. Now I have a problem of where to stash it so it won't be found. I put it into the breast pocket of the scrubs, hoping the pin won't slip out while I am asleep. I rest my head on the pillow, and my heavy eyes close.

Chapter Eighteen

The first thing I am aware of is a loud clank of the cabin door as it hits the bulkhead. Quasi has come for me and I yawn and sit up on the bunk. I would have liked another few hours' sleep, but I'm not going to put off another shower and change of clothes.

"You ready to get up?" Quasi poses the question like it is my decision to get out of bed.

"Yes, I am." I swing my legs over the side of the bunk. I notice the shoulder pain is much improved this morning.

"Mr. Winther wants to see you after you have showered and have breakfast."

"Breakfast too! This is like a real cruise." I make this small joke with a smile in my voice. Quasi doesn't get it and goes to work taking off the ankle and wrist restraints. When he finishes he takes my upper arm and bids me to stand. I noticed last night and today Quasi has a very firm grip. He must workout. I pick up the toilet kit and let him lead me out of my cabin to the shower. Once there he opens the door and holds it until I step in. He remains in the hall holding the door. He tells me a change of clothes will be back in my cabin, and I should shower and go back when I am finished. I tell him I will do so and he lets the door go.

I see a terry cloth robe hanging on a hook by the shower. There is also a towel underneath the robe on the same hook. I turn on the shower and start to remove my scrubs. I almost forget the cotter pin in the breast pocket of the tunic. I stick my fingers in to snag it and it is not there. A moment of panic hits as I whip the tunic over my head. I turn the pocket inside out and there is no pin.

It must have fallen out during the night. I need to go back to my cabin and don't know what excuse to use. I am sure if I don't get back soon someone will find the pin while cleaning the cabin. I tell myself to calm down as I start thinking of what to do. My first thought is hopefully no one will clean the cabin until I am out for the morning. I have no evidence that anyone will clean anything on this ship. After all, this is not a luxury cruise; this is a boat full of criminals. I decide to take a chance and simply finish the shower and go back to the cabin as instructed.

After the shower I dry off and put on the robe. I look in the mirror and try to do something with my hair. The comb goes through the hair easy enough and since I have no spray my careful coif will fall out after it is dry. Still I'm not a pretty picture with no way to improve it.

I return to the cabin thinking how nice it is without the restraints to be able to walk like a human and not some swamp monster. I push against the cabin door and step over the threshold. My heart is beating faster as I try to determine if anyone has been in the room since I left for the shower. I immediately see that the room has been visited. There is a pile of clothes near the pillow which were not there when I left the room. I go over to the bunk, and, mindful of the camera, sit down and turn slightly to conceal my right hand from the camera lens. I run my hand around the top of the covers to determine if I can feel the pin. I don't feel anything unusual. I then get the idea to get dressed and then make the bed so I can give it a real good look. Probably won't look as suspicious as sitting here trying to feel up the bed while trying to keep the lens off my actions.

I get up and with my back to the camera and still wearing the robe I pull on a pair of boxers. I throw off the robe and it hits the floor. I pick up the shirt which is on the bed and look at the label. It is a large, which is my size. It is a Hawaiian made out of silk. I put it on and button it up while thinking someone went to a lot of expense on my wardrobe. There is a pair of walking shorts and a belt. I put these on and slip into the deck shoes which are placed by the bed.

I then turn toward the bunk and grab the blanket which is on top of a sheet. I pull it off and the sheet as well. There is no pin in the bed. I put the sheet back on and tuck the corners like I learned at camp. I throw the blanket over the top and casually tuck the corners and sides as well.

I am thinking and hoping maybe it fell under the bed. I get down on my knees and look under the bed. By now I am not caring a lot about what the folks behind the camera are thinking. I look as carefully as I can with no flashlight and cannot see the cotter pin anywhere.

Crap, I am thinking as the door opens. I am not reacting to the door but the disturbing fact I have lost one of the two tools which might help me out of this mess. The other is the pin in the public rest room, which will not be easy to flitch. Quasi comes in with his restraints and chains, making noise like the ghost of Christmas past.

I sit on the bunk and wait patiently until my ankle and wrist bracelets are in place. Quasi takes my arm again and I get up. We leave the cabin and I then notice he is more quiet than normal. I am wondering what is wrong.

"So, cat got your tongue?"

"I can't say much, but Mr. Winther is very angry and whenever he gets angry it is not good for the crew."

"What is he angry about?" I am hoping it is not the cotter pin.

"I have heard he has been told by the higher ups to hold his course and to slow the ship down in preparation for the arrival of a VIP."

"Do you know who it is?"

"I have said too much already. We will just have to wait and see. We are going to the bridge to meet Mr. Winther. Maybe you can find out from him yourself."

Quasi talks no more as we make our way to what I suppose is breakfast. We come to the elevator and Quasi punches the button for up. After a short wait the sound of the elevator's arrival is heard. Quasi pushes the door open and we go inside. He hits the one marked "three." The door closes and we start the slow move to the third level. We finally arrive on the third level and Quasi holds the door for me. I go through the same double doors as last night and the room is set up like a buffet. There are silver-looking food covers on a long table. This is not the general mess and appears to be a place for the elite to gather. Last night's event is obviously one of many uses for this room.

Quasi tells me to wait and he unlocks my handcuffs and guides me to a chair. He locks one handcuff to the back of the chair and then I sit. Quasi pushes my chair under the table and asks me what I want for breakfast. I let him know that anything would be good. He takes exception to my suggestion and goes to the table with the food. He carefully lifts each cover and calls out what is in the tray. He mentions scrambled eggs, eggs benedict, sausage, ham, bacon, hash browns, toast, french toast, pancakes, and various kinds of fruit. He describes the juices and coffee as well. He again wants to know what I would like and I tell him eggs benedict, coffee, and orange juice.

Quasi lifts and lowers several covers as he gathers the food. He returns to the table and puts the eggs in front of me. He places his plate on the table across from me and then goes back to the food. He pours two cups of coffee out of a silver pot and places them on saucers. He puts them down on our table and returns for the orange juice. He pours two large glasses from a huge pitcher which is on a bed of ice. He puts the two glasses in one hand and grabs some flatware wrapped in a cloth napkin with the other. He heads back to the table and dispenses the juice and flatware. His plate is full of almost everything offered.

"No pancakes?"

"I'll get them on the next course."

We pretty much eat in silence except for an occasional comment about the fresh-squeezed juice and good coffee. Quasi goes back for three more visits before he leans back in his chair with a satisfied look on his face.

"You guys eat like this all the time?"

"Pretty much."

I decide to shut up since I don't believe Quasi wants to discuss anything right now. I think he is worried about the high-level visitor and the fact he already said too much. I assume he is wired like Jason was, so he needs to watch every word.

"What happened to Jason?" I decide to hit it head on.

"Working in another part of the ship," is the quick reply.

"What part?" I feel I should be a big pain in the ass.

"Dunno," is all I get.

I finish my coffee and Quasi puts the handcuffs back in place. I get up and we head for the double doors and out to the hallway. We walk back to the elevator and Quasi hits the up button again. The lack of sound indicates to me that the elevator is already on our level.

Quasi slides the door open and we get in. He closes the door and presses the top button on the panel. After the ride up, we get off on the sixth level of the ship. We are in a hallway which seems to end in a blinding light. We walk toward the light, and as my eyes get used to the brightness I can see the beautiful blue ocean which appears to join up with the sky somewhere beyond a mostly glass door.

Quasi opens the glass door and we step up one step and enter the bridge. The brightness is from the sun which has started its assent into the morning sky. It is obvious we are heading northeast since the sun seems to be just a little to the right of the expansive glass which completely covers the far wall of the bridge. We approach the glass and are met by Winther. He dismisses Quasi.

"Good morning, John." I anticipate he is going to see how I like the accommodations.

"Just fine." My answer is as if he already said the words. Since he has not, Winther looks a little puzzled at my response.

"Well, that's good enough for me." He replies to me with a smile. "I want to introduce you to the captain."

Winther steers me toward what appears to me as the biggest control panel I have ever seen on a ship, boat, or otherwise. There are hundreds of dials each reading out details regarding the performance of this large ship. Looking out the window gives the impression of what it is like looking over a very large Bay Class container ship. The deck seems like it goes on forever before it reaches the bow. I see the boat is equipped with cranes and remembering my classes in seafaring school which I attended right after I bought *My GRL*, this type of ship is called a geared feeder and runs over nine-hundred feet in length.

I am trying to see as much as possible when Winther and I come face to face with an iconic man dressed in white with four gold striped epaulets on his shoulders. This must be the captain. He has a glorious white moustache and white hair. He is tanned, as if he paid someone to pick out a perfect shade in a spray-tanning booth. He gets up from his chair and reaches out his hand.

"Captain Wycliffe, and welcome to my ship." He grabs my right hand and, since they are cuffed together, shakes both.

Winther speaks as if I have no mouth. "Captain, this is John Cannon, he has loaned us the boat that is currently in the hold."

Captain Wycliffe smiles and I am again taken back with Winther's information flow. What does he mean by the boat in the hold? I decide not to find out by a direct question, but I do want to know.

"Can I get a briefing on that?" I speak up with all seriousness.

The Captain and Winther burst out laughing. I look at each as if I don't understand what is so funny.

Winther speaks while still chuckling. "You absolutely come out with the funniest things, John. Of course we will give you a briefing as you call it."

Captain Wycliffe excuses himself, pointing out with an air of self-importance he has a lot to do before the arrival of Jacobs and his team. I am not sure I was supposed to hear the comment about Jacobs yet Winther does not seem affected. He tells the captain to go ahead and we will find our own way. The captain wonders if we will need someone to accompany us around the ship. Winther lets him know we do not need anyone. The captain leaves us. The bridge is packed with people working at various sets of instruments. There are a couple of officer-looking types walking up and down among the workers. They are providing advice, answering questions, and seem to be competent in their work. Winther suggests that we will be able to talk better if we go below.

"Would you like to see your boat?"

"I really would like to do so."

We leave the bridge and get on the elevator which brought me up here. Winther pushes button number two. He explains the hold has an access elevator on the second level. We go to the second and enter a hallway. A short walk brings us to another elevator. Winther pushes the down button.

"This ship is amazing. The hold is divided into cells built to hold those containers you see stacked up in harbors. They are the same containers which are put on trucks and delivered right off the boat. This container type configuration was only invented in the 1950s. Before then, cargo had to be individually loaded and unloaded. It could take up to two weeks to unload a ship. This ship can be unloaded in two days. Ah, the elevator is here."

He slides the door open and we get on. He looks at the panel and wonders aloud if he has the right level, then punches the lowest button. We move down what I estimate to be six levels although I have no way to validate other than by using the other elevator running time as a gauge. When Winther slides the door open and turns on the lights I can hardly believe my eyes. We are at the absolute bottom of the ship and I am looking up at my sixty-five-foot boat.

It is sitting on blocks and looks like it could be on a library shelf. There are a number of spot lights focused on *My GRL*. It is very disconcerting walking along her hull and viewing her from the bottom up so to speak. I have a concern we might hit a big wave and *My GRL* will roll out of control over on top of us. Winther assures me she is not going to move until she is lifted out of the hold and placed back in the water.

I walk from her bow to stern. I look at her transom expecting to see the *My GRL* logo. To my amazement she has a new name, and for the first time I notice a slightly different color on her upper hull. "Our Surprise" is painted on the stern. The city has also been changed from Port Aransas, TX to New Orleans, LA.

"I suppose 'Our Surprise' means something," I observe with some bitterness.

"Yes, it means something special to our cause. This is a nice surprise gift to the American people. Death, injuries, and panic; all the things that we have felt over the centuries."

"Please forgive me. I still don't see why it is necessary to hurt innocent people in the name of an ideal."

"That's because you have never been hurt for an ideal."

Before he can continue the propaganda I interrupt, "Is there a way to leave me in my cabin. I don't see why I need to be exposed to this lunacy."

Winther remains calm and carefully explains I have pissed off a very important man and the man wants me to suffer for my sin.

I decide to tell Winther what I think, "I will not suffer no matter what you do to me. I have nothing to be ashamed of, and Jacobs is the one who tried to take advantage of others. He can be as pissed off as he wants, but I will not be intimidated by him."

Winther is silent during my tirade and when I am spent he speaks, "You may change your tune when you are sitting at the helm of your boat as it is heading for those forty-five or so Navy cadets and a half a billion dollar warship."

Another surprise by Winther. "What makes you think I will guide my boat into that situation?"

Winther smiles his patronizing smile. "You won't have a choice. We will simply lash you to the wheel and you will have a bird's eye view of the carnage."

"You really enjoy doing this, don't you?"

"I do get a charge out of your continued belief that you are in charge and will somehow alter the outcome of this grand plan. Look around you, John. This ship and full crew were not cheap. The retrofit of the container ship to accommodate the only cargo, your boat, took millions. This plan will be successful because men of means want it to be successful. You are naïve if you think anyone is going to stop this mission. Oh, by the way, here is your cotter pin. I think you might find it useful to unlock your cuffs." He begins laughing like the proverbial madman near a sawmill and tosses me the pin.

The pin falls to the deck. I bend over and pick it up with both hands. "You know, Ralph, you just made a big mistake. I will figure out a way to get loose. Once I do you will be the first person I visit." I try to sound as fierce as I can.

Winther laughs and shakes his hands in mock nervousness. "I will keep my door locked and bolted. I am so afraid."

I decide this game is over. I remain quiet and let Winther talk. "We will get within forty-five miles of the New York/New Jersey harbor. We will then, under cover of darkness, crane your boat out of the hold. We have installed a remote guidance system on *My GRL,* which will allow one of our people to sit at a monitor and guide her to the target. I think of this system as the moral equivalent to the Predator drone, which has killed many of his kinsmen. The boat will then cover the distance and enter New York Harbor in time to meet up with the Missile ship, *New York,* and the *Intrepid.*

You will be at the helm and will be martyred for the cause I want to give you a few prayers which may help you to enter heaven."

"Uh no thanks Ralph I think I will get to heaven on my own."

"Also your boat is loaded with C4 explosives and because there is a lot of it we can get the job done without the need to get too close."

I am prompted to think about the fact the shuttle *Enterprise* will be on display at the *Intrepid* and the explosion will in all probability destroy this artifact as well.

"Don't you think someone will challenge an unresponsive boat in the harbor?"

As usual, he seems pleased. "Good question. We have the radio set up so that our controllers can answer any challenge with an innocent response. We chose New Orleans as the city of registration because it is far enough and different enough from New York to justify any confusion in communication. We will only need a few minutes of confusion to achieve our goal. I can only imagine some New Yorker on the radio trying to understand the Cajun dialect. I can also imagine the Cajun talking to the New Yorker forcing a repeat of every instruction or question. On top of that, who is going to challenge an innocent boat like yours? Besides a boat like that belongs to someone with money. When authorities challenge money they are always careful. Being careful takes time. Time is on our side. Any more questions?"

I have to admit I have no more questions. I just have this hurting place in my stomach coming from beginning to believe these guys might just pull this off. What really adds to the hurt is that I am the only person on this earth besides this band of pirates who knows the plan. I am standing here, squeezing my cotter pin, and feeling pretty helpless.

I wish I could get word out to someone. Of course Ned is the only one who could possibly understand a message connected with something as weird as this situation. My hopes of reaching him are really remote. Also, I would have to get past his belief I am dead. I am not very confident I will have the time to explain I am in fact alive and also these guys intend to blow up a ship with Annapolis midshipmen aboard. I am now feeling I have been handed too much to overcome.

"You ready to go back?" Winther snaps me back.

"Yes, I am more than ready."

We get back on the elevator and return to the bridge. There are a number of activities going on all at once. I can see one of the radar screens and notice a small white dot showing up with each green sweep of the screen. The blip is being tracked.

"Would you like to listen in?" Winther, the quintessential host, holds out a pair of earphones. "We are in contact with Jacobs' helicopter and it is getting ready to land. It is quite interesting."

I figure I have nothing to lose and maybe can pick something up which may be useful. "Sure," I respond.

Winther tosses me a pair of wireless headphones. I catch them with two hands. I give him a look and he comes over and puts the phones on my ears. I hear sporadic communication between the helicopter whose call sign is "Blue 17" and the ship uses the sign "Avery Afloat Control." The ship control requests a heading of One-hundred and eighty degrees.

"Roger control, turning to one-eight-zero. Blue17" the helicopter responds.

"Blue 17 report visual." control orders.

"Roger, control, we have visual, Blue 17."

"Blue 17, you are cleared to land."

"Cleared to land, Blue 17."

The communications channel crackles a few times and there is no more conversation. One of the workers at a station gives thumbs up sign, which I take to mean the helicopter has landed. Winther lifts the earphones off the top of my head.

"Jacobs has landed and he would like to see you." Winther speaks in a matter of fact way.

"This can't be good." I express this out loud without even thinking.

"Oh, come on, John. Think of the fact that one of the richest guys on the planet hates you so much he is willing to forgo martyrdom for one of his followers in order for you to possibly be blamed for this whole disaster. I myself have volunteered to steer your boat into New York, but Mr. Jacobs is adamant you and your family need to suffer throughout history. If a man is known by his enemies you are a world-class celebrity. You should at least feel good about that. Can you imagine what public opinion will say about you when the world finds out you drove your own boat into that harbor? You will make Lee Harvey Oswald look like a saint." Winther makes his observation with a nice degree of sarcasm.

"But I am dead remember?"

"Oh don't you worry we have ways to bring you back to life. Think video pictures of you on your boat with a time stamp. Think sworn confessions of a few of our followers that you did not die in that ambulance, but arranged it to look like you did. Believe me we can sell it.

Well we had better go below to the dining area. That is where we will meet Jacobs." Winther takes a hold of my arm.

We step away from the beautiful view and hubbub on the bridge and enter the elevator. We do not talk as we head down to the dining room.

The third floor arrives as I am deep in thought. Winther opens the elevator door and I mechanically step out. My thoughts have turned to Jacobs and can't help wonder what kind of person has the ego, and at the same time, the insecurity to hold a grudge against a person like me. If I had billions I would certainly not think about an incident which, in the grand scheme of things, is insignificant. If I wanted to plan an operation like the one currently being executed, I would not give two thoughts to getting revenge on a powerless person named John J. Cannon. Of course, this may mark the difference between a person who is rational versus one who is clearly insane.

Chapter Nineteen

We go through the double doors to the dining room and come face to face with a huge guy dressed in a tight fitting black t-shirt and black slacks, frowning and making a hurried motion we should raise our arms. He looks like he belongs in a WWF death cage match and Winther and I do not want to disappoint. I look at him apologetically and show him my restraints. I think I caught a hint of a smile in the corner of his mouth yet he is still insisting Winther and I raise our arms. I do the best I can, and Winther puts his hands over his head. I can see Winther has a perturbed look on his face like I guess I would if my boss did not trust I was not packing.

The big guy goes over Winther from shoes to armpits. It looks like he touched every inch of his body. He orders Winther to remove with two fingers what turns out to be his wallet and cell phone. Then he turns to me. He gives me a rough pat and seems satisfied I have not hidden an Uzi under my clothes. Once finished he mumbles something into his shirt like the character Brick on *The Middle* TV show and steps to the corner of the room.

The service door opens and another guy dressed in black with the WWF look comes into the room. He looks around and nods to the other. He also talks into his shirt and joins the other guy in the corner. After a few minutes the service door coughs up another similarly dressed guy. He holds the door for the arrival of Jacobs.

Jacobs enters the room and pauses for a moment. Unlike Winther, he is not dressed casually. He is wearing a Seville Row light tropical wool suit with a handmade white cotton shirt and a tie which had to cost several hundred dollars. He looks me straight in the eye, and I don't want to take the chance of checking out his shoes since, if I did, it would appear as if I blinked. We continue to stare at each other until he speaks.

"Let's all have a seat. Mr. Cannon, I would like you to sit there." He then points to a chair directly across from where he is standing. "I will sit here." He pulls out the chair across from mine.

My thoughts tell me, so far so good.

Winther takes the chair next to Jacobs and the entourage sort of moves in closer while staying standing.

"I took the liberty of ordering some coffee. Would you like to join me?"

Since he is only addressing me, I answer, "Coffee would be lovely."

"Coffee would be lovely," he repeats in a lightly mocking tone. "Where did someone in your position get the cheek to believe 'coffee would be lovely,' is acceptable like we were on a pleasure cruise?"

"I only answered your question, and I really believe coffee would be lovely."

Jacob sighs. "I guess the severity of your situation has not sunk in." He tells one of the goons the coffee should be served. The goon relays the order.

Almost immediately Jason enters the dining room carrying a huge tray with silver coffee service. He sets the tray down. He does not look at me as he goes about serving. He places my cup on the table along with a napkin and spoon. He also places a small ramekin of sugar, Sweet & Low and Equal, as well as a small pitcher of cream next to the spoon. I decide not to ask for Splenda. The coffee smells delicious and I help myself. After a two-handed stir I pick up the hot cup and take a sip.

"Purer than any Columbian you will find on the planet. Dare I inquire as how you like it?"

"Best coffee I ever tasted." I reply to Jacobs with the whole truth.

Jacobs seems pleased. "I grow it myself and it is hand-picked and sorted. Only one bean in one hundred makes it to my cup. It is fitting that you should have tasted the finest coffee in the world before you need to leave."

I know what he is telling me and I think this whole casual attitude is somewhat frustrating to Jacobs so I decide to proceed. "Leave to go where?" I look at him with wide eyes.

Jacobs may suspect I am putting him on but decides to play it straight. "Has no one told you that you will be blown to smithereens in the company of several of your country men?"

Winther looks very nervous and jumps in, "I told him all that per your orders."

"Then why in the hell isn't he a little more bothered by the whole thing. Did you people drug him or what?" He looks accusingly at Winther.

Winther speaks quickly. "He has not been drugged. I really do not think he understands the reason for his demise and therefore does not accept it."

I remain silent since it seems the experts are doing my talking for me.

Jacobs looks at me again. "Is it true? You do not understand?"

I glance at Winther, and it is clear he is not going to answer for me. "I understand that you are angry because I beat your lawyer in the Taft vs. Avery case."

"You did not beat my lawyer, and anyway that would not make me angry."

"Okay, then I humiliated you on the stand."

"Now you are getting close. Do you know how you humiliated me?"

"By exposing your weakness in written English?"

"Do you know why this was so humiliating?"

"No, I really don't."

Jacobs takes another sip of coffee. "Let me give you the ways your tactics caused me immense trouble. First of all, several of the company boards on which I serve were appalled with my lack of writing skills and the knowledge that I was not born in America but rather in Palestine. One seriously tried to get me to step down for the so-called 'good of the company.' Secondly, I was repeatedly investigated by immigration authorities since there was an assumption that my lack of written skill and my heritage could mean I was not in the country legally.

Finally, our dear homeland security folks dug through my past with the idea that I could be connected to terrorists. I had the FBI all over me for several months. They were joined by the IRS, whose sole objective was to find a tax irregularity, which could be used as a reason for further suspicion and detention. In short, you made my life a living nightmare and I need revenge."

"But you are a terrorist."

"I need you to shut the hell up." Jacobs is now trembling with rage. His eyes narrow to slits, and his voice sounds like his throat is shaking as well. "This operation is set to begin tomorrow. I will be glad to tell you goodbye today. I do not want to have any further contact with you. In fact, if I see you again I will personally throw you overboard." He stops and gains his composure. He turns to Winther and sort of spits out an order. "Take him to his cabin and don't let him come anywhere near me."

Jacobs stands up and, without another word, walks to the service door followed by his guards. Winther lets out a whistle and Jason is busy picking up the coffee service.

"You are lucky he did not have you thrown overboard today."

"Yeah, so so very lucky."

Winther looks at Jason, and then orders him to take me to the cabin. I guess the mistrust of Jason is a thing of the past. Or could be as simple as Quasi has more important things to do. Jason stops what he is doing and takes my arm. I notice he is very gentle. I immediately get up and respond to his touch as if he was giving me the strong-arm treatment. He seems to appreciate my acting. We leave the dining room and go to the elevator. Once on I make a sign to Jason and silently mouth the word "wire." Jason nods indicating he is still wired.

I clear my throat and make small talk about what he has been up to. He tells me to be quiet. I make a sign of writing, and he nods and holds up his finger giving a sign we need to wait and I am thinking he means until we are in the cabin. I make a charade sign of a motion picture camera trying to communicate the fact there is a camera in the cabin.

He waves me off which I take as we are not going to the cabin. He also points down to his groin. I get it. We are going to the head. I am guessing he believes there are no cameras in the head. I give him a nod of understanding, and he holds his finger in front of his lips with the classic shushing sign. The elevator reaches the bottom floor and we get out. As we walk, Jason again points to his groin. I take his sign as a cue for me to bring up the need to use the head.

"Excuse me, Jason, but before we go back to the cabin may I use the head?"

Jason sighs as if he is put out. "If you must." He answers me with some shortness in his voice.

We walk past the cabin and reach the head. Jason holds the door and I go inside and he follows. He immediately pulls a pencil and a small notebook from his breast pocket. He quickly scribbles in the book and holds it for me to see.

He has written, *I am a hostage. Don't talk; go to the bathroom.*

I walk over to the toilet and with some difficulty unzip my pants and begin to make the usual falling water noise. While I am using the toilet, I can see Jason writing quickly in the book. I finish and flush the commode. Jason holds up the book again. He has written, *Wash hands. We must get away. I do not have a key to your cuffs but can get one. We need to meet again and make a plan. They are holding my sister hostage in New York. If I run they will kill her so the plan needs to protect her as well.*

I turn on the water and finish reading the rest. I nod to Jason letting him know I understand. I also silently mouth, "I'm sorry," referring to his sister. Jason tears out the pages of the notebook and puts them in his mouth. He chews and swallows them as if he does this all the time.

Jason takes me by the arm again and guides me to the cabin. He opens the door and directs me to step inside. I go inside, and he lets me know he will be back at lunchtime. He also tells me that the door to the cabin will be locked from the outside and I am not allowed out. With that, he slams the door and I hear the tumbler turn to the locked position.

I now have a lot to think about. How in the hell did it become my job to save the midshipmen, the *Intrepid* museum, the shuttle *Enterprise*, Jason, and his sister? I lie down on the bunk bed and begin to think of the possibilities. I could work on Jason to get a key to the cuffs and then when I have the chance, I get free and go into the radio room and send an SOS message. That sounds like a doable plan with only one problem. What will the SOS mean to those outside the ship? Certainly not a warning there is going to be a big boom in New York Harbor. Once the message is sent I'm sure I would be taken captive again, and who knows what would happen to Jason. His sister would be in jeopardy if they put it together he unlocked my cuffs. No, that plan won't work.

The plan will need to include both Jason and I making a clean break without being discovered. I also don't believe a clean break will mean simply getting away. A clean break means no one suspects we are gone and we also have enough time to warn the authorities of what is going to happen. In the back of my mind a troubling thought is beginning to make its move forward to the more conscious front. I am beginning to see the closer the escape scenario is played to the actual planned event, the more the probability of success goes up.

An example would be if Jason and I could be on *My GRL* when she is launched; we could take control of her and maybe prevent her from reaching the target. I am scheduled to be on her lashed to the wheel anyway. If Jason could somehow be on the boat as well and not missed on the freighter it could work. The key will be to figure out a way to have Jason disappear and not be missed. I wish I could talk to him without his being wired up. I will have to assume it is never going to happen. I am going to see if he will give me writing materials so I can communicate the plan to him.

So here is where I come out. I get lashed to the wheel. Jason is stowed on board as well. Once *My GRL* is in the water, Jason comes out and sets me free. Jason and I override the guidance system. We steer *My GRL* away from the harbor. We get on the radio and warn the coast guard to the fact *My GRL* is, for all intents and purposes, a floating bomb. We then head to open ocean in case the thing goes off. The last thought just turned my blood to ice. If *My GRL* blows, Jason and I go with her. There must be a way to override the detonation system. I wonder if after *My GRL* is in the water there will be enough time to figure out how to disable the bomb.

This whole plan does rely on Jason getting on *My GRL* as well. I guess in proper order I need to determine if Jason will be able to get on *My GRL*. If so, I guess everything else will work out. I close my eyes and try to relax. I don't know when it happened, but I guess I fell asleep since the tumbler turning in the door woke me in what seemed like minutes after Jason left.

"I'm back Mr. Cannon." Jason calls to me as he swings the door open.

"Hello, Jason." I can hear sleep still in my voice.

"Would you like to wash before lunch?"

I catch the hint and immediately tell Jason I would really like to do that. I get off the bunk and Jason takes my arm. We go to the door and he holds it for me. I step over the transom and we go down the hall to the head. Once inside I make writing signs and Jason hands me the notebook. I go to the sink and turn on the water. I write quickly and show Jason the message. *"Is there a way for you to get on the boat with me when they put her in the water?"* Jason reads the message, and I make sounds as if I am washing my hands. He nods affirming he would be able to get on. I write, *"Without being missed?"* He nods "yes" again. *Damn,* I think, *we may make this work.* I write again, *"I need paper and pencil to detail a plan."* He reads the message and looks down. He shakes his head "no." *"Why?"* I write. He takes the notebook and writes while signaling me to continue to the toilet. I don't have to go, so I take a mouthful of water from the running faucet. I turn the faucet off and go to the toilet. I let the water fall out of my mouth in an approximate imitation of going to the bathroom. I save a little for the final finish. I flush and turn to Jason. He holds the notebook and I see his message. He has written, *"Too dangerous. Might be found. We will meet like this and do the best we can."*

I cannot argue with his logic. I nod I understand and agree to proceed. He seems relieved and tears out the pages of his notebook and eats them.

He then talks out loud, "Your lunch is being delivered to the cabin. We will go back there."

I decide to try a little communication under the wire, "You mean, Jacobs doesn't want to have lunch today? We so enjoyed talking at coffee."

"Mr. Jacobs has left the ship. Besides, he said he never wants to see you again."

"Yeah I heard that. He could have changed his mind."

"No more talk. I mean it."

We talk no more as we go back to the cabin. Jason lets me in and locks the door after he leaves. I see lunch has arrived. For some reason I have worked up an appetite. Must be all the planning and the good news Jason thinks he can slip away. I go over to the desk and lift the napkin on the tray. There is a salad and what appears to be turkey rolled up in a tortilla. There is ice water and a pot of coffee. Not bad, I think as I put some Italian dressing on the salad from a large foil packet. I take a bite of the turkey roll and see it needs some mayonnaise. There is a packet of that as well. I tear a corner off with my teeth and squirt some on the turkey. I roll it back up and take another bite.

It is very good. It seems to be mesquite smoked turkey with

shredded Fontina cheese. I pour some coffee from the pot and add some Sweet & Low and cream. I pick up the coffee to take a sip. I cannot feel the cup in my hands. I see it there and can't feel the heat. I can't even feel the porcelain. The coffee falls from my hands, and as hard as I try I cannot stop it from falling. In fact, I am falling as well. I have walked off a cliff and I'm free falling into a very dark place. I cannot see anything except darkness, and finally the darkness disappears as well.

Chapter Twenty

I remember Jason and the walk back to the cabin. I remember the lunch, a salad, and a turkey roll-up. I remember the salad dressing and mayonnaise. I do not remember being lashed to this wheel. I am fully awake with the thought now I am on *My GRL* and sure enough my wrists are literally tied to the helm. I cannot pull them away. I try to steer the boat and the helm is locked. It is also pitch black, so I know *My GRL* and I are still in the containership.

Shit I never got the plan in place. I can feel the fear rising in my gut. A quick review of my situation leads me to believe I'm certainly in a high degree of trouble. I was drugged and I don't how long I was out. I try to calculate from what I know how dire the circumstances are. First of all, Jacobs said at coffee the launch and beginning of the operation was taking place tomorrow. That was about ten a.m. I had lunch at about twelve-thirty and since *My GRL* is still in the containership, I am betting it is sometime the next day. I must have been out for twelve hours or so.

I am afraid to call for Jason in case he is still wired. If so, then the masters will know we are up to something. I don't know what to do but wait to see if Jason is here somewhere. I cannot imagine he would wait too long. If he is not here, he still has time to get down to the hold and on *My GRL*, or whatever the hell they have named her.

I totally forget the name. I am trying to think. It was something with a double meaning.

It comes to me: *"Our Surprise."* I guess the mental effort was worth it. I will need the name of the boat if I get loose and am able to communicate with the outside world. I note they have taken off the handcuffs and shackles. I am sure they don't want an investigation to turn those up should this boat be blown to bits. I imagine an investigator finding my body or at least some pieces wrapped up in shackles. A little rope would not raise too many questions. It could have been accidently wrapped around the wrist. The same cannot be said for cuffs. I have at least some respect for these guys. They certainly think in the smallest detail about everything.

I must have been awake for about ten minutes when it hits me hard I really need to go to the bathroom. Oh now this adds insult to injury. I am lashed to the helm and now it looks like I might have to pee my pants. I try hard not to think about it, but the thought of water building up in my bladder becomes my sole obsession. I finally decide I can't hold any longer and begin to talk myself into the fact of wet pants not being the worst thing in the world. Although I am willing to let it go, for some reason nothing happens. It is like someone put a plug in the place where the urine needs to run out. I am now concentrating on letting go when I hear a "psst," behind me. That is all it took for the dam to break. I hear my water falling on the deck after its run down my leg and over my shoe.

"Mr. Cannon, it is Jason."

"Shit, Jason, I just wet my pants." I want to warn him to avoid getting wet himself. "I could not wait one more second."

"Shhh," he cautions. "I do not have the wire on, but you never know who is listening."

Jason moves very carefully until he touches my arm.

"Can you get these ropes off my wrists?" I whisper.

He touches them, and then whispers into my ear, "These ropes have been frapped so there are no knots to untie. Someone knew what they were doing. I have a knife and I can hardly see my hand in front of my face. I am afraid I will cut you."

I whisper back, "What the hell does *frapped* mean?

"They have taken a smaller cord and have weaved it around your wrists on top of the rope so there are no knots."

"The rope winds around the wheel in such a way I think you

can cut the rope without getting near me."

I instruct Jason to feel the rope on the wheel and see how it is connected to my wrist. He runs his hand down my arm until he comes to my wrist and then goes over my hand to the wheel.

Jason continues to whisper. "I can feel what you described. I believe I can saw through the rope. It will take some time since the only knife I could safely take was a steak knife from dinner."

"It is still a knife and is more than I have."

Jason begins to work the left hand. He is grunting with the effort.

"How long have I been here?"

"It's two-thirty in the morning. So more than twelve hours."

No wonder I had to pee, I think. "Do you know when the boat will go in the water?"

"I think about daybreak, which should be in three and a half hours."

That is all the time he and I will have to disarm this bomb and figure how to override the remote guidance system. First he will need to make a little more progress on the ropes.

"How's it going?"

"It is very slow." Jason sounds frustrated.

"You are doing a great job." I try to encourage him.

"I am quite complimented. I do have to remember, this is from a man who pisses his pants."

"Touché."

Jason keeps working, and I can't tell if he is making progress or not. I know he is putting a lot of energy into the task. About the time I am going to request a progress status, I feel the rope fall away from my wrist.

"Hot damn," I whisper.

Jason sits down on the deck and I hear him breathing very heavily.

"You okay?" I inquire a little louder than a whisper.

He doesn't answer for a minute. He then stands up again and comes close to my right side.

"I am asthmatic," he whispers and wheezes at the same time. "I don't have my inhaler and this hold has something in it causing me a problem; might be dust."

"What can I do for you?"

"Nothing, I will just have to keep going. I never leave without my inhaler and for some reason I left it in my cabin."

As Jason continues to work on the right hand rope, I whisper to him, "How did you get away."

"I audio recorded sleeping one night. I have an eight-hour recorder, and when I got out of bed an hour ago I turned on the recorder to replay the sounds of myself asleep. I believe we will be well on our way before anyone knows I'm gone since the room is too dark to see any video. My last assigned duty was to drug you at lunch and then having successfully done the job I was told to stay in my cabin. I don't expect that anyone will check on me until after the mission, which will of course be too late."

"I must say you are very good at drugging people." I cannot see his face and think I hear a smile in his voice. I also hear his breathing is becoming much more labored.

I whisper, "When I was at camp one summer we had a kid who had an asthma attack and he was without his inhaler as well. We gave him some aspirin and it seemed to help. It had to do with relaxing the air passage. I know there is a first aid kit on this boat so I think we should try it."

"I will try anything." Jason answers me, sounding like he is whispering through a wet cloth.

"Maybe the aspirin should be our first stop. Now that we can talk freely, I should let you know the plan."

"I think I figured it out, but go ahead."

"You and I find the electronics connected to the remote steering and figure out how to override it without giving a warning to the operator. When the boat is put in the water we steer it to a different location."

Jason interrupts, "Different location?"

"Yeah, away from the Port of New York."

"You are aware this boat is rigged to be detonated remotely."

"Well, yes. I figure there is enough time to disarm the detonation device as well."

"I hope you are right," Jason wheezes. "If not, you and I are on a suicide mission."

"Well, at least those innocent people will be kept out of it."

"Yes, but Winther and his bunch are free to do this all over again. Jacobs has gone back to his office and is in the clear. I'm sure they will put together another attempt. All we will have managed is to create a really big accidental explosion which will take years to investigate. If I had a choice, I'd rather not die without inflicting damage on this container ship as well."

He makes a good point. Since he was actually involved in the mission, he may have some information which can be useful.

I decide to probe, "Let me put this to you. Is there any way you and I could survive the explosion?"

His answer comes back more disappointing than his point, "I really did not get involved in any part of the actual mission plan. These guys needed a medic, so they grabbed my sister and then conscripted me. They did not let me in on the plan nor did they give me any insider information."

"Okay, so we have to assume that we will be toast."

"I would think so." I wish I could see his face.

"So if we are toast anyway, why not direct this boat right back at the container ship if we can't figure out a way to disable the trigger?"

"I don't see any other way." Jason sounds weaker, and I can't tell if it is the asthma or the realization that these may be our last hours on this earth.

I feel the right rope drop away. "You have done it. Good man."

"I need to rest a moment."

"Sit here. I will be right back with that aspirin."

"You need to be very quiet."

"I know every inch of this boat. I can find the first aid kit blindfolded. Come to think of it, this is like I have a blindfold on."

Jason does not answer so I believe I have made my case. I very gently place my hands on the helm, then turn and walk the several steps to the stair ladder leading to the main cabin.

The staircase ends at the aft cockpit where there is a door leading to the main salon as well as the hatch entrance to the engine room. The first aid kit is in a small cupboard in a partition which separates the main room from the galley. It will be an easy matter to simply follow the wall to the closet. There will be a couple of lounge chairs to avoid, but that should be no problem. I start down and work my way to the cupboard. I feel the edge of the door, and then I slide my hand on the face of the door until I feel the knob. I move around so I am facing the door and open it and I reach inside and feel for the kit.

I will know it since it has a metal clasp on the front and hinges on the back. I soon feel the metal box and pull it out of the cupboard. The box has a handle and I am very sure it is the right one.

I am not going to risk opening it here since I don't want anything to fall out.

While feeling the box I also remember there is a mag flashlight in the cupboard as well. It should be clipped to the inside of the door at about the halfway point. I feel the inside part of the door and find the clip and no flashlight. It could have popped off at some point, and if so will be lying in the cupboard on shelf two. I reach in and walk my fingers around shelf two. Sure enough, the mag light is lying on top of some dish towels. I pick it up and shove it into my pocket. I sure don't want to drop it since I will never find it again.

Since we are still in the hold of the container ship I don't dare turn on the flashlight since someone might see it through *My GRL*'s main salon windows. I am not sure how we will be able to use the light quite yet, but it is nice to know we have it. I also think we could use the dishtowels. I am also not sure how, I will take them anyway. Before pulling them out of the cupboard, I feel them to make sure there is nothing else sitting on top which could fall to the deck. I find nothing and I pull them out. There are four neatly folded cotton towels. I recall when I bought them and they have never been used. The macabre thought of bandages comes to mind which I quickly shake off. I would like to proceed to the next level below to take a look at the steering set up but I think I had better return to Jason.

I reverse my path and come back to where Jason is sitting. I reach out and touch him, and I guess he was asleep since he jumps what seems to be a foot in the air. I give him the shush treatment.

"You really surprised the shit out of me."

"Now we are even. Of course I don't think your pants are full are they?"

"Of course not. Did you get the aspirin?"

"Yes, and I got a flashlight as well. I think we should head below where there are no windows and see what is down there."

"Are you sure you can get there? One loud noise and we are cooked."

"Don't you worry, Jason. You are in my world now. We will get there."

I sit down crossed legged on the deck and place the box so it rests on each thigh. I feel for the front and turn the box around so the clasp is facing me. I pull it up and it unlocks. I open the box and feel three bottles I know one is aspirin, one is an antacid and one is a calcium supplement. The next elimination is a bottle with a pop-off plastic cap.

There is only one of those. I pop the cap, being careful to hang on to it and take a smell of the bottle opening. I tip the bottle and one of the pills falls into my hand. I put it in my mouth. There is no mistaking the taste and smell of aspirin. I shake out two more into my right hand and put the cap back on the bottle.

I touch Jason and let him know, "I found the aspirin. Here are two. You will need to swallow them without water unless you brought some. Give me your hand."

Jason reaches out and connects with my left arm. I use my arm to guide his hand to my right where the aspirin is waiting. We make the connection and I am thinking a docking with the space station could not be more difficult. I hear Jason make a connection with his mouth and I believe he chewed the tablets. Now it will be a matter of time to see if the aspirin works. We should get moving. I put the bottle in my pocket in case we need more.

I grab Jason by the arm and notice for the first time how hard his bicep feels. He must work out a lot. I caution him to follow very closely and to keep one hand on me at all times. I offer to tie one of the dishtowels to my belt for him to hold onto and to my surprise he accepts. I take one of the towels and tie it on my belt with a small knot at the top. The towel is long enough for Jason to hold. I put the end in his hand and can feel his fist around it. He seems to have a tight hold and so we move out.

We descend the staircase. I am glad Jason has the towel to hang onto; otherwise it would be really hard to lead the way on this steep staircase without falling. When we reach the bottom I whisper. "We will need to move to our right and feel along the bulkhead until we feel the hatch which opens to the engine room." He whispers, "Okay," and we move again.

I feel the hatch release and pull it to the open position. The hatch door pops inward. I caution Jason to watch his head since the hatch is quite short and you only can stand straight up once inside the engine room. We descend the three steps and both remain crouched. I reach back and shut the hatch. Since there are no port holes visible to the outside I turn on the flashlight, which causes us both to flinch. I point the light to the ceiling and stand up and Jason follows suit.

We have our back to the hatch as I make a sweep of the engine room. Normally there is a walkway between the two big engines and it is now blocked with two-foot stacks of what look like bricks of plastic.

"You are kidding me!" I blurt my comment without a whisper.

"This is the C4 Winther was talking about."

"This looks like a lot. Is it?" I needed to pose the question yet feel I already know the answer.

"My God, there is enough here to blow up Manhattan Island let alone the *Intrepid* museum and the midshipmen. I used to handle this stuff when I was in the Navy."

I brighten, "You were in the Navy?"

"Yes, I served in Afghanistan. Before I went in the country, I took a counter insurgency course and they taught us about C4. The good news is it will take a detonation device to blow this stuff."

"What is the bad news?"

"I am sure these guys have a sophisticated redundant detonation system which can be remotely set off."

"Can't we just pull out all the wires connected to this pile?"

"We can but they probably have a detection device rigged up that will divert the charge to another pile which will set this off."

"Another pile. Where?"

"Might be under this one or behind the engine, or it might simply be rigged to blow if anyone disturbs the sequence."

"Is there a central control box?"

"Yes, we should spend some time looking for it."

"What will it look like?"

"Might be a shoebox, a fishing tackle box, or a wall phone. No way to tell."

"I don't feel too good sitting on all this destruction."

"Don't feel alone, neither do I."

We agree to start looking for electronics which don't belong on this boat. I suggest we go over to the central electric panel. The panel is enclosed in glass for easy reference. There is only one light blinking red. It is the stand-by light normally blinking red until the boat is powered up, and then it will turn green if all is normal. The rest are all in the green indicating systems are normal. The engine instruments are all at a state of rest, which is normal given the engines are not working now.

I speak up, "Looks like they have the external power hooked up. I don't see anything out of synch here."

Jason agrees, "We need to look around for anything out of

place."

We start to systematically go over every foot of the engine room. Since we only have one light, our chore is a little clumsy since Jason and I have bumped heads more than once. We are about halfway to the back of the room when I see a black cord leading away from the explosives. It is snaking to a point just behind the port engine. I pick it up and hear Jason suck in air. It appears to be a few wires wrapped in electrical tape. We follow the cord with the light and see a black box on the floor under the struts holding the engine in place.

"What do you make of that?" I question Jason as if he knows any more than I do.

"I think it looks like a control box." His answer has no more information than I had already concluded.

"Can we move it?"

"I wouldn't. Sometimes these things are rigged to detect motion and go off if disturbed."

I am not in agreement so I offer, "Let's think about it for a minute. If this was a bomb at the side of the road there would be a reason to booby trap it. I don't see why they would do that when the bomb is sitting in the hold of their own ship. If it blows they would all be in trouble, wouldn't they?"

Jason sits with a thoughtful look on his face. "You make a good point. Okay, let's move it out where we can look at it."

I smile at the thought of putting our lives on the line with simple logic. If I am wrong and have underestimated the planning these guys have put into the placement of the bomb we are breathing our last. I figure the worst case would be a fireball in the night and end of story. I still hold my breath as I pick up the box to move it closer to us. I put my hands under it and lift as if it were a baby. It weighs more than it looks like it would weigh. Being about a foot square, I did not expect it to be heavy at all. The box moves without any encumbrance, which is a good thing. I pause and wait for any sign I have disturbed anything. All is quiet and I exhale while moving the box fully out from under the struts. I put the box on top of the explosives being careful not to dislodge any wires. After setting it down I realize my hands are shaking.

"Nice job."

"I am too old for this shit." I shake my head to clear it.

I try to see if Jason knows how we go about opening the box.

He does not give me a degree of comfort when he tells me he has never seen this kind of control box before.

I look the box over. It looks like it was hand made for this use. It feels like plastic and because of its weight I think it is black enameled wood. It has two latches on the front also painted black. There are hinges on the back, so it appears it was designed to be opened to load. The cord comes out of a hole in the back. It looks like whoever built the box took care since the cord seems to be locked in place by some kind of rubber grommet. I decide to unhook the latches. I take it slow, one at a time. The loud click of each latch has Jason and me on edge, since such a click could be followed by some alarm or worse.

The latches are now disengaged. I pause getting ready to open the box.

"Here goes nothing." My words sound as if I am bungee jumping off a cliff.

I pull the top of the box open and pause, holding my breath waiting for any reaction. There is nothing. Jason and I squeeze together trying to see in the box. There are several elements all tightly jammed into the space. There's a cell phone attached by twist ties to a board and two AA batteries attached to the board as well. There are wires running from the batteries and connected to the phone. The wires all converge to the hole in the rear of the box. It is now clear the cord is made up of the wires all wrapped in electrical tape to form what looks like a black rope. The colors are red, black, green, white, and yellow.

"Damn. I understand red, black, white, and green. I don't get yellow." Jason expresses his thoughts, "I think yellow can be either a dummy or the trigger wire. The black and red are power conduits. The green is a ground, and the white could be like the red on another detonation device."

"So can we just cut them all and be done?"

"Let me think about that." He is sounding like the answer is probably no.

"Do you have the time?"

Jason looks at his watch. "Half past five. If we cut them all we may have some sort of problem with any other feature of the bomb."

"Half past five? If they decide to launch at daybreak we only have a half hour to render this bomb useless and to find how the boat will be operated from the container ship. What other feature are you talking about?"

"I honestly don't think we will be able to figure out how to disable the bomb. There are just too many variables. This particular box is a very simple device. When someone calls, the cellphone's vibrator will make the connection to the electrical charge to trip the detonation. This cannot be the only device. I am sure there is a radio controlled trigger somewhere else. The guy who rigged this bomb was brought in from some secret group. He probably covered the bases enough to make sure if these wires were cut there would be an alarm somewhere. They would come aboard and find us and probably get rid of us. Then those guys would simply rewire the whole thing after they killed us. We should concentrate on finding out how to control this boat."

"This is a nightmare."

"I agree, but I think we need to talk about what happens when they do decide to lower the boat in the water."

"What do you mean?"

"I am sure they are going to have people come on board to check to see if everything is as expected. You tied to the helm for example, me not being here for another."

"I get it. Also the box back where it should be."

"Yes, so let's return the box. We can always drag it out again but understand once we are away from the container ship, this bomb might have been built to have a number of ways to detonate. I don't believe these guys take chances, so we could well cut these wires and then set off an alarm, which would not bring people running and could trigger another way to detonate. They probably would just abort the mission and blow the boat up if they thought the device was compromised."

"Not comforting." I continue a grumble as I close the box. "I think you are telling me there is not much we can do with the bomb. Is that right?"

"If we had ways to test each line and had some other safety equipment we would have an even chance. The way we are now, there is no chance. I think the only way to prevent an explosion is to gain control of the boat and steer it next to the container ship. In the meantime we send out maydays and hope someone is listening."

I place the box back where I found it. "What makes you think these guys won't blow the boat anyway? They seem crazy enough."

Jason thinks a moment then responds, "They may be crazy, but they are not stupid. If they blow the boat the container ship goes down, they have not completed the mission, and they are dead men even if they survive the sinking. Jacobs won't stop until they all pay for their mistake."

"What will they do then?"

"I think they will try to re-board your boat and take us. All we have to do is stay close enough without letting them get on board."

"Sounds easy to say and tough to do." I hope Jason has some experience in this area.

"The key is being able to control your boat. It is much faster than the container ship and more powerful than any small boat they might launch. If we stay on our toes we can probably ram little boats and maneuver around the container ship."

"You have experience in this kind of situation?" Right now I need a ray of hope.

"Served on a pirate task force in a past life." This is his understatement.

"Pirate task force?" I am talking way too loudly. "You're a Navy Seal?"

"Um yeah," he answers with no fanfare at all.

"You mean to tell me these guys grabbed off a Navy Seal and hold his sister hostage?"

"Well," Jason pauses. "They did not know I was a Seal. They thought I was just a medic since I was working at a hospital when they took me."

"So you are not on active duty?"

"No, I am in the reserve. I started my civilian life about five months ago."

"How did they run into you?"

"Winther actually spent time in the hospital where I worked. He was having some stomach trouble and I was on the same floor working as a nurse. I made a mistake during some idle conversation of telling him about my sister in Virginia. He said he traveled there and would not mind passing on a hello and taking her to dinner. I gave him her telephone number. I also called her and told her he was a good guy. I really thought he was a good guy. I learned a lesson too late."

"Okay, now I know your background, I think your advice can be taken to the bank. Let's go aft and see if there is any kind of control device on the tiller."

Jason agrees and we make our way back out of the engine room. Once in the rear cockpit, I lift a hatch in the floor and jump into a pit. The steering mechanism looks normal to me. I don't think anything has been attached on the gear itself. I come up out of the pit and ease the hatch closed. I report my findings to Jason and he nods.

We then go back up the ladder to the enclosed bridge. Once there I can see there is some kind of electrical device sitting up by the windscreen next to the depth finder. It is giving off a glow which causes us to cross the bridge so that we can get a close look in the dark.

"Look at this." I tap the device.

Jason looks closely at the device including running his hands gently over it and offers an opinion, "I think this is a wireless receiver and it is probably hooked up to the autopilot and throttles."

"We screwed?"

"I think once underway we can simply cut this puppy free with no consequences. It would let the control think all is in working order, and then cut it off. We can allow a few minutes of testing and then take over."

I am relieved, "This is good news then."

"Yup. It looks like they were not concerned anyone would be actively trying to override the system so they made it pretty simple. Could be one of the few mistakes these guys have made."

"To your other point, should we tie me back onto the helm?"

"I think we can make the ropes look like they are tied and you should be able to break away if necessary. I will also need to hide where I can't be found. Any ideas?"

"I would go back into the engine room to the crew's quarters. The door is hard to see, but when you get close there is a little handle on the right. Pull it and the door opens into the room. Once in, there are a number of places to hide. I don't think any of these guys will go in there. I'm pretty sure they do not know a crew quarter even exists."

"That sounds perfect. Let's get you strung up again."

"By the way, how does a person with asthma qualify for the Navy Seals?" I question him while Jason fashions pretty convincing restraints.

"I developed the asthma while serving in the desert. Never took disability though. The aspirin seems to be working. I feel pretty good."

"I am glad it is helping. When you go below be sure to take the flashlight. I don't need you making noise as you trip over things."

When Jason finishes lashing me to the helm he declares he is going to make his way to the crew quarters. He thinks it is almost daylight and had better get moving so he is not caught above decks when the lights go on. I hate to see him go since he unknowingly gave me a sense of courage which leaves as he does.

I am forced to stand at the helm, and in the darkness I feel a little weak in the legs. I guess it is all the tension now coming to roost in the quiet. Before I get a chance to really feel sorry for myself there is a bright light appearing above the boat. I have to squint to keep the light from blinding me totally. I can hear voices from below the boat, which lets me know there are men starting to ascend the rope ladder attached to *My GRL*.

There are grunts and noises of men straining to pull themselves up to the deck. There are also noises behind me of metal clicking on metal, and I am sure the sound is of great hooks being connected to rings on the deck to be used to hoist *My GRL* into the air, up and out of this ship.

I catch a glimpse of someone moving forward on the deck and can see him attach the hooks forward as I had supposed. There must be four or five men all shouting orders at each other in preparation for the launch. No one has even looked in my direction and to my knowledge no one has gone below.

I am startled by the voice of Winther, who has entered the covered bridge from aft, "How was your nap?"

"Slept like a baby." This is my original, and I might add humorous, reply.

Winther comes closer so I can see him by turning my head, "Well, it won't be long now 'till you can sleep forever." He is smiling, obviously enjoying his attempt at humor. "I don't want to keep you, so I'll just wish you goodbye and hope you have a good trip to the other side. Are you sure you don't want some prayers to take with you?"

"I'll go by myself, thank you very much. I certainly hope you have the great faith in your religion that you will be delivered to a grand eternal life for the loss of life which you will be responsible for inflicting. While we are in such a collegial mood maybe you can tell me why you had Gerry killed and why it was necessary to involve me?"

"As you know she was getting out of control. She was starting to get real nasty with one of her clients. We were using two people to buy boats. You met Mr. Stans who had no idea we were using him and another who worked for us. We needed to cut her off right away before she got too irrational. We talked to her about her responsibilities, but when she told our agent to get someone else for the deal, we knew her time had come. We tried to warn her but made the decision she would probably bolt. When she started talking to you in the bar, we knew we had made the right decision. We were sure she would eventually tell you we were holding her brother and we had her wired, on a misguided belief you could help her. She did not know why we wanted the boats, but we could not afford to have her start talking. You two made a good target when you left the bar, but we couldn't kill you otherwise we would have never been able to consummate the purchase of your boat. We knocked you out so you could deny any involvement. I am sorry about the gun under you but it was an unauthorized joke by one of my men. He has been punished."

I can't believe evil like this exists. "In my religion you would be sent to eternal damnation, and so I feel strongly that I will be redeemed without using any of your prayers. I think killing an innocent person like Gerry is not forgivable and you will suffer for it. I am curious to know how you tried to control her."

"I appreciate your belief you are covered by the right religion, but think whoever survives this mission will have chosen the right religion in the end. As to your curiosity; we controlled her by kidnapping her brother in Washington and telling her he would be killed if she didn't co-operate. We wired her up so we could keep track of everything she did. We told her to buy two boats and she got sideways on the one by asking too many questions and then deciding to abandon the deal. It really was her own fault after all. Sorry but, it's now time for me to go and I really don't have time for more questions. Goodbye, John Cannon. You are a brave man, misguided yet brave."

Winther laughs, turns and disappears from my limited peripheral sight. Soon the noise of the workers slows down until there are only two or three voices on the boat. I hear a muffled loudspeaker announcement and what seems to be a train rumbling along a track.

In a short time I can see the sky out of the bridge window. It looks like it has been framed in a metal rectangle but blue sky never the less. It is clear the cover to the container hold has been rolled away. After starts and stops, I also feel the boat lurch as the cable slack is taken up and the cranes begin the task of lifting *My GRL*.

The coordination of the lifting to keep the boat level shows the skill level of the operator. Whoever has his hand on the cranes controls knows what he is doing. The boat rises smoothly with neither bow nor stern exceeding a one degree difference in level. We rise above the cargo cover, and I can see we seem to be pretty far out to sea. *My GRL* is suspended above the great ship, and I almost feel like we are flying.

The suspension does not last long, and the cranes start the move to position *My GRL* out over the ocean. There is a slight sway reminding me of being caught sideways in a swell. It's kind of a sickening motion all boatmen endure and seriously try to avoid when the swells get big enough to jeopardize the stability of the craft. Bow into the wave is a natural tendency, so this side motion is quite unnatural.

The boat is suspended over the water on the port side of the container ship. The swaying eventually stops and once it does the slow descent to the water begins. I look over to the ship and watch as the boat descends along the huge hull of the container ship. It is almost like being in an elevator with a gray wall on one side and an open wall on the other. *My GRL* finally comes to rest on the sea.

I did not realize there are still two crewmen on the boat with Jason and me until I hear them. They are talking loudly to each other, and it is obvious they are releasing *My GRL* from the cranes as there is much swearing over the difficult task. Not only am I surprised about the crewmen, I am also startled to see the gauges on *My GRL* come to life and to hear the sound of the engines starting. This is a very weird feeling. I look at the tachometers and see the operator is revving the engines to warm them up.

The crewmen seem to have finished and have been hoisted on the crane hooks back to the container ship. In an instant I can feel the acceleration of the boat as the instruments demonstrate the addition of power and a forward gear. I feel the helm jerk slightly to port as the invisible captain steers *My GRL* away from the container ship. I am attached to a large wheel, and if the unseen operator decides to make a hard turn I am going to be yanked off my feet. I am hoping hard turns are not on the agenda. I yell for Jason to make his way to the bridge while I struggle to release the ropes as he told me to do.

I get my right hand free and use it to free the left. I back away from the helm and I'm really at a loss of what to do next. I look behind me and I see the container ship is beginning to appear smaller as we start to get further apart. I have to remain on the bridge so as not to tip my hand to anyone on the container ship who could be watching. I am getting a little concerned about Jason and why he has not made an appearance yet. That concern coupled with the feeling I need to stay here is causing another stomach pain.

Chapter Twenty One

I finally decide to go find Jason. I figure the boat is far enough from the container ship and no one will notice me being off the bridge. I duck down and move aft to the ladder leading to the aft cockpit. I look out over the stern to make sure I cannot be seen. The container ship is slightly behind and to the right of *My GRL*. It looks like we are running in parallel and I count this as a good thing. At least this will give us some time to figure out how to gain control over the boat and not be too far away from the containership. If we were too far away those guys could simply hit the detonator and we would be gone.

As I was about to descend the latter I hear Jason call up. I tell him it is safe to come onto the bridge. He quickly comes out of the engine room and up the ladder. I feel better immediately with him present.

"So what do we need to do?" I look for direction as soon as Jason is on the bridge.

He looks around, "It looks like the container ship is planning to stay with your boat at least for a while. This is good. It means we have a free ride until they decide to put some distance between us."

"Do you think they will know they have no control over *My GRL* if the distance becomes so great that they can't see the boat anymore?"

"*My GRL?* Who is *My GRL?*"

"It's the name of my boat."

My GRL? I thought the boat's name is *Our Surprise.*"

"That's what Winther named it. It is his little joke."

"Oh some joke. As to your question about can they control the boat over distance? I'm not sure. Why do you ask?"

"I was just thinking if we got out of sight it might be a good thing. We could then divert *My GRL* to another location and warn everyone."

"Sounds good, but as I think of it they do not intend to have this mission go south. I am sure they have a GPS device warning them if this boat deviates from the course to New York Harbor. If they detect deviation, then boom we are toast. Our only chance is to somehow get the two boats close enough together so any action to blow this boat will jeopardize the container ship."

I tell Jason of another concern, "I am worried we won't get the opportunity to get that close. Right now it looks like we are too far away."

"Once we figure out how to override the remote control system, I think we could pull the power on the engines, and when these guys pull in close to figure out the problem we could take over control of the boat. That's when the rodeo will begin."

Maybe Jason has a plan in mind, "It looks like you have a plan."

"There are two things I know. One, surprise is an ally. Two, delay can be good. Right now we are in a delay. I think we should use the time to look at the box on the control panel and see what we are dealing with right now. Once we understand the box we can figure out how to override it. Then we can surprise these guys with our own maneuvers. If you call this a plan then that's it."

"Sounds good to me. By the way I don't know how close you Navy Seals are but did you ever hear of a Ned Tranes. He was in the FBI?"

"Ned and I go way back."

I am taken aback. "You do? How far?"

"He was my section leader on a couple of missions on loan from the bureau."

"Have you kept in touch?"

"Not really, but I can tell you he really knows his stuff."

I look at Jason to see if he is telling me the truth because what are the odds he and Ned know each other. I look him straight in the eye and he has a very non-committal look on his face. I can't tell one way or another. It looks like I am going to be forced to draw any information I want to learn one piece at a time.

"When is the last time you talked?"

I can tell Jason is getting a little perturbed, "I don't remember," he snaps. "Maybe two years ago. Why?"

"Ned was the last person I talked to before I got grabbed. He is the Police Chief of Port Aransas."

"He told me he was the head of a small town force. They are lucky to have him."

"Is there any way we can get in touch with him?"

"What the hell for? He is several thousand miles from here."

"I am not sure. I just think he is the kind of person who can help no matter where he is. There are two SAT phone systems on the boat. I just thought we could call him."

"First of all, we cannot call anyone until we get control of this boat. Secondly, once we are in control we don't want to waste time calling Ned. We will need to get in touch with Navy operations. I still have my operating codes, so we will be able to get an alert out quickly. Let's look at the box, and then figure out how we are going to get help after we understand how the remote control works."

I agree and we cross the bridge to the box sitting on the shelf under the windshield. The box looks like a standard Simrad Auto pilot screen and appears to have a cradle with a phone sitting next to it along with an iPad. I want to know what Jason thinks and he wastes no time. He explains what we have here is a Simrad AP50 and it is connected to the system on the boat. The phone is actually a satellite phone and is resting on a high-speed modem which is connected to the iPad.

The iPad is connected to the remote control device for the AP50 and by using high speed Internet through the satellite phone the operator on the container ship can control *My GRL*. He further explains when the AP50 was installed they set it up to control steering, power, and thrusters. The operator is getting the readings we see on the display and can operate the boat from a pretty good distance since they are using Internet and not electronic guidance systems.

"*My GRL* has a Simrad AP20 auto pilot. I guess they installed their own Simrad AP50. Can we take control?"

"This will be as easy as hanging up the phone, except we need to have a coordinated maneuver. I will go below and interrupt the engines while you stay above and get ready to apply power at my signal. The key will be turning and getting as close as possible to the container ship. You will have to be careful and not get too close because I am sure they have hand grenades which they can lob onto our deck."

"Won't the grenades set off the explosives?"

"That's the beauty of C4. It needs a jolt from an actuator to set it off. It could happen but not likely. Besides, these guys would be using high frag types. They won't be interested in blowing up anything; they would just want to shred everything on the deck."

"I guess that would include me." I interject what I think is some humor.

"Especially you when they find out you are free and in charge of your boat."

"Okay, so what is the plan?"

"I will go below and call you on the intercom which I saw in the engine room. When I pull the engine power you will need to keep an eye on the container ship. Once they get within fifty feet we will need to unhook the satellite phone and fire up the engines. You will then steer close to the ship. I will come back to the bridge and take the satellite phone and place some calls. At the same time you need to get on the radio to announce an emergency situation and keep repeating our location. You checked out the Nav gear on this boat, right?"

"Yeah! I got it."

"Any questions while I am still here?"

"I really can't think of anything. You afraid?"

"Scared shitless."

"Makes me feel better."

"Okay then I'm going below. I'll call you in a minute."

Jason disappears down the ladder. I am standing by the controls waiting for his call. Looking at the Nav-net monitor, keeping in mind that I will need to read out the longitude and latitude on my mayday call. I glance at the AP50 screen and see we are currently at lat 40°20'47" N, long 73°23'19" W. I don't want to hit the key giving the distance to New York since that may alert the operator someone is messing with his gear. I am assuming we are around forty-five miles out.

I will need to turn on *My GRL*'s system since once we disconnect the satellite phone the readings on the AP50 will stop. I will also have to power up the Icom VHF and shortwave radios and turn on the class B transponder. I am hoping all of them will function. I know the coast guard stands by twenty-four hours a day on the VHF and the transponder will send our location continually. I don't know if anyone disconnected this equipment so it may or may not work. I make a mental note to get Jason's input on if we should power all this stuff up before disconnecting the satellite phone.

I look at the magnetic compass and see our current heading is two-hundred-eighty degrees. This means we are heading for New York moving from the southeast. While I try to figure out where we are, the intercom phone on the conn rings and the light above blinks red. I pick it up.

"Hello." I realize I sound as if I don't know it is Jason on the other end.

"Hello yourself. You ready?"

"Yes, I am ready and have a question."

"Go ahead."

"Should we power up the Nav gear and radios before we start?"

Jason is quiet for a moment. "Damn good idea. Do all except the transponder. If you power it up before we are ready those guys will know it is powered since it will give them a danger warning since we are within six nautical miles to them, which is close enough right now for that safety feature to kick in."

"I did not think of the transponder giving us away, so I will wait until we are under control to activate it."

"Okay. I am looking at the engines right now and I think the best thing to do is manually take control of the throttle. I wanted to shut them down, but I am worried they may cool off and it will be hard to start so I will just hold them back to idle. It could be done from the bridge, yet I am not sure how much the auto control can override the bridge controls. Down here I can pretty much guarantee I will be able to intercept all control commands."

"I could try to bring the throttles to idle from the bridge." I offer the alternative, thinking if it works it will be the easiest way to go.

"I think I better do it." Jason gives his opinion in a way that I know took a lot of thought so I let it go.

"I am going to power up the radios now." I talk into the phone wishing Jason would talk me out of it.

"Go for it." He didn't bite and is being no help to a coward right now.

I hit the power buttons on the Nav gear as well as the radios. I also turn on the monitors. The Nav-net twenty-inch monitor comes to life first. I tell Jason the Nav-net monitor is on. He tells me to enter a waypoint to see if it works. I hit menu and scroll through a listing of North American ports until I come to New York and highlight it and hit enter. The system comes to life informing me we are forty-two nautical miles to the southeast.

The current course is dead on. At our current forward speed we will be there in about three hours. The radios both begin making familiar noises of other boat traffic. I report to Jason everything seems to be working. He is satisfied and gives me the heads up he will begin slowing the boat. I confirm I am ready.

Jason reduces the power very gradually. I think he is trying to imitate a mechanical problem rather than someone in control of reducing the speed. Almost immediately the containership slows to match our speed. I can also detect a small correction in direction which will bring the ship closer. Since *My GRL* has slowed to no more than two or three knots the container ship has cut power in an attempt to intercept us. I report the response to Jason and he seems satisfied with the results.

"Just hold on a little longer." This is his encouragement to me.

"It looks like they are getting ready to lower a boat. Oh Jesus."

"That would not be good." Jason's reply is the understatement of the decade.

"I can tell you that is exactly what they are doing. They are loading it with some guys who have what looks like AK47s from here."

"Okay, tell me the relative position of the container ship to us."

"If we were at cruising speed we would hit them amidships in about two or three minutes."

"All right. I am going to turn on the power again for about a minute. This should get us close enough to take over control of the boat."

"Shit, do it, but hurry."

Jason hits the power again. *My GRL* lurches forward and I almost hit the deck with the acceleration force. He obviously has the throttle wide open. I can see the men getting into the boat looking over in complete surprise. They must think we are going to collide. This may be why they have not lowered the boat yet. Hitting the container ship would be no big deal and not a worry for them. Having to deal with a sixty-five-foot boat at twenty-plus knots while in a small skiff causes them to pause. After a minute, Jason cuts the power again. The wake catches up with *My GRL* and causes a swell that carries us even closer to the ship.

"I am coming up there. Pull that phone off the modem."

I manage to snap into action. I yank the phone off the modem and put it in the captain's chair. I grab the throttles and throw them into full forward. I steer the helm gently to the left. *My GRL* responds beautifully to the commands. She comes up to speed and the gentle turn places her heading more toward the bow of the container ship where I hope there are few crewmen for now. Jason comes into the bridge. He complements our heading and makes note the guys further astern have started lowering their boat. He picks up the phone and starts dialing. While dialing he tells me to turn on the transponder. I do it while he is talking to someone who seems to have a lot of questions the way Jason is answering. I make out some of the conversation. He is talking in some kind of code so I don't understand all he is discussing.

I start to pay more attention to navigating *My GRL* around the bow of the container ship. I give us about twenty-five feet separation as I cut across the bow. It is clear the container ship has picked up speed. I have to think a little but I believe the best he can do is eighteen knots. This means I have a ten-knot advantage. I have never been this close to a huge ship like this. The sight of the bow chewing up sea coming right at us is not at all comforting. I check the throttles and there is no more forward speed possible. I am thinking twenty-five feet might have been a little too close. I start screaming "Come on, come on," as I hope to apply speed with my mouth.

The speed of *My GRL* is enough to carry us by the bow of the container ship with a few feet to spare. I immediately crank the helm to starboard and set up a course which will run parallel to the container ship. I pull back on the throttles since I really don't want to reach the stern quickly. The boat lowered has two choices. The first is to head for the bow and chase us around the ship. The second is to head for the stern and intercept us as we come around the stern. I would rather be intercepted somewhere amidships of the container ship. This will give me maximum flexibility in maneuvering away for

JOHN W. HOWELL

the little boat.

Jason has finished his calls. He grabs the microphone on the VHF radio. He starts calling mayday. He repeats our position, which he picks off the Nav-net monitor over and over. He tells the airwaves there is a terrorist threat underway. He gives *My GRL's* new name as well as the container ship's name of *Container Wind.*.

As I am navigating alongside *Container Wind* I ask loudly how the calls went.

"It will take about ten minutes for my security credentials to clear. Once they do I expect we will see some relief!" Jason yells back.

"How come it takes so long?" I am like a kid in the backseat of a car.

Jason smiles. "I called for a level one response. You can't just do that without having someone check out the caller. Level one is a request for armed interdiction. They have all my codes and my credibility should hold up."

"What do you mean should?" I shoot back almost as a joke.

"Of course if my membership has expired we could be in trouble." Jason pokes me in the ribs.

I see any more questions about being saved and the effectiveness of the US government will be met with the same evasive answers. I believe Jason has no idea if we will be rescued or not, so it is silly to keep on with dumb questions. It will be much better to drive the boat and shut up.

I look out the windshield and see we are almost at the three quarter mark moving along the hull of the ship. A small boat is coming out from behind the stern with four men aboard. The scary part is the number of automatic rifles I see pointed in the air. I'm sure these guys are not in the mood for any discussion, and sooner or later the rifles will be pointed at us. Jason is still calling mayday on the VHF. I decide to seek his council.

"Jason, look at what is coming around the stern. Looks like we have a small problem and it has a bunch of rifles I take to be AK47s."

"Keep on course. They won't start shooting for another hundred yards or so. Our best bet is to get down on the deck and try to ram them."

"If we are on the deck how to we keep up with their maneuvers?"

- 210 -

"We will hit the deck when the rounds start raking the bridge because that is what they will do in a few minutes. You take the remote from the onboard autopilot and get into the rear cockpit. Cut the power now so we have a little more time. Once you get to the cockpit get ready to gun her again on my signal."

Jason gets down on the deck and moves to a point where he can see ahead out the door on the left of the helm.

"I see them." Jason's voice sounds excited. "Get moving to the cockpit."

I pull the throttles back to idle speed, set the autopilot, then grab the *My GRL*'s AP20 remote and clamber down the ladder and almost jump into the cockpit. I hear Jason yell up to me and wonder if I can hear him. I tell him I can.

Jason yells to me, "Hold on, I think the rain is about to begin."

No sooner did he raise his voice then showers of glass, wood, and fiberglass fly over my head as if propelled by a burning rocket. Some of the debris bounces around the cockpit. I can feel small cuts on my face where some of the glass splintered and hit me on rebound.

"Hold her steady," came Jason's warning. "I think these guys are through shooting so wait for my command. You okay?"

"I am okay. How about you?"

"Right as rain." Jason lowers his voice. "We better not talk anymore they are getting close and I want them to think we are dead."

I am thinking I am good with that. I really don't have any more to add anyway. I brush some of the scraps of the bridge out of my hair and wish I had put on a hat. I wonder how many rounds went through. Feels like it could have been a thousand. I snap back when Jason screams "Now!"

I jam the remote control into full throttle position and feel *My GRL* lurch forward.

"Maintain one sixty degrees," Jason yells.

I look at the remote and quickly adjust the heading. I see the indicator come to one sixty degrees just as I feel what seems like an explosion in the bow. *My GRL* shudders slightly and I call out to Jason. "What the hell was that?"

"You just cut their boat in two. Come up to the bridge quickly."

I spend no time trying to understand Jason's request. I run up the ladder as fast as I can. Jason is at the helm pointing down to the

water. A part of the little boat is floating in the surf near *My GRL.*
We pass the piece and I look back to see more pieces of the boat in
the water.

"Where are the guys on the boat?" I really don't want to see
them again.

"I think they got sucked under and given a haircut on the props.
Look at the blood and junk bubbling up." Jason stops talking and is
almost laughing.

I look around the bridge. The damage is massive. The
windshield is completely gone. The Nav monitor and VHF radio are
gone. I am surprised the ceiling has not caved in given all the bullet
holes in the supports. I get Jason's opinion on how bad the damage
really is or does it just look really bad. He tells me the helm is
responding and the throttles work fine. He believes we will get
another set of visitors soon and is not worried about being able to
control *My GRL.*

"These guys must have heard the maydays and I'll wager they
need to get rid of us and get on their way soon. They are making a
gradual turn and are now at three-hundred-forty degrees and I
believe they will head to thirty degrees. This will take them out to sea
again. So, if nothing else, we have altered their plan enough to save
the midshipmen and the museum."

"That's good and we still need to survive this expedition." I feel
the need to add this in case Jason has forgotten.

He laughs, "I have not forgotten."

"How about the transponder? Do you think it still works?"

"It looks okay and there is no way to tell for sure. The screen
looks fine. I still have a danger close traffic warning being registered
on our big friend out there." While talking he nods in the direction of
the container ship.

"Do you expect a call on the satellite phone?"

"Not really. If all is good we should see some Blackhawks with a
team of Seals aboard. There is no other way to effectively take care of
these guys since surface ships would take too long."

"Do you think they will come?" I keep hoping for a guarantee
from Jason.

"We will just have to stay alive long enough to see. Speaking of
that, we need to keep an eye out as we move toward the bow. The
stern is where most of the crew is located. I am still worried about
grenades. I have pulled away a little from the ship. If they want to hit

us with anything they will have to shoot it, not drop it."

I look up at the ship. There are about ten crewmen high above us. They seem to be working on something on the deck. It doesn't take long to see what consumed their attention. One of the men stands up with a shoulder mounted rocket launcher.

"Hell, that's no fair. I'll bet that puppy is guided by wire as well."

"What the hell are they trying to do?" I scream at Jason. "You can't tell me that a rocket won't set this stuff off."

"You bet it will." Jason's response is what I had hoped not to hear.

The guy lets the rocket fly, and we watch as its smoky trail spirals down toward us. At the last second it takes a hard left turn and it hits the water in front of us. The plume of water washes over *My GRL* and I instinctively duck.

"They want us to stop." Jason reads the signal.

"What should we do?"

"Not stop, that's for sure! I am betting they are bluffing. They know if this boat goes up they will have some serious damage as well. They need to do something quick because they will want to get the hell out of here. I think they thought we would stop thinking we could talk our way out of this. We should keep moving."

"I'm with you. I don't trust Winther at all."

As we are talking a new barrage of bullets tear into *My GRL*. Jason swings a little wider and the bullets start tearing up the water beside us.

Jason tells me, "We are out of AK47 range and still close enough to be safe. I hope they don't have a sharp shooter on board. A high-powered rifle would not be good."

"Let's not curse ourselves by talking about that." Sounds superstitious of me yet I really mean it.

"We are on a thirty degree heading," Jason calls out. "They are heading out to sea."

"Isn't there a way we could just jump off *My GRL* and get away?" I suggest as a possible way out of this mess.

"I was thinking about the same thing. If they set their course and hold it there is no reason why you and I could not set the autopilot and slip off the back. It would take them a while to figure out we were not longer with the boat. They could then do one of two things; either pick up the boat or blow it up. I'll bet they will come back for us though."

"Yeah, but by that time our help will be here."

"You hope and I have to believe you are right."

"I believe we have done our part and now it is time to get off."

"Okay, let's drop back and shadow the container ship and see how long she stays on the same course."

Jason pulls the throttles back and we watch as the crew on the ship yells at each other. Jason and I look back toward *My GRL*'s stern where the crew seems to be pointing. Closing in are two airplanes. They are dots in the sky at this point. It is clear they are on what could be considered a final approach to attack and they look like military planes. I turn to Jason and he is squinting to try and make out the type of aircraft. His eyes narrow as it looks like he has made them.

"Those are P51 Mustangs. They are World War II vintage propeller planes and my guess is the pilots are private mercenaries. I think your Jacobs contact is trying to even the score. I believe we are going to get a good old-fashioned strafing. The bullets won't blow the C4, but they will certainly tear hell out of you and me. Get two life preservers quick."

I jump to the locker on the side of the bridge. There are four life jackets stowed there. I toss one to Jason. He tells me to go to the aft cockpit and be ready to jump overboard. He sets the auto pilot, grabs the remote, and descends the ladder right behind me. We both look out the stern and see the planes are making a wide turn, which will bring them in over the bow of *My GRL*. We both seem to be fascinated at watching the planes finish their maneuver. He and I both suck in our breath as we see small sparks on the wingtips and watch as the fifty-caliber bullets stich small geysers in the water as they work their way to *My GRL*.

They finally get here. Chunks of *My GRL* jump up from the large holes made by the ammunition. I imagine the bullets passing completely through *My GRL* into the hull and out to the sea again. I do hear strange noises like steel hitting steel and figure some of the shells are hitting the cast iron engines. The two planes finish their pass and *My GRL* looks like an insane person has taken a large pick and worked her over. The only distinction between that vision and reality is the real holes are somewhat well spaced and follow what look like a well laid out course.

"You think they will make another pass?" I shout over the engine noise.

"Take a look." Jason is pointing back behind us.

Sure enough the two planes climb, bank, and turn for a return match. I don't know why I am thinking *match* since the sides are definitely uneven. Again they take a slow, wide turn and line up to come over the bow.

"Jump over the side!" Jason yells at me and points to the low spot on the gunnel. "Hold on to the rope there." He is still pointing.

I grab the rope and do a small roll over the side. I'm immediately pulled under by the force of the boat's forward motion and the pull of the rope on my injured shoulder makes me scream out loud. I am hanging on for dear life and feel if I continue I will be dragged to death or at least pass out from the pain. Just when I was thinking of letting go, I feel Jason's strong arm around my waist and the upward motion carrying me to clean air. I gasp, choke, cough, spit, and finally get a breath worth the effort.

Jason has us positioned so we are not so much being dragged but more like we are riding the wake. It is all a matter of shortening the rope to the point we are on the crest and more like part of the boat rather than part of an anchor. I see he still has the remote in his hand and wonder how he does it all. My reverie is cut short with a series of small explosion sounds which are the fifty caliber shells ripping up the deck and below. *My GRL* seems to shudder with each hit and I am sure there won't be the need for too many more passes.

"Can you see the container ship?" I scream to Jason, thinking in the excitement she may have made a drastic maneuver and might be pulling away.

"She is still with us," Jason shouts. "I think these guys are waiting for your boat to go under and then will hit the detonator when she is a quarter of a mile or so underwater."

"Does their system allow that? I mean, how can they communicate under water?"

"They just drop a small antenna over the side. Would be good up to two or three miles. For sure the cell phone will be useless. I'm glad we did not count on that being the only device."

"Do you think their receiver may have been damaged in the strafing?" I shout still grasping for straws.

"I think not. If so, they would have bugged out already and then hit the cell phone for a big finish. I now see how much genius they have on their side. They have all contingencies covered. Even if they can't set off the explosion your boat will sink out of sight and they are hoping with us aboard. Hold on, the planes are on their final again."

The sound of the bullets hitting *My GRL* has become pretty standard after the three passes. There is a sound like chopping, followed by a sound like trees crashing, followed by complete silence. After the silence the secondary sounds start. They are the sounds of *My GRL* living out her last moments on the surface. Creaks and groans and the sound of rushing water tell me the end is near. I am at a loss as to why the engines are still running. It is clear *My GRL* has taken on a lot of water since the boat has slowed to half speed even though the throttles are wide open. The engines are straining against the weight and can't last too much longer.

I call out to Jason, "It looks like she is almost done. What do you think?"

"I think you are right. I see smoke, so I think the fuel has started to burn. You and I need to find a nice piece of debris to hide under and let her go."

I look around and the only thing I can see which might do the trick is the very large cushion on the aft bench. I reach up and pull it over the side. Jason seems to approve.

He yells, "We need to time this with the sinking of *My GRL* or the big fire, whichever is first. You and I will stay afloat and we will need to go under the cushion and stay as flat as possible. We need these guys to believe that we went down with her."

"I think we can do it." I offer this as encouragement I know Jason doesn't need and is really meant for me. "Let me know when you think it is time."

As I finish I hear and suddenly feel a major rush of air followed by a hot blast. I put my head down in the water to stop what feels like an instant sunburn. Jason yells the fuel has erupted. He tells me to get ready to let go of the rope. I uncoil it from my arm. I feel like I am letting go of a loved one and know I can no longer stay with *My GRL.*

"She is a boat," I tell myself as I hold the end of the rope.

"Get ready," Jason yells in my ear. When we let go, put the cushion over your head and arch your back. Try to keep your legs under you. I will be right beside you. On my mark . . . one, two, three, let go!"

I release *My GRL* and do as Jason said. The life jacket makes it hard to arch my back. It keeps trying to get me more upright. I am having some trouble breathing under the vinyl cushion. I am able to hold onto a strap which runs under the cushion so holding on is not a problem, but it continually presses into my face cutting off my breath. Jason finally comes under the cushion and the increased space allows a little more free air. I take a deep breath.

"Where have you been?" I am not meaning to sound like a nag.

"I threw the remote on board. I think the engines will stop soon. She is on her own now."

"Do you think the planes will come again?"

"I think they believe they have finished her. No, I don't."

"Well, we won't have to worry about being strafed some more. We were lucky to escape without getting hit."

"Well, it's not over yet. Let's hope they don't come back because this large white cushion makes a dandy target."

"Can we look out?"

"I think we can take a peek. We are so far away from the container ship they won't be able to see us."

With that, Jason picks up the side of the cushion. He describes the scene.

"My GRL is still afloat and is totally engulfed in flames. It looks like she will burn to the water line and then go under. The container ship is still with us. It looks like it may have moved closer but it is hard to tell. Oh my God!"

"What is it?" I now exhibit panicked impatience.

"They are strafing the boat again. This means they think we are still on her."

"Well, that's a break."

"She is going down, stern first. She could not survive another attack. We should try and put some more distance between us and where she is going down. I don't know the extent of the blast area under water if they decide to blow her."

Jason and I begin to sidestroke away from the scene. It is slow work carrying the cushion along. I am fully exhausted in what seems like a few minutes.

"We gotta keep going." Jason sees me pause.

I am totally out of breath yet continue to swim. Something like a second wind comes over me. I suppose the prospect of being blown up gives an incentive to forget one's weakness. I continue and make up my mind not to stop again until Jason does. After what seems to be an hour Jason finally takes a break.

"Let's take a break." Jason is clearly out of breath. He is wheezing as well as heaving and it is clear the aspirin has worn off. I should have given him another dose but it is too late now.

We are both trying to get enough air to replace what has been expended. Jason lifts the side of the cushion to take a look at how we are positioned.

"Your boat is gone John." He announces her demise with a proper tone of respect. "The container ship is dead in the water."

As he drops the side of the cushion, a wall of water rushes up at us from below. It picks us up and surrounds us with a cone of dark blue mixed with green. A punch is delivered from an unseen hand, which blows the precious air stored right out of my lungs. I see the white of the cushion at least ten feet above in a tunnel of water silhouetted against the bright sky. I do not see Jason and realize I no longer have a grip on the cushion.

I continue to rise in the tunnel and know I will not catch the cushion since we are rising at the same rate. I am thinking this might be how I will die since I don't think I can hold my breath any longer. I think of my life and decide it was lived as I wished. I close my eyes and all goes black.

Chapter Twenty Two

I open my eyes and am blinded by a light whose heat seems to have taken up residence on my face. "Where am I?" I talk through lips too dry and not sure there is anyone near to answer.

"You are in the naval hospital in Corpus Christi." It is Ned's voice. "You were airlifted here from New York."

"Ned, how are you?" I am very pleased to hear Ned's voice again. "That sun is so bright I can't see you."

"John, you have some bandages on your eyes. The room is quite dark. When you were in the explosion the doctors tell me you have had some injury to your eyes."

"What kind of injury? What explosion?"

"You were in the water under that cushion, remember?"

"Yes, I remember. Where is Jason? He was with me."

"Jason is fine. He is in the next room."

"What do you mean fine?"

"He has two broken legs but otherwise is fit for duty."

"Ned?" If I could see him I would look him in the eye. "Tell me the truth, how bad is it?"

I can hear Ned shuffling as if he is being given a question he doesn't want to answer. He clears his throat. "They don't know for sure yet; there is a good chance you will be good as new."

"Thanks. You don't sound convincing."

"Sorry, that is all I know. Not to change the subject but since you seem like you are fully awake, care to hear what went down after you and Jason hit the water?"

"I sure do. You are telling me the truth about Jason right?"

"Yes I'm telling you the truth." I can hear the sound of a chair being pulled closer to the bed. "I talked to the security guys at the Towers and they told me a girl came in and gave them some coffee and cookies. I asked them if she worked for the Towers and they said she didn't, but they thought they could recognize her again. I gave them some pictures and after they reviewed them they agreed her picture was not among them. Guess where they saw her again and pointed her out to me?"

"Geez, Ned, I have been pretty busy, just tell me."

"They saw her at your memorial."

"My memorial. What memorial?"

"Oh yeah," Ned chuckles. "You wouldn't know. We had a memorial when we thought you burned up on the Kennedy causeway. Well anyway, these security guys are at the service and come up to me and point out the girl who had distracted them while the security camera was blacked out. Guess who she was?"

"Ned, you are driving me crazy. I have no idea."

"That girl you took out a couple of times. The best friend of Gerry Starnes, Sarah Barsonne."

"What?" I exclaim. "That means . . ."

"Yes. She worked for that lowlife Winther. After I picked her up she confessed to her involvement and told us you were in fact still alive. She did not know all the facts, but enough to be useful. I immediately got in touch with Homeland Security and we attempted to locate you. As it turns out, without the call from Jason we never would have found you or him."

"Did anyone call my parents and tell them I was not dead after all."

"Yeah, I got on the phone immediately and gave them the news. They were really happy but a little in shock."

"They okay now?"

"Oh yes the government flew them here. They are in the coffee shop downstairs. I told them I needed to talk to you and then I will send them up."

"That's great Ned. Thanks. Why did the government fly them

here?"

"You are a hero. That's why."

I wanted more information, but I let his comment go for now. "So tell me, how did you find us?"

"Well when the call came over the satellite phone the section leader of Team Six got in touch with Homeland. We immediately honed-in on the transponder on the boat. We were not able to scramble in enough time to prevent your boat from being destroyed and got there just as it was blown."

"What happened to Sarah?"

"She is in a lock up. She needs to testify at Winther's trial."

"You got him?" I am now excited.

"We sure did. We jumped off some Blackhawks and found him hiding like a baby in a stateroom. His team gave up mostly without a fight; seems they were all geeks except a few of the armed ones."

"Let me guess, did you come across a big guy who looks like Quasimodo?"

"Yeah, he went down with guns blazing."

"Figures. Were you there?"

"I was. They let me participate since I spent time as the bureau liaison to Team Six."

"So how did you find Jason and me?"

"After the explosion, and when we could not find you on the container ship, we took one of the Coast Guard zodiacs and crisscrossed the area where the explosion went off and found you first. You were out like a light and your preserver worked to keep your head out of the water. Jason was second and he started yelling at us so we found him right after you. I think he kept quiet until he knew we were friendlies."

"Is Winther doing any talking?"

"Naw. He has not said a word."

"Do you guys know anything about Jacobs?"

"The fact he put up all the money for this fiasco, yes."

"Who told you about him?"

"Jason was completely debriefed and he gave us the whole story."

"Are you going after Jacobs?"

"The feds are investigating now. I am not sure what they have. All the physical evidence has no track to Jacobs. The only other person who has any information about his involvement is Winther. I am sure Winther knows if he talks he is a dead man. So I don't know how far the feds will get."

"What about all those people on the container ship? He landed in a helicopter. They must have seen him on board the ship."

"Yeah, well seeing and telling are two different things. Jacobs has a way to keep people quiet."

"Did Jason tell you about the P51s which strafed us?"

"He sure did. There is no trace of them. The FAA is investigating and has a flight plan filed for two acrobatic pilots who requested and received permission to do some maneuvers out at sea. None of the traffic controllers had 'em officially since they were operating under visual flight rules with no supervision. We suspect even though they filed a plan, they kept pretty close to the deck unobserved. Once they took off from New Jersey no one talked to them again. They used a small airport which had no traffic control. We think they came back to New Jersey but don't know for sure. It's like they never existed."

"You think Jacobs will walk?"

"No charges have been filed yet, so my guess is yes."

"Did you find out who was in the EMS vehicle that blew up on the Kennedy causeway?"

"One of the people was a homeless guy, and we think the other two were the EMS personnel who picked you up. Their DNA results have not come back yet. They had disappeared about the same time. We know they died before the explosion though. We think they were en route with you to the hospital and were then forced to stop. We believe they were shot. The final tests will give us answers, but I don't know anything will change. We won't know who did this as I am sure it was a professional hit."

"It sounds logical. Any guy who can hire a container ship and P51 Mustangs could certainly hire professionals to take out two EMS workers. Ned, this just makes me sick to think that the mastermind may get away with it not to mention I will need to be very careful since I think he might keep coming after me."

"I know what you mean. I would try not to worry about Jacobs getting to you. You have a lot of security looking after you so try to rest easy on that. Anyway do you have any more questions because I need to go back to work and let your parents come up. It is never quiet in a beach town."

"I would like to know more about what happened to Sarah."

"She is being held as a material witness. Not too much else to hold her on right now. She has denied any part in her friend's killing. I suggested to the Federal DA she be charged with accessory to terrorist activities so he is looking into that. She does not have a bail hearing until next week. I doubt she will be able to come up with ten percent of ten million, which is pretty standard for terrorism."

"Did she offer anything about why she was involved?"

"Nope, she has been pretty mum since we read her Miranda rights. I suspect Winther or Jacobs have something on her. She seems too nice to be running with this pack."

"How about Jason's sister and Gerry's brother? Were they released?"

"Unfortunately, Gerry's brother has not been found. We had no idea where they were holding him and I suspect he was killed right after they took him. Jason's sister was rescued by a SWAT team in New York. It appears while you two were swimming around in the ocean she was able to make a 911 call on an old cell phone which was in the bedroom where they were keeping her. She actually knew she had the phone and needed to find the charger before it would work. It took her several days of quiet searching to find it in a box in her closet. By the time she made the call the city cops had been notified by the SEAL team to be on alert as a result of Jason's satellite call."

"Wow! That is really good news. I bet Jason is thrilled."

"He was very happy. Also you should know you and Jason are being hailed as quite the heroes. After you are feeling better there is going to be a meeting at the White House and a presentation to you and Jason of a commendation medal for preventing what could have turned out to be a real catastrophe."

I feel my face flush and know I am several shades redder. "I don't deserve anything; it was Jason who did all the brave heroic stuff."

"That's not what he is telling me, so you might as well sit back and enjoy being famous cause that is what is going to happen. As for me, I gotta go."

I hear the chair move away from the bed and know Ned has stood up. I press Ned for when I will be able to see Jason and he tells me in a day or two maybe he will be well enough to come into the room. Ned takes my hand. I want to squeeze his and find I do not have the strength. I assume the explosion has caused some temporary interruption between my brain and hands. Ned leans close and whispers everything will be all right and I believe him. I do not want to let him go, but know I must. He puts my hand back on my chest.

"Take care, Ned, and thank you." He moves away as I am talking.

"You take care and I will see you soon."

"Yeah, I will see you soon."

I lay back against the pillow. I should have found out from Ned how long I was unconscious and if anything else was wrong but it did not occur to me. I move my legs and they seem normal. My arms feel like lead weights. I have a small pain in my side and for whatever reason I don't seem to care.

I think of the FJ and wonder if she still runs. I make a mental note to get a report from Ned when he comes back.

I feel really badly about Sarah. This is a person I thought would be sharing my future. I guess the only sharing will be in court. My dread about letting her know we should get to know each other better was again validated. She was the only one who knew I was heading to Ned's the day I was shot. She must have told Winther's gang where I was going to be. I was really surprised she said she liked the intrigue when she visited Mexico under a ruse to collect information for a deposition. I guess she liked leading a double life so much she got lost in it. She sure fooled me. So much for love, I'm thinking.

I should have gotten Ned to let me know if I need to be a witness against Winther. I am sure I will be but will need to check.

I also should find out when I need to report back to work since I am not sure how long my leave has left on it. I had not thought of it until now, but the office probably thinks I am still dead from the EMS accident. I can imagine all the paperwork has been cut and my parents inundated with lawyers asking them to sign as my beneficiaries. My parents will be relieved, but I'm not sure how Peters and the rest will take this little miracle. I'll have to get the story from mom and dad and then see what to do.

I have all these thoughts and they seem to rush in all at once. I guess it will take me some time to process all which has happened.

Right now I am glad to be here. The rest will need to take care of itself until I feel better. I can't help myself in wishing the bandages will be coming off soon. I think I will ring for the nurse and try to get some more information. My brain tells me to reach for the buzzer, which should be near my pillow. I am surprised my arms reject the command from my brain. I want to call out to someone and then stop.

"The hell with it."

After I said it, I have to be honest with myself and admit I don't really mean 'the hell with it.' I wish I could do more than accept I may never be the same again.

I lay back into the pillow and think maybe I'll plan and build a new boat in my head. I also make up my mind to somehow bring Jacobs to justice. I don't think it is fair for a person like him to be able to control others to do his bidding, and then when the time comes to "pay the piper," to be able to simply walk away. Big thoughts for a guy who is lying in bed and unable to reach for a buzzer to summon help, which by now he must acknowledge he definitely needs.

END

About the Author

John's main interests are reading and writing. He turned to writing as a full time occupation after an extensive career in business. John writes thriller fiction novels and short stories. He also has a three times weekly blog at **johnwhowell.com** where he writes about author and reader view points on stories which make a difference.

John lives on Mustang Island in the Gulf of Mexico off the coast of south Texas with his wife Molly and their spoiled rescue pets. He can be reached by e-mail at: johnhowell.wave@gmail.com

50671507R00125

Made in the USA
Charleston, SC
05 January 2016